MW00463476

PLEASE WRITE

a novel

Janette Byron Stone

Copyright © 2019 by Janette Byron Stone

This novel is a work of fiction. Any references to real people or locales are intended to place the fiction in its historical setting. Other names, characters, places, events, or incidents are either the product of the author's imagination or are used fictitiously. Any resemblance to actual persons, living or dead, events or locales is entirely coincidental.

Permissions have been granted for the inclusion of letter excerpts. The search continues for the authors who have not yet been found.

All rights reserved. No part of this book may be reproduced or reused in any manner without written permission of the copyright owner except for the use of quotations in a book review.

Author website: www.janettecatherinestone.com

Cover design by Juan Carlos Negretti Briceno
Author photo by Michael Procaccini

DEDICATION

This novel is respectfully dedicated to the men and women who served in Vietnam, their families and friends who waited back home, and to my mother who reminded me that World War II was her generation's war.

It is necessary to write if the days are not to slip emptily by. How else indeed to clap the net over the butterfly of the moment? For the moment passes; it is forgotten; the mood is gone; life itself is gone. That is where the writer scores over his fellows; he captures the changes of his mind on the hop.

~ VITA SACKVILLE WEST

Note to Reader

This book was inspired by the time I spent, the experiences I shared, and my subsequent correspondence with American soldiers who spent their R&R in Sydney, Australia, during the Vietnam War. The particular file in my memory cabinet that housed those days would have remained sealed if it hadn't been for the letters I received during that time.

Like the authors of the letters, I had locked my memories away. But with time, the letters circled back around, engaging my attention. It began at the University of Alberta with a class where letters were acknowledged as sources of information. For the first time in over twenty years, I tentatively unlocked that drawer. I researched the letters and wrote my master's thesis with the premise that what was important enough to write from a warzone would correspond with what's important outside the warzone. Themes emerged: friendship, the concept of time, love, authority, sincerity, humour, and the importance of family. The common thread within and without the culture of war was communication, the desire to be heard and accepted without judgement.

Who were the young men who unknowingly captured and recorded a time in history? They were Australian and American soldiers, sailors, and airmen drafted, conscripted, enlisted, and commissioned. They were sons, brothers, uncles, and friends. They were the poets, philosophers, intellects, and comedians who expressed themselves in words and created an opus out of the living truth of their thoughts at the time.

Long after I completed my thesis, my heart tugged at me to set the record straight about the often maligned men who served in the military during the Vietnam War. I realized I could incorporate my firsthand knowledge of them into a novel that would allow readers to see them through the eyes of a young woman coming of age during turbulent times. It is my hope that readers will recognize the "letter writers" for who they were: young men thrown into an unpopular war and branded with that legacy. Events in the story developed because a word or a phrase in those almost forgotten letters triggered a snippet of memory that generated a thought that set in motion a plot line that shaped a chapter, and ultimately a book.

ACKNOWLEDGEMENTS

Writing this novel engulfed days, weeks, months, and years of my life. It wouldn't have arrived at this point without the support of family, friends, readers, and editors in Australia, Canada, and the United States, who jumped on board with flags waving.

My daughters Jes, Erica, and Kelly, thank you for listening and for your infinite support. Jes, Erica, and Leif, you have journeyed this story with me and know it without ever having to read. Thank you, my sons Leif, Jeremy, Kyle, and Ross, for the confidences we share and for the next generation view you bring to the table. My husband Tom, your patience and tolerance—while I sat for hours and wrote—are true gifts. I'm proud of your military experience and commitment, and grateful you share information about details outside my realm. Mostly, I am grateful that you were there as my go-to reader when I just wanted the reassurance that it was "working."

Dr. Jean D. Clandinin, thank you for encouraging me to write an "out of the box" thesis all those years ago and for still being with me as a reader and supporter. Thank you for being a ground-breaking advocate for the value of digging into the past and present through writing, and for your intelligence, vision, and calm assurance. This book would never have happened without you.

My extraordinary editor Betsy Beard—a Gold Star mother with a commitment to the respectful acknowledgement of the men and women who put their lives on the line for the rest of us—trimmed, tightened, refined, rearranged, and begged me to reinsert phrases after I did my own trimming, tightening, and refining. Your clarity, honesty, and wit are invaluable. Thank you Bob Doerr for introducing us.

Australian journalist, Alan Reid, thank you for your meticulous fact checking of Aussie details. And thank you William New for your detailed tailoring of sometimes lengthy sentences and for telling me that anything you suggested was just your opinion and in the end, it was my decision.

Meeting with fellow writers is like therapy. Thank you June Osborne for initiating those meetings the year I took my first leave to write. I'll never forget the feeling of elation when I finished what was to be only the first of many more drafts. Thank you, Rusty Hodgdon and the Key West Writers Guild, for providing a place to read, listen, and comment in the company of skilled writers with diverse interests.

GLOSSARY

Please Write is written with Australian English spelling, which sometimes differs from American spelling. In addition, the following terms may be unfamiliar to American readers.

ABC: Australian Broadcasting Company
Anzac biscuits: coconut oatmeal cookies
Banister brush: a small brush for sweeping up crumbs and
    dirt into a dustpan
Bikkies: sweet biscuits or cookies
Boot: trunk of the car
Brollie: umbrella
Chook house: chicken roost
Daggy: blah, not stylish
Docket: receipt
Docket book: receipt book that records sales
Drongo: mild insult meaning idiot
Ex-students reunion: high school reunion
Fibro: fibrous cement sheet

Flat: apartment

Fourth form: Grade 10

French roll: an up-do hairstyle

Funnel web: an aggressive deadly spider native
to Australia

GPO: General Post Office

Higher School Certificate: exam at the end of sixth form
(grade 12)

Housie: bingo

Jumper: sweater

Kapooka: an army base not far from Wagga Wagga

Larrikins: a mischievous young person

Lemon Delight: lemon flavored soda pop

Mactac: a patterned plastic covering with
a sticky back

Pinny: short for pinafore which is an apron

Prang: a crash involving a motor vehicle

Pull on the pokies: play the slot machines

R&C: Australian military term for a two day leave

Redbacks: venomous spiders related to the black widow

Redhead box: an Australian brand of matches

Results: results of the Higher School Certificate exams

RSL: Returned Servicemen's League

Salad sandwich: raw vegetables on a sandwich e.g. beetroot,
grated carrot, lettuce, onion, tomato

Serviette: napkins

Shytie: Scottish for "shitty"

Singlet: undershirt

Slacko: somebody who avoids responsibility

Slippery dip: playground slide

Smith's Crisps: a brand of potato chips
Sunset Sip: red soda pop drink
Tea: dinner
Thongs: flip flops
Waratah: a shrub native to Australia

PROLOGUE

Melbourne, Australia, February 1956

Once she came to terms with the fact that her marriage was over, my mother donned her green and pink floral frock and a pair of black patent leather flats. She grabbed me by the hand and with long, quick strides, pulled me to Moorabbin Post Office. There she sent a telegram to her mother, requesting enough money to purchase one-way tickets on the Spirit of Progress.

With him out of the house, she had a few days to survey the collections of her short marriage, deciding they would stay right where they were. Leaving no room for a change of heart, she sparsely packed the brown suitcase her parents had given her as a wedding present six years earlier. She threw in a few clothes for herself and chose a pair of corduroy overalls, a practical dress for playing in the yard, and two frilly dresses for me. The fact that her mother was a dressmaker reassured her that a new wardrobe was imminent.

On Saturday morning, she booked a taxi to pick us up at five. With the brown suitcase in the boot, my mother in the front seat, and me in the back, the taxi driver pulled away from the curb. The house on Glenmer Street and all that had taken place within its fibro walls in the last six years were left to fade into our wretched past.

Sadly, neither of my parents seemed to care about the legacy of abandonment and confusion their booming finale had left behind. My mother's desperate order to "turn off the bloody waterworks, for Christ's sake," shoved those pitiful tears and illegitimate feelings to the pit of my stomach where they gurgled, fermented, and did the best they could to deal with themselves.

At six o'clock we pulled up outside Spencer Street Railway Station, where Melbourne had enthusiastically welcomed Anna Pavlova—the famous Russian ballerina—the year my mother was born. Although ballet and tap dancers were show-offs in her opinion, my mother envied celebrity, which her looks and singing voice could have achieved had she not been tricked into the marriage cage.

My mother wasted no time bustling us onto the train scheduled for Albury, where my grandparents would be waiting. Not long after the Spirit of Progress had taken us away from the platform, my mother and I swayed our way along two corridors to the buffet car where she ordered shepherd's pie and a pot of tea for herself and a ham sandwich and glass of milk for me.

By the time Mum finished her cigarette, the city lights had disappeared, and the darkness of night had settled in. Stars danced through the window and mesmerized me with their magic until sleep closed my eyes on their brilliance.

Then, without warning from behind the glittered veil, I heard my mother's anxious voice. "Wake up, Catherine, we're almost there. Come on!"

The conductor who had collected our tickets at the beginning of the journey popped his head into our compartment and offered to carry the brown suitcase for my mother. I could hear her excitement as they chatted, and she hurried me along to get first in line behind the bolted door.

The train slowed down and finally ground to a halt, puffing and huffing like an exhausted beast. The conductor stepped onto the platform and held out his hand for Mum. I peered down between the bottom step and the platform to the rusty steel rail and the rocks on either side.

Then out of the dark and the steam and the filtering light, the familiar musty smell and the trademark greeting, "Hello, dearest," heralded the arrival of my grandmother. She bundled me up and scooped me out of the train. I buried my face into her faux leopard-skin coat and slipped back into my blissful sleep amongst the stars.

* * *

Grandpa packed the boot of his Holden sedan early the next morning while his wife and daughter lingered over another cuppa. This gave my mother an opportunity to elaborate on my father's lying and cheating. I sat quietly, as expected, and ran the tablecloth's lace edging back and forth between my fingers and tried not to listen. The kookaburras laughed outside.

When my grandfather returned to the dining room, he announced it was time to get on the road. My grandmother paid the bill while Mum and I walked out to the car. Once again, I sat in the back, and even though my mother joined me this time, I felt buried in its grey cloth upholstery.

"Home, James, and don't spare the horses," announced my grandmother. She slammed the car door tight, placed a cigarette in her mouth, and struck a light along the side of her Redhead matchbox. The sound reminded my grandfather to take out a roll-your-own from the tin he kept in the breast pocket of his shirt, and my mother to reach over the seat to grab one of Granny's. It was uncannily quiet as the smoke-filled car left Albury and headed for our new home in Sydney.

Mother, father, and prodigal daughter had all decided it was best not to stop at Wagga Wagga. The situation would be difficult to explain to nosey family members and anyone else who might see us if we stopped at a café for a spot of tea and a sandwich. Instead, it was decided we'd take a break at Snake Gully, five miles from Gundagai, so I could see the Dog on the Tuckerbox. The story of how that puppy died waiting for his daddy to return rumbled up some of those waterworks I wasn't supposed to turn on, so I swallowed hard and dreamt about him scorching in the hot sun by day and basking in the stars by night.

Although the bitter fights between the two people responsible for my existence ended the day my father dropped abruptly out of sight, my mother's subsequent laments, regrets, and strange longings for "that bloody bastard" and their unfortunate mismatch kept him absently present.

Regardless, life became more tolerable for my not yet six-year-old—but already bruised—soul the day my mother and I moved to Sydney. If Granny felt resentment about her daughter and granddaughter adding our second and third generation presence to her home, she never voiced it to us directly. And yet, I still hear her times-of-darkness lament: "Sometimes I wish we were like the birds. We raise our young and when they're old enough to fly, they leave the nest."

Chapter 1

BREAKING NEWS:
THE SUMMER JOB

Sydney, Australia, November 1967

After she'd swallowed the last mouthful of her tea, it was customary for my mother to shuffle from the kitchen to the lounge room. There she'd park herself in front of the television and sink into her night-time coma. I was startled then when she leapt from the table and packed Granny off to watch the six o'clock news.

"I'll do the dishes," she announced.

"No need for that, love. You've been working all day. You deserve to take it easy," Granny murmured.

"Go on, now," Mum insisted. "I've got some good news for Catherine. I'll tell you about it later." She grabbed Granny's cigarettes from the table and shoved them into the pocket of her mother's floral apron. "Go on!"

With Granny out of the way, Mum sat down, put her elbows on the table, and clasped her hands. She pointed two red fingernails at my chest. Only three feet of table separated us in the tiny kitchen booth.

"I saw Maureen at the ex-students reunion yesterday," she said, as Brian Henderson's muffled voice in the background read the headline of the day. "They need someone to work in the record shop for a few months. And!"—this was the high point before the bomb drop and the end of Brian Henderson's report on our troops' latest clash with the Vietcong—"I told her you'd love to do it."

The humidity swelled the kitchen clutter to dripping. The bare forty-watt bulb that saved on electricity irritated my tired and strained eyes.

"You could have asked me," I said, scraping a fork around the few dollops of food still lingering on my plate.

"Ask you? You should be grateful."

A forkful of potato and gravy gagged its way into my mouth as Mum jumped out of the booth. She swiped the knife and fork from my hands and grabbed the plate. On her way to the sink, she stopped at the garbage can by the stove and slammed her foot on the pedal. The lid swung open. She scraped until my uneaten dinner fell in. At the sink, she splashed the plate into the soapy water and tore at it with the faded blue and white striped dishrag. Satisfied with her effort, she stacked the plate so hard it froze my breath while I waited for the crack—and for her to say, "Shit!"

It was only when she took up one of the glasses and swirled it around in the water with loving care that I began to breathe again.

"It'll be good for you. You won't know yourself." She turned on the tap to rinse away the bubbles. "Besides, it's about time you started chipping in, giving Granny something for room and board. She hasn't had much to go on with since Grandpa died, and I can't do everything, can I?" Her upswept hair had begun to droop around her neck and face, with the weight of day turning to night. "You can't expect me to pay your way forever, you know."

She held the glass up to the greenish light that shone like a beacon from the next-door neighbours' television. As the light and dark of other lives flickered in their lounge room just above the fence, Mum scrutinised the rim for stubborn spots.

"Where's the record shop?" I asked.

Mum detected a lipstick smear. "Kings Cross," she replied, just as I was about to repeat the question.

"What?" I gasped.

"You heard me," she said, as if Kings Cross—known locally as the Cross—was just another suburb.

"Isn't Kings Cross the sleazy part of town where the pros hang out?" I shrieked.

"There is that side to it." She paused for a moment. "But if you don't look at them, they won't bother you."

"Oh great, what do you mean by *they*? Do you mean the pimps, the pros, or the other creeps? I'd have to walk around with my eyes closed."

"Don't be ridiculous," she said.

She placed the second glass beside the other on a carefully laid out tea towel and threw the washed knives and forks into the rack where their steely metal greeted each other in a loud clatter.

"Maureen will keep her eye out for you." She wiped the counter by the stove. "You'll be fine."

She turned to the opposite counter and skimmed the cloth over a small open surface, the rest of it cluttered without apology by the yellow breadbox, old opened envelopes, a progression of four empty canisters, and the last three editions of the *Daily Mirror*.

"I asked Jake for the day off tomorrow so I can take you to meet her. We'll catch an early train to the city, and afterwards we'll have a bite to eat at Woolworths." She hurried back to the table for a final wipe. "No, we won't. We'll make it a special occasion and have something lovely to eat at the cafeteria in David Jones. I'm getting a bit sick of grabbing just a plain old sandwich from Woollies."

Back at the sink, she peered again through the textured glass louvres. She stared at the family of three—mother, father, and son—gathered around the television while she scrubbed each dinner plate with the dishrag. Perhaps she longed for a home of her own. Possibly the one she left. She couldn't look at her own choices, it seemed. It was easier to blame my father and me for her pitiful situation.

"I think it's great," she reflected with pious satisfaction. "A job for the Christmas holidays. Who knows? You might want to stay on until you get married." Her words sat poised above the sink while my life passed before me. "Oh well, never mind. I still think you should have left school after fourth form and taken that secretarial course."

"I don't want to be a secretary," I protested.

"Sometimes it doesn't matter what we want. It'd be a nice job for you." She opened a drawer and pulled out a neatly ironed tea towel. "Here, swing yourself onto this and make yourself useful. When do your results come out?"

"Sixteenth of January."

"That's a long way off. We're still in November. Gives you plenty of time to make some good money."

She squeezed out the excess dishwater with the same ferocity she'd used on my hair once a week until I was fifteen, then folded and draped the tired rag over the cold water tap until next time.

"You'll be able to support me soon," she said, grabbing the tea towel to wipe her hands. "Your father promised to do that," she added. "Just another one of his lies."

She had relived her resentment so many times it was etched into the walls like a graffiti display of boring times tables. "Anyway, I don't want to talk about him anymore," she said.

And neither did I.

Mum set the alarm for six-thirty and sprang out of bed the next morning, still high on her success at forging a productive future for me. It was a stark contrast to other mornings when she dragged herself around in her petticoat, plastering on her face, and manoeuvring into her starched uniform only seconds before storming out the front door.

"Now, let me look at you." She lingered before the mirror and patted the beige powder puff with more than usual care on her forehead and cheeks. I stood behind her in the bathroom and waited for the inspection. She stroked the tube of red lipstick back and forth across her lips and then drew them back to admire the white, straight teeth that gave her the perfect smile. "Where's that lovely butterfly brooch Granny and I gave you for your sixteenth birthday?" she asked, catching my reflection in the mirror so she didn't have to turn around.

"You're not going to make me wear that, are you?" I closed the bathroom door so Granny wouldn't hear.

She stuck the final bobby pin in her French roll, turned her head from side to side so she could pick up the overall effect in the mirror, and then aimed the aerosol can for a shower of spray.

"It'll look lovely on that pink dress. Now go and get it."

A cascading halo of sticky muck clung to her hair, face, and shoulders. I got out before the droplets could assault mine. I went to the bedroom we shared and opened the cedar jewellery box Grandpa had brought back for her from the Middle East during World War II. I shifted around a string of fake pearls and earrings and rummaged through an assortment of sparkling brooches until I found the ugly one in the shape of a butterfly.

The November sun hadn't yet had a chance to burn through the concrete footpath on the walk to Belmore Station. Mum prattled on to the fences and rosebushes amidst the early morning music of nature's hum—a sound that would escalate into a deafening clatter with the heat of day.

"I'm going to have veal and chips for lunch. We should go to the pictures while we're at it. I wonder what's on at The Royal," she mused.

The cut glass rhinestones on the wings of the brass brooch sparkled. It sat on my left shoulder like a sideshow alley prize, a ridiculous antithesis to the smooth, velvet patterns found on real butterfly wings.

"No uniform today, Brenda?" asked Mavis as we walked by her fruit and veggie barrow tucked in neatly beside Belmore Post Office.

"Taking the day off to go to the city with my daughter," said Mum.

"Lovely, darling. You might want to pick up some string beans on your way home. Got a great special going today," she said, tightening her apron strings.

Mavis had provided the neighbourhood with fresh fruits and vegetables for the past ten years. She loved to tempt her regulars with a good bargain, displaying her produce with care and pairing colours to highlight their freshness.

"Nosey old bitch!" Mum said when we were well out of hearing range. "She's the biggest gossip shop in Belmore."

"She was just being friendly."

"Friendly, my foot! Before the morning's out, the whole of Belmore will know I'm not working today."

"Do you think the whole of Belmore cares if you're not working today, Mum?"

"Don't be smart with me, Catherine Mary Moreton, or I'll just turn around and go back home." She picked up the pace and lengthened her stride. "You don't know what they're like around here. There's always some old nosey parker ready to bloody well pick you apart for this thing or that." She swung a quick look right and then left before crossing Burwood Road to the bridge over the train track. "Nothing better to do with themselves." With a break in the traffic, she grabbed my arm. "Hurry up before one of these idiots bowls us over."

We caught the eight-thirty train to St James Station and the bus to Darlinghurst Road. Maureen and Ed's shop, the Crescendo Record Bar, angled a corner of the main road and an alley in the heart of the Cross. It took a while to adjust to the artificial dim of four neon ceiling bulbs after being in the bright sunshine.

The Crescendo was a poky little shop, with rows of yellow wooden bins jammed tight with LPs in plastic jackets. The smaller sage-green bins along the side and front walls had been constructed to accommodate 45s. A dark grey cash register stood like a mini bank on the counter at the back.

"They're busy," Mum said. "We'll just look around until they're ready. Smile. Don't look so down in the dumps. And get that hair out of your face."

I flinched as she pulled handfuls of hair behind one ear, then the other.

"I'm not down in the dumps," I said, squirming away. "I just don't know about this whole record shop thing. Especially here in the Cross." I folded my arms and lowered my head. "It gives me the willies being in this creepy place."

"Didn't I tell you, you'd be perfectly fine?" she said with the loudest volume she could afford in such a small space. "Your problem is you think too much. Now just give it a rest for a change."

"Hello, Brenda. Thanks for coming," said Maureen from somewhere behind us. "And is this Catherine? My goodness, you've become quite the young lady. You must have been about seven years old when I saw you last. How old are you now?"

"Seventeen," I replied.

"She'll be eighteen in April," Mum interjected.

"And you'd like to work in a record shop, your mother said?"

"Yes," I lied.

"Well, we're opening a new shop in the little arcade beside the Crest Hotel in a few weeks. We could do with some extra help. One worker will be enough down there, but we need two in this shop. Can you start tomorrow?"

My mother jumped in before I had a chance to open my mouth. "She'd love to."

"Mum! I've already made plans to go to the beach with Monica tomorrow."

"You'll have to change them." The increased lines on her 37-year-old face threw my hopes and plans out the door.

"I suppose so," I said.

"Are you sure?" asked Maureen.

"Perfectly sure," chimed my mother.

Maureen turned towards me. "Then I'll see you at half past eight tomorrow morning."

Back on the street, we waited for the bus while lunch hour in Kings Cross bristled on the footpath and in and out of doorways.

"Well that went well, didn't it?" Mum said. "I'm feeling a bit peckish now. I think we'll head straight to the cafeteria at David Jones. What do you think?" she asked, as if my response was worth anything.

"Was that her husband?" I asked regarding the rather short man who'd observed the goings-on in silence from behind the counter.

"Don't worry about him. Ed's a bit funny," Mum confided. "They've had a few problems over the years. He's okay. He doesn't say much. Just stay out of his road. Maureen runs the business. She's the one you have to worry about. Make sure you do as you're told or she'll fire you, and then you'll be stuck without a job."

"Then all I'll have to do is get married, and I won't have to worry about it, will I?"

Mum ignored me and fumbled in her bag for a cigarette.

"What about all these strip joints?" I asked. Pink Pussy Cat. Dive. Girls Galore. Nude Peep Show. Les Girls.

"They're just night clubs." She shook her head and grabbed my arm. "As the name suggests, they do their business at night. You're working in the day, so leave it alone. Besides, Les Girls is a female impersonation joint. That means they're blokes who dress up as showgirls. Bit sick, if you ask me."

Two well-dressed ladies, their transparent blue hair crimped close to their skulls, limped by. Arm in arm, they held each other up.

Mum let go of my arm. "How many times do I have to tell you there's nothing to worry about?" She dropped her plastic lighter on the footpath. "Dammit!"

She brushed my hand away when I held the cracked lighter in front of her. "I've got a box of matches in here somewhere." She rummaged around in her bag while the cigarette hung from the left side of her mouth. "God! I've got to clean this damn bag out one of these days. Give me that thing." She grabbed the lighter and threw it in.

"Why are those body-builder types standing in front of that place across the road?" I asked, looking at the burly, muscle-bound suits framed by a string of flashing lights running around the doorway.

"Thank God, there's one left." She struck the match along the side of the Redhead box. The cigarette bobbed up and down as she spoke. "They're bouncers. They get rid of people who cause trouble, and they keep the unsavoury types out."

"Who goes in if the unsavoury types are kept out?"

"Never mind," she snapped. Then, as if to offer some advice and salvage her motherliness, she said, "See that cheap-looking piece across the street?" A girl walked back and forth in front of the bottle shop. Her hair hung down her back. White hot-pants clung tight and short, and a drawstring top hung off one shoulder. "Well, that's one of those ladies of the night. She's the type I meant when I said if you don't look at them they won't bother you."

The next day Maureen put me to work within minutes of hiding my shoulder bag under the counter. "Time is money. Retail is not just sales, but also the maintenance of a clean and tidy shop," she said.

So in the morning I dusted the record bins with a rag soaked in Mr Sheen. After lunch, she showed me the alphabetical order to the records and modelled being a good saleswoman.

"First rule is to keep busy. There's always dusting, sweeping, unpacking, familiarising yourself with titles in the quiet times. Things like that. It looks bad if you just stand around. The customers will leave. No one wants to do business in a place where the salesgirl looks bored. Be confident and aggressive." She stared through the doorway and frowned. "What I mean is, be enthusiastic. You don't want to be annoying, but you don't want to be standoffish, either. Always ask the customer if you can be of help. And smile even if you don't feel like it." She winked. "If you can't find a record, just ask Ed or me. It might be out the back."

Ed looked up when he heard his name. He gave me a nod and went back to studying packing slips.

Many of the customers who wandered in and out during the day were boys about my age or a little older. They spoke with American accents. Overseas visitors were common in Sydney, but the ones who came into the shop that day all had the same kind of clean-cut look. I asked Maureen if they belonged to a youth group or something.

"Heavens no! Crikey, that's kind of funny. No, they're soldiers on leave from the war in Vietnam. Rest and relaxation I think they call it. R&R for short. Lots of those young fellas around here. Maybe a couple hundred come into Sydney every day. Here for about six days, I believe. Then gone again. Nice blokes on the whole. Well mannered. Not like those rich Texan loudmouths who complain that we're backwards and brag about how much bigger and better it is back home." She went to the front entrance and stared out beyond the pedestrians to the traffic. "I'm going to put you down in the new shop we're opening in the Crest Hotel. I've decided on the name already. The Concerto Record Bar. And you'll manage it."

"Manage it?" The very word startled me to near unconsciousness. "Do you think I know enough? I only have a little fory-five player at home and just a few records. Not even one LP."

"Of course you don't know much right now, but after a few weeks you'll know everything you need to." Her confidence shone a spotlight that focused somewhere off to the side, certainly not where I stood. "I'm sure you like music. The Concerto will cater to a younger crowd. We'll cater to the older lot, the ones that like the classics, jazz, the old-time dance tunes." Her face betrayed a distant longing. She looked at it then shook it off. "You can play whatever music you want down there. That will draw those young blokes in off the street. I don't like the psychedelic stuff. It's too boisterous. But these young fellas sure like it, and some of them are willing to buy lots of LPs to take back to the war with them."

I didn't like the psychedelic stuff either. I liked the lyrics and gentle tunes of ballads and folk music; the connectedness of pop; the beat, rhythm, and texture of Motown; and the beach images of surfer music. But being able to listen to whatever I wanted was as good as having my own record collection.

On my way home, the train roared through the tunnels that wove around the underground stations. When it emerged from the bowels into bright sunshine at Circular Quay, the beauty of Sydney Harbour struck me like the magnificent dawn of a new day.

The sun, reflected in the blue-green water, peered through the steel beams of the Harbour Bridge. Ferries carried commuters back home and others to the shops, events, and nightlife of the city. A moored ocean liner suggested dreams of exotic adventures, as it prepared for the next Pacific Island cruise.

The train plunged into the depths of darkened tunnels again to complete its city loop before emerging in the suburbs, where endless rows of red-roofed houses huddled one step back from the track. As the train settled into its familiar rattle, speed, and predictable stops, it established a mantra.

One thing the path ahead seemed to indicate was my escape from the captivity of well-meaning females.

Chapter 2

THE CONCERTO RECORD BAR

December 1967

During the first week of December, I became the manager and sole worker at the Concerto Record Bar. It took a while to realise that a new sensation, painted with pastel tones, was making its way into my general wellbeing. No uniforms, no rules, no nuns, no prefects, no assignments, and no exams translated into eight hours a day, from Monday to Friday, of pure and utter freedom—except when Maureen made her visits at three o'clock to remind me that I was neither alone nor the boss. On Saturdays, she turned up at eleven due to midday closing.

She checked that the Concerto was operating smoothly—that is to say that I was doing my job as an efficient salesgirl: friendly to the customers and presenting the business in the way she'd explained the first day. Although Maureen's stern demeanour posed a bit of a threat to my confidence, her clear expectations spared me from having to work procedures out for myself. She expressed her approval when things ran to her liking, and she wasted no time pointing out my shortcomings when she saw fit. Besides inspection, the other purpose of her daily visit was to clear the till, bag the money, and take it to the ANZ Bank before closing at three thirty.

Maureen was right. Americans on R&R were interested in perusing the latest releases. When it was all said and done, there would have been no sales at the Concerto without them. The majority of the R&R customers were guests at the Crest Hotel. The music of our generation called them as they walked through the tiny arcade on their way to Darlinghurst Road.

The word *friend* is not a usual term when referring to a virtual stranger. Yet in a sheltered upbringing, teenage sense of the word, friendships were made. We had no history, not even that of growing up in the same country, but more often than not, a feeling of familiarity and comfort swaddled our conversations and spilled over into letters once they got back to Vietnam.

They were told during their briefing upon arrival at the Chevron Hotel that they were representatives of the United States and, as such, to behave themselves. The Americans I met and observed on the streets, in the restaurants, and in the night-spots obeyed that order. Sometimes our relationship consisted merely of a few snatched moments in which we exchanged some thoughts and ideas. Other times it went deeper.

Just as stepping onto the plane after five days was the con-sequence of their R&R, asking for my address before they left was the consequence of our meeting, and writing letters when they returned to duty was the consequence of being soldiers in war. And so began my introduction to Vietnam when I was seventeen.

So absorbed was I, thumbing through the dockets and making a mental tally of the sales—and thinking how pleased Maureen would be—that I didn't notice him enter the shop.

"I like this song. It reminds me of my girl back home," he said.

At the sound of his voice the dockets flew off the counter. I dropped to the floor to gather the bits of paper that recorded the day's date, record titles, costs, and totals.

"Sorry, I hope I didn't frighten you."

"That's okay," I replied, emerging from behind the counter clutching the jumbled pieces of paper in both hands. "Can I help you?"

"You must be Catherine," said the stranger.

"How do you know my name?" I asked, quite convinced that my clumsiness had identified me to a perfect stranger.

"Billy wanted me to say hi and give you this." He handed me a folded sheet of paper that was sealed end to end with a single strip of sticky tape folded in the middle to secure each side. Directly below my name, THE CONCERTO RECORD BAR was printed in neat blue pen. "I just arrived this morning and since I didn't have anything else to do, I thought I'd drop it off." He looked at me through crystal-blue eyes. "I sure threw you off, huh?"

"It's fine, really." I tried not to sound flustered. He was handsome—movie star handsome—with a charm and accent to match.

"Mind if I take a look around?" he asked. "What else do you have by the Box Tops? I definitely want this one," he said, referring to "The Letter" coincidentally playing on the turntable. "Got anything by the Young Rascals? I really dig their music, too. By the way, I'm Tom."

"Hello, Tom." I pointed to the bins along the wall.

"Say, what's there to do in this town?" he asked, flipping through the LPs.

"There's quite a bit." His question heralded the response I'd rattled off several times before. "If you walk down Williams Street and turn right on George, you'll eventually get to Circular Quay. From there you can see the Sydney Harbour Bridge and our Opera House that has been under construction since 1959. You can also catch a ferry over to Manly Beach, Taronga Park Zoo, or Luna Park. You could walk to Centre Point, take an elevator to the top floor, and view the whole city."

I stopped to take a breath and noticed the camera slung over his shoulder. "You can get some great photos from up there. There's an amazing fountain in Hyde Park at the end of Williams Street. Lots of people go there to eat their lunch, sit and feed the birds, and just enjoy the brilliance of its sculptures. The Archibald Fountain is a tribute to the alliance between France and Australia during World War I. Also, there's a great museum diagonally across the street from Hyde Park on your left as you go down Williams Street, if you're interested in Australian culture."

His eyes had glazed over. He stifled a yawn. "I really want to buy a boomerang."

"There's a souvenir shop a few doors down and a larger one on Pitt Street. I can draw you a map if you like. They both sell kangaroo skins and stuffed koalas, if you're interested in meaningful souvenirs."

"Maybe," he replied. "What about the night life? I've heard Sydney is a pretty swinging town."

"Well, first of all, Sydney is a city, not a town. Three and a half million people, in fact."

"Hey, it's cool. Where I'm from we sometimes call a city a town, a term of endearment kind of thing if you know what I mean." He tried to smile but it turned into more of a nervous grin.

"Bourbon and Beefsteak is back up the street on the corner by the fountain," I continued. "You've probably noticed the fountain. Looks like a dandelion gone to seed. It's not the Hyde Park fountain, of course. This one's called the El Alamein Fountain and is dedicated to Australian soldiers who died in battle in 1942 while serving in Egypt."

"Oh?"

"Then there's the Texas Tavern just down from there," I said. "Finally, if you turn right when you leave here, and right again down Williams Street, the same Williams Street I was talking about before, you'll come to the Whisky A-Go-Go."

"Now we're talking. I heard the bad girls go there." He winked.

My cheeks took on a fiery glow. "I wouldn't know. I haven't been there myself."

"I've heard about some of these places from guys who've already been here. They all come back with stories of where they went, what they did, and who they met on R&R."

"Oh, there's one more spot. Martinz Place is on Martin Place in the heart of the city, across from the GPO. It's tamer than most of the nightclubs around here. It has a telephone on each table."

"Any chance you'd like to show me around?" he asked.

"No," I said, forcing back a "maybe."

"Well, I guess I'll see you later. Thanks for the help." He raised his eyebrows, smiled, and headed towards the door.

"Excuse me!" I called out, anxious to avoid a discrepancy in the day's take.

Tom stopped and turned.

"The record?" I said.

He snapped his fingers and walked back to the counter. "Geez, I'm sorry. I forgot all about it. I'm not used to being back in real life," he said. "Sure allowed myself to get distracted, didn't I?"

"I suppose so."

He leaned forward to take out a wallet from his back pocket. His aftershave caught my attention.

The rest of the day was steady though uneventful. Maureen, during her afternoon patrol, expressed her appreciation of the tally and suggested that perhaps it was time for a raise.

After work, the walk to the station took me down Williams Street and past Whisky A-Go-Go. It had never occurred to me before to venture into its darkened entryway. But tonight I wondered what it was like inside and if Tom would go there in a few hours.

On the train ride home, I thought for a moment what the *perhaps* meant in Maureen's talk about a raise. Then I reached inside my pocket and took out Billy's letter.

Dear Catherine,

I hope you received the roses by now. Were you surprised? I enjoyed every minute of your company, and thank you again for being nice and talking to me while I was there.

I got back to our base camp, but the tents were all deserted. They looked lonely and sad. Our company moved to a new area. We live on a hill now. It looks better, but the sleeping quarters are too crowded and congested.

I'm going to give this to one of the guys in my unit who is going to Sydney in a couple of days. His name is Tom. Hope you don't mind, but I think you'll receive this faster with him delivering it than if I send it through the post.

Bye, Billy
PS. I'll be waiting for your letter.

Chapter 3

AND SO IT BEGINS

Tom slipped into the record shop the next day as smoothly as ice cream melts on a warm day. He was still there chatting about American radio stations when Maureen walked in to collect the money for her afternoon deposit. She hardly said a word but was visibly disappointed at the takings this time. She glanced at Tom on her way out. Just inside the door, she stopped, ran her fingers over some plastic covers, and shook her head. Tom didn't seem to notice.

"Would you like to have coffee after work?" he asked.

"Yes, I would," I surprised myself by saying.

"What's a good place around here?"

"La Tête-à-Tête," I said without hesitation. "It's on the other side of the street about half way up the block."

"See you then." He turned and walked out the door. His aftershave stayed behind and this time made me anxious for the workday to end. I was yet to learn to be wary what I wished for.

Maureen returned just before closing and marched from one end of the shop to the other. She pulled out the wooden stool, sat down, and slapped both hands on the counter. "We're closing this shop. I know it's early, but if the Christmas trade is this bad, imagine what it'll be like later."

"People don't know about the Concerto yet, Maureen," I protested. "It's still new and it's out of the way. Just wait until the word gets around. Customers will come flocking in from all over."

"I can't wait that long, I'm afraid. It's already costing us money. Unless…unless I send Ed down here." Her eyes darted from wall to wall. "Oh forget it, that won't work either. I don't trust him on his own. Well, whatever I decide—Ed and I decide—about the future of this shop, I have to let you go. I'm sorry, Catherine. I don't have a problem with your work, and I know I talked yesterday about a possible raise. But this place just isn't supporting itself, let alone making a profit. Saturday will be your last day."

Stunned, I began the preparations for closing. I cleared the docket book and pens off the counter and ran two flannelette bed sheets over the bins to protect the covers from overnight dust. Maureen remained on the stool.

"I suppose we could give it another month." She seemed to be talking herself into something. "See how it goes. Give you one more chance to see if you can build up the business."

"I really don't know anything about running a business, Maureen, let alone one in the record industry. I told you that the first day."

"We'll stay open another month," she continued, ignoring what I'd said. "We'll decide what to do then. Besides, I need someone to do the odd run to Double Bay, Bondi Junction, and the City to pick up records. I'm too busy for all of that."

Clouded and bewildered, I locked up for the day and walked to the traffic lights in front of the Goldfish Bowl, a bar attached to the Crest Hotel with a view in and out, as the name suggested. As I waited for the light to turn red, a whoosh of air from a thunderous blue streak pushed me back from the curb and blew my knee-length skirt in a condensed Marilyn Monroe version—minus the flaring white billows and shy though flirtatious giggle. My eyes shut tight in response to another whoosh, followed immediately by another. I squinted through the percussion of warm air to see the fourth bus zoom by and caught fleeting glimpses of weary Americans in khaki shirts and pointed caps.

"Four busloads just arrived from the airport," I said, pulling out a chair opposite Tom, already waiting at the coffee shop. Once again the brilliant blue of his eyes caught my breath.

"They're late, poor bastards. The plane is scheduled to arrive in the morning. I wonder what caused the holdup," he said, mostly to himself.

La Tête-à-Tête, situated on Darlinghurst Road, sat between a fruit shop and a florist, making its location ideal for attracting passers-by as well as a reliable flow of regulars.

Tom had chosen a table by the door. Grace, the waitress, and Paul, the cook—her boyfriend—sat at the back table on their cigarette break. Paul leafed through the *Daily Telegraph*, occasionally commenting on an article or headline. Grace rested her chin on the palm of her right hand and stared down the aisle through the door, taking a breather during the lull before the evening rush.

"What's wrong?" Tom asked.

"Nothing," I said.

Grace appeared at our table, pen poised on the docket pad, ready to take our order.

"Two cappuccinos. Lots of froth, thanks," I said, without bothering to ask Tom for his preference. "They make the best cappuccinos in Sydney here."

Paul had sauntered to the entrance where he could look out at nothing in particular. He stopped at our table on his way back.

"How's business over at the Concerto?" he asked.

"Not good," I replied. "Maureen's probably going to close it at the end of January."

"So that's what's wrong," said Tom.

Grace gave Paul a slight elbow before placing the cups and saucers on the table.

"Is Lara serious about getting someone for the weekends?" he hollered after Grace as she stomped to the kitchen. "Or is she too cheap?"

"She's serious," Grace snapped. "We're both getting tired of working seven days a week. Incidentally, if you keep chatting up the customers like that, you just might have to find yourself a new job. Lara's been pretty good to you, don't forget."

"Okay, okay," he said, shoving off her remark. "I was just thinking that Catherine should talk to her since Maureen's closing the Concerto."

"Not for sure," I corrected, "but there's a good chance."

"That's fine, but it wouldn't hurt to meet her," said Paul. "She should be here any minute now."

On cue, a tall woman in a black pantsuit strode past our table. Eau de Toilette lingered in her wake.

"Well, speak of the devil," Paul said.

"Watch it, mouth!" threatened his boss.

"Wait here," said Paul as he left.

"Striking woman," said Tom.

"Is she?" I asked.

Tom was in the middle of explaining that he preferred black coffee when Paul reappeared at our table. "Her majesty will talk to you now," he said, clearly pleased with his effort.

I stood and straightened my skirt. "This won't take long," I said to Tom. "Watch my bag for me?"

An elegant, older woman in her mid to late thirties (not quite *striking* as Tom had said, I thought), Lara wore her blond hair swept up in a French roll. She pointed to the table and signalled me to sit.

"Paul said you're interested in weekend work." Her voice was stern, even more so than Maureen's. Its threat, though, was softened measurably by a slight lisp.

"I'm waiting for my Higher School Certificate results," I said. "If I go to university it won't be until March. I'd like to work as much as possible until then. I'm still at the Concerto 'til the end of January. But I could work Saturday afternoons as well as Sundays. And Monday to Friday after January."

Lara placed her right elbow on the table and tapped her finger on her lips. "All right then, you'll work Saturdays and Sundays, ten 'til six both days to start off. If things work out, I'll put you on through the week. I'd like you to wear a short pleated skirt. Any colour will do as long as it's not orange—too much of a clash with red table cloths. And a white top. It gets pretty busy in here and you'll work up a sweat. You won't want to wear anything too restricting. Do you have any questions?"

"But I just said I could only work Saturday afternoons and all day Sunday until the end of January. After that I can work whenever you need me. At least until I know what my schedule is in March."

"All right then. Twelve thirty 'til six on Saturdays, until the end of January. On Sundays you'll work the ten-to-six shift. You'll start Saturday, January sixth, at twelve thirty." She stood. The interview was over.

Tom insisted on walking me to St James Railway Station. A dozen or so Americans from the war, and perhaps their father's dairy farm before that, stood under the lighted awning outside Whisky A-Go-Go, seemingly disconnected from each other—apart from their ubiquitous short hair. Two of them, dressed in dark suits and new shoes, stepped off the curb into the traffic bustle, hoping to outdo each other in their bid for an approaching taxi. Another one engaged in serious conversation with a girl who appeared to have the upper hand. A few stood as though waiting for the order that would direct their next move. A board on a pedestal announced free cocktails from six until seven.

"Great! It's only six thirty. You really should check this place out," Tom said.

"I thought you said the bad girls go there."

"I did. Let's go."

Dusk spread out its backdrop for the streetlights, head-lights, and flashing neon signs that announced evening on Williams Street, the corridor between Kings Cross and the city. Tom put his hand on my waist and moved me into the foyer, the effort so smooth it felt like I'd stepped onto a mov-ing footpath. We slid by one of those bouncers whose job Mum had said was to keep unsavoury types out. A coat check counter to the right provided a recognisable spot to wait for friends, if there were any.

Granny's warnings whispered in my ear as we entered the dazzling cave. Spotlights lit up a small parquet dance floor, and sparkling cages glittered along the walls. Half a dozen men in suits hung over the bar. A smattering of eager patrons occupied five or so tables. They sat, sipped, and waited. Although there was nothing in particular going on, anticipa-tion hung in the air, lit up by a taped recording by the Four Tops, "Baby I Need Your Lovin'."

"What can I get you?" asked Tom. This was the fit of a comfortable chair for him, just as the coffee shop had been for me.

"Nothing, thanks."

"Oh, come on, I drank cappuccino with you. Now it's your turn to have a drink with me."

"Okay," I said, feeling a bit prudish. "I'll have a Coke, thank you." The thought of a soft drink—especially Coke that I'd only been allowed to have on school excursions to the Coca-Cola bottling factory once a year—felt rebellious and daring.

"With bourbon or whisky?"

First Granny and now the nuns marched into Whisky A-Go-Go like bright shining stars reminding me that if I failed to say no to alcohol, I would either become pregnant or get a disease, and possibly both.

"Coke is all I want, thanks."

"You're kidding me!" His eyes widened.

"I'm not kidding you. Three years ago I took a pledge not to drink until I turn twenty-one," I said, as though nothing was out of the ordinary. "By not drinking 'til then I'll get a soul out of Purgatory. I even have a certificate on my wall to prove it. This is how the pledge goes: For Thy greater consolation, O Sacred Heart of Jesus; for Thy sake to give good example, to practise self-denial, to make reparation to Thee for the sins of intemperance and for the conversion of excessive drinkers, I promise in honour of the Sacred Heart and with the help of the Blessed Virgin Mary to abstain from intoxicating drink until my twenty-first birthday."

"Poor girl. How long have you got before you can have a drink?"

"Three years and four months."

"You're gonna get awfully thirsty."

"Maybe." I felt silly. The security of Granny's hot and humid kitchen called me. The familiar aroma of her meals would overpower its clutter and stale cigarette smell, and protect me from temptation. "I should be getting home," I said, without looking at him.

Tom offered no objection. I was surprised when he insisted on walking me to the station.

"Maybe I'll drop in to see you at work again tomorrow," he said as he stood beside me in front of the turnstile.

"I'll tell you about all the bad girls I met at the Whisky," he teased.

My breath escaped in a rush as he leaned over and placed a gentle kiss on my cheek before turning to walk away.

"Wait," I said. He stopped and faced me. "When do you leave?"

"Christmas Day. I'll see you tomorrow," he said. Then he turned towards Hyde Park and back to Kings Cross.

While jostling with other commuters at the turnstile, I glanced back. He had already disappeared. My hand reached up to capture the kiss where he'd left it.

"Ticket please, miss," barked the ticket collector in his most official *thought you were going to get away with it but you're not because I'm on duty* voice.

City workers bumped past as I stood off to the side and fumbled in my purse for the weekly pass that allowed me to avoid queues and long waits. As he checked other tickets, he kept one eye on me in case I was one of those nasty types who'd try to sneak through. As I searched for my pass, thoughts of Christmas and what this one meant for Tom crept in. An oversized lady decorated with a beehive hairdo squeezed through the turnstile, flailing festive gold and red bags. She lost her balance and leaned towards me. I found my yellow pass just in time to help her steady. The ticket collector, satisfied it was the right colour for the week, gave me the nod to go through.

The spices and smells that announced Friday night's usual dish—tuna curry and rice—greeted me at the front gate. Granny was the one who assembled the meals, and as a rule she was also the one who cleaned up the mess afterwards.

If Mum ever cooked a meal, the memory, together with its taste, was long gone. After standing on her feet all day as a dental assistant, Mum was excused from household responsibilities. Besides, a call into the club for a pull on the pokies before going home meant she'd be too late to participate in dinner preparations anyway.

Often while the vegetables boiled, Granny and I would sit at the kitchen table and share our day. We'd resume our tales and weave them together as if creating a quilt of memories with our words. On other evenings our together time would take place after the dishes were cleared. She'd light up a cigarette and deal out the cards for a game of Patience, preparing to listen. The table, covered with the same stone-patterned Mactac that covered the counters, was secured to the wall at one end and supported by a fixed leg at the other. Immovable benches with lift-up seats ran the length of the table on either side. They housed *Women's Weekly*, *Woman's Day*, and *New Idea* magazines dating back at least ten years.

"Tell me about your day, love," Granny said, hungry for the crumbs of life outside her narrowing world. She'd been active as a young person, sewing for others, playing tennis and lawn bowls, taking on executive positions. In her later years, she was satisfied to spin her yarns of days gone by and make the odd bet on the Saturday trots, as well as soak up my present-day versions of youthful discovery.

"I had coffee with an American after work. He's going back to Vietnam on Christmas Day. He's a really nice fellow, Granny, and I was wondering if he could spend Christmas Eve with us. Some of the boys from Housie are going sailing on Saturday. A few of us girls are going along to watch. We're planning a picnic and I'm going to ask him to join us."

"Where did you meet this fellow?" she asked.

"He came into the shop looking for some records to take back to Vietnam, and we just started talking," I explained.

Granny, her grey hair turned blue with a regular Saturday morning rinse over the kitchen sink, continued to rotate her cards in hopes of completing all four suits.

"I suppose that would be all right," she said after some consideration. "I could do a leg of lamb and roast some veggies. Are you going to make that fruit cake?" she asked. "It's almost too late. The flavours won't have a chance to work their way through."

I smiled. "I'll make the cake right now, Granny."

"He could come to Midnight Mass with us and then catch a taxi back to the Cross," she said. "What's his name again?"

"Tom."

"That's a nice name."

For the past few years, it had been my responsibility to bake the rich fruit and nut Christmas cake. I dug through the many scraps of tattered paper and magazines kept in the drawer by the stove and finally found the *Barossa Valley Cookery Book* that Granny's cousin, Peter Lehmann, had given her on one of her visits to his winery. I never remembered the right page, but every time I leafed through, I found other tempting recipes I'd like to try some day. When I found my favourite Christmas cake recipe, it felt like opening the lid on a rare treasure.

"Soak the fruit and nuts in brandy first," she said. "It's supposed to be overnight, but some of the recipes in there don't even require you to soak them at all. They just throw everything together all at once."

"Well, we won't be soaking them this time. It's going to be the last-minute throw-it-all-in-together version. Can you get me the brandy, Granny? I'll get everything else."

"That's funny," she said after rummaging through the cupboards above the fridge. "I could have sworn this bottle was almost full. You'll be lucky if you can squeeze out half a cup."

"That's all I need," I said. "And one more thing, Granny. Would you mind cutting the brown paper to line the tin?"

Together we cut, measured, mixed, and sampled the batter.

"You didn't think I'd get it done this year, did you?" I said once it was in the oven.

"I knew you'd pull through. Now, clean this mess up, you little stinker. Or I'll be tanning your hide."

"Did the postie come today?"

"I forgot to look. He's been coming a bit later with the extra Christmas mail."

"I'll check."

Letters from Vietnam were like surprises that I came to anticipate.

Dear Catherine,

It was really good to meet you. My records made it back here safe and sound.

There isn't much to say about having to spend the first Christmas in my life away from home and without snow. I suppose you are used to no snow at Christmas time but it will be a first for me. It was about 100 degrees here yesterday.

I'm now what's known as a two digit midget, meaning I'm so short that I have less than 100 days left in the Army!

Thought I'd give you something to do until school starts. It's a short timer's calendar. On December 13, I had 97 days to go, so when you receive it you can fill in the days that were missed in mailing. Don't get ahead because it's very unlucky. Happiness really is being short.

Your friend, James

Chapter 4

INFATUATION

Christmas Eve 1967

Christmas Eve closed in like a sauna. Even without the sun burning in the sky, summer nights refused to cool down and guaranteed a scorcher the next day. The odd southerly buster brought gusting winds and buckets of rain that drenched the city, giving dried up petals, leaves, and dreams a second chance.

Since Christmas Eve fell on Sunday, Granny and I were duty-bound to attend Mass twice. In the morning we walked the familiar route to St Joseph's Catholic Church on Canterbury Road. The footpath was well worn where pilgrims past and present had etched their passage into the concrete slabs. Every gouge and every bump conjured up a memory of experiences past.

Inside the large light-brick church, the congregation fanned themselves and each other with missals, handkerchiefs, gloves, hats, and whatever light paper or fabric would break up the heavy air. As faithful sinners, we focused on the Christmas message that Father O'Connor would more than likely repeat at midnight. It was something to do with last-minute gift giving, spending unnecessarily, presents jumping out at him in shops as he walked the aisles. And of course, the greatest gift of all, which I thought he said was love.

On the way home, Granny and I walked arm in arm and planned for our guest. Our feminine desire to nurture hoped to provide the warm memory of being in a home at Christmas that Tom could take back to the war. The cicadas screeched from their vantage point in neighbours' trees, annoying every nerve in my body.

Once inside, Granny whipped off her hat and gloves, placed them on top of each other on the grey lowboy in her bedroom, and proceeded to the kitchen. She tied on her favourite Christmas pinny, the one patterned with white bows, green ivy, and red berries.

She took the knife out of the drawer and sharpened it on the stone she kept by the stove. Granny often reminded visitors how proud she was of her little green Metters. "One of the best electric stoves ever made," Laurie, her electrician nephew, had told her when she and Grandpa moved into the house in 1950.

She opened the bench and pulled out one of the newspapers kept for collecting peels, shells, seeds, and cigarette ash. She knelt on one knee and clutched the counter by the fridge. Green and grey veins poked through sun-spotted skin. She bent lower until she reached the potatoes she kept in the porcelain bowl. Then she assembled the things she required— including cigarettes and ashtray—and sat down at the table to peel the potatoes and shell the peas. My mouth watered when she said, "Roast potatoes and peas with mint sauce and gravy. That's what we'll have with the leg of lamb."

Mum had enjoyed Sunday morning solitude in her pink dressing gown, sipping tea and eating buttered toast burned to her liking. Our reappearance inspired her to contribute to the household in some way other than just being civil. After vacuuming the carpets in the lounge and dining rooms, she opened a beer to cool off. She had another and then declared she was going to have a bit of a lie down.

"Get out the Christmas tablecloth, dearest, and set the table, will you?" Granny asked me. "We'll use the good cutlery. Have a look under the sideboard. I think that's where I put the box last time I moved things around. Oh, and set out the wine glasses."

Something in the word and in the loving way Granny called me *dearest* warmed my heart every time she said it. In a profound but subtle way, she introduced me to the power of words and their ability to lift or bury another spirit.

"Are the matching serviettes there?" she called from the kitchen. "Do they need an iron?"

"They're here. And yes, they could do with a bit of an iron," I replied.

"Ask your mother to do them for me then."

"She's sleeping," I said, already setting up the ironing board in the back-room extension beyond the kitchen. "Better not disturb her."

Granny dolloped the leg of lamb with lard she kept in a silver-ridged tin that once contained raspberry jam. The drippings, as she called it, had been poured into the tin from previous roasts and kept on the counter beside the stove. She scooped up generous amounts of salt to season the fatty meat. After sixty years of smoking, her tastebuds demanded a substantial amount of salt beyond what was normal or acceptable. Despite the fat and the salt—or perhaps because of it—the aroma of a leg of lamb cooking in Granny's oven promised the nourishment our bodies and souls craved.

"God, I didn't realise it was that late. Completely went out to it," Mum slurred in a groggy voice. "What can I do?"

"It's all under control," Granny said in a forgiving manner. "Just get yourself ready."

Mum took a wine glass from the table, pulled out an opened bottle of cheap Riesling from the fridge, and filled her glass to the top.

"I'll just have a quick smoke and then I'll get ready," she announced.

I cringed with too many memories of occasions ruined when Mum drank beyond her limits, and could only hope it wouldn't happen this time.

With the food and the house preparations under control, each of us, according to our own generation's model of self-beautification, prepared our hair and our faces and decided what to wear. Granny touched up her red lipstick, a regular habit she'd practiced over the years, even before going to bed. "Just in case I die in my sleep," she'd say. By six o'clock we anticipated Tom's taxi pulling up outside.

Three generations of women drifted into the lounge room and sat by the Christmas tree, mesmerised by the coloured Christmas lights.

"I wonder if he lost the address," I said at six thirty.

"Can you get hold of him? What's his phone number?" Mum asked, sipping her third glass of wine.

"I don't know where he's staying. I forgot to ask."

"What do you know about this bloke anyway, Catherine?" Mum demanded.

"Not much. Just that he's a really nice guy. He's fun. He's—"

"He's late is what he is," she said. "You can't trust these blokes. They're here today and gone tomorrow. You'd better start watching yourself or you'll end up in all sorts of trouble. I spoke to Maureen yesterday, and she's not happy with that new record shop you're supposed to be running. She's closing it at the end of January. What are you going to do then?" She lit a cigarette. "I think you're spending far too much time talking to these American fellas. And not enough time doing what you're supposed to be doing," she lectured. "You're damn lucky I got that job for you. And now you're going to lose it. You've got to work; I can't do it all by myself anymore." Mum paused her diatribe to take a sip of wine. "I think you'd better get out of the Cross. You seem to be distracted up there."

"It's fine, Mum. I've already lined up another job." Without allowing her time to process the idea, the next words—which probably should have stayed locked away—flowed effortlessly out of my mouth. "I kind of like it at the Cross. It's interesting."

"Another job?" she charged. "Doing what?"

"Waitressing—"

"Waitressing up there? No bloody way! I won't have it." She gulped down the remainder of her glass and stood up to get a refill.

"You're the one who took me up there in the first place and said I'd be fine."

"That was different," she yelled. "Maureen was going to look out for you."

"I don't need anyone looking out for me. I can look out for myself quite well, thank you."

"Don't you cheek me, miss. You have no idea what you're talking about."

Granny rose from her chair and headed for the kitchen. "Well, let's eat. There's a perfectly good dinner getting ruined. I think he'd be here by now if he was coming, don't you? I'll do up an extra plate and keep it in the oven, just in case he turns up later."

"A taxi just pulled up out front," called Mum, interrupting her trip to the kitchen in order to check her hair in the bathroom mirror.

I watched through the screen door as Tom opened and closed the wrought iron gate and walked up the path to the veranda. I could feel myself beam. The awkwardness I felt when he first walked into the record shop was gone.

"I'm so sorry, Catherine. I'm not ready to meet your folks yet. I want to explain what happened. Can we go for a walk?"

"Tom's here," I called. "We'll be back in a bit."

I pushed past him and grabbed his hand. We bustled down the steps ahead of the tirade of objections sure to be fired through the screen door.

"It's difficult for me to put this into words. But I want to try so that you'll understand." He took a deep breath. "I was kind of stupid. I was going to make up this lie about forgetting the time, but the truth is I didn't want to come here tonight. I didn't want to spend my last night and Christmas Eve with you and your folks, so I went to the Whisky."

"No one was forcing you to come here. You could have just said you wanted to do something else," I said.

He stopped under a streetlight and grabbed both my arms. "The truth is I was scared to see you. I tried to tell myself that it didn't mean anything. But I feel like the GI in the movies who falls in love and has to leave. I never imagined meeting someone like you and having the feelings I do. I wish I could just pack you up in my bag and take you with me. I know it's crazy, but the fact of the matter is I feel like I've known you all my life."

"Even though I took that pledge?" I asked.

"Even though you took that silly pledge," he answered. "Let's go back to the house so I can meet your folks."

The evening happened around us. Tom and I, lost in our togetherness, captured and attempted to freeze time. We soaked up every bit of the relationship as we knew it—an interlude together provided by the hours, minutes, and seconds we had before he would leave. Granny served the leg of lamb. There was enough wine left for each of them to have a sip. I filled my glass with water from the tap. After the meal, I served the cake. We drank tea and played cards. Mum talked about her husband, referring to him as "Catherine's father, who was in the Air Force when we met."

"Nineteen years it will be this coming New Year's Eve," she reminisced, with a glow of the youth she'd say was taken away from her by "that bloody bastard" who'd promised the world and then left her with a child to raise on her own.

Nevertheless, she spoke as though the day was a legitimate anniversary, even though he'd been gone so long I had no recollection of his physical presence.

Granny made up a tin of Anzac biscuits she'd baked especially for Tom to take back to Vietnam. At eleven thirty, we walked—Granny and I for the second time that day—to St Joseph's Church to attend midnight Mass. This time it was Mum and Granny arm in arm while Tom and I followed hand in hand.

Solemn spirits housed in their temples' best finery lined up in the pews outside the confessionals to purge themselves of all evil before the Birth.

"Would you like to go?" I asked Tom.

"Where?"

"Confession," I said.

"No thanks."

Father O'Connor, as far as I could tell, repeated his morning sermon. But I couldn't be sure.

With the closing down of Christmas Eve, Granny sliced potted meat and served it on toast. A Christmas and Easter tradition, potted meat was one of those unwritten recipes that had been passed from mother to daughter through the generations. So far, it had only got as far as Granny.

Tom and I sipped more black tea tempered with milk, as the inevitability of separation closed in around us.

"I've got a second wind. I'll drive you back to your hotel," Mum announced out of the blue. "Let's go, mate. You can come too, Catherine."

Granny got up from her chair and in her grandma way of moving, quickly darted to the kitchen.

"Don't forget your bikkies." She handed him the tin she'd been saving for such an occasion and gave him a good-luck-and-look-after-yourself hug.

Mum insisted that Tom take the privileged position beside her in the green Morris Minor, relegating me to the backseat. As we waited to turn left onto Canterbury Road—ribboned with revellers making their way back home—I leaned forward and grabbed his fingers, squeezed between the door and the seat.

Tom and I talked about life and what's important as though we had forever to figure it out. Mum listened or was lost in her own world. We dropped him off outside his hotel, and he waited at the curb while I scrambled out of the back to occupy the seat of privilege. A final hug and we were gone. He was gone.

"Well, he was a nice enough fella," said Mum. "A bit on the quiet side for my liking, though. And I didn't like the way the two of you took off when he arrived, either. What was that all about? Did he tell you why he was late?"

I shook my head and turned away. Tears blurred the parade of houses, darkened in anticipation of the joyful morning the seasonal hymns proclaimed. The passing parade served to dull the blade of my mother's tongue. In the early hours of Christmas Day, we turned and snaked along deserted roads in the dull roar of silence.

Unlike some families, we didn't put our gifts under the tree until Christmas morning. It was a carryover from childhood days when Santa Claus included our house in his around-the-world trip. The Southern Hemisphere, we believed, was last on the list. It was forbidden to get up early, poke, prod, shake, or search for hidden treasures in the branches. For the first time, I was not tempted by the decorated packages. One gift, though, would spark a feeling of warmth and gratitude. A diary from Granny.

Uncles, aunties, and cousins came for Christmas dinner in the late afternoon. Friends dropped in to offer good cheer. I wondered how Granny managed to keep going, preparing oven-cooked meals in a cramped kitchen when outside it was so hot.

The bustle of Christmas day finally subsided and Mum passed out on the couch. Granny and I finished washing up the last of the dishes. With a loud sigh, she announced, "Well, dearest, I'm calling it a day. Hope you had a lovely Christmas. I've done my best but now I must lie down. Before I fall down."

I hung the damp tea towel over the bench and turned to give her a hug. "Are you shrinking, or am I growing?" I asked.

"Probably a bit of both, I'd say. You're my blossoming dearest and I, I'm afraid, am starting to stoop and droop from years of bending over a bloody sink. Just getting old. The sewing hasn't helped the situation either. Remember to keep a good straight back. Don't slouch or you'll shrink and end up just like me."

"I'd be proud to end up just like you," I said.

"That's the best Christmas present I could ever receive, apart from the little griller you gave me, of course, which will come in handy. Are you going to bed now?"

"In a while. Is there still some of that fancy writing paper I gave you for your birthday?" I asked. "Could I borrow a couple of pages and an envelope?"

"Check the top draw on the right of the sideboard. I think you'll find it there. Try not to be too late. You don't want to over tax yourself," Granny whispered before disappearing behind her bedroom door.

Now that the house was quiet, I sat down at the kitchen table, stared into the emptiness of nothing, and began to write.

December 25, 1967

Dear Tom,

You might still be on the plane flying back to Vietnam. I don't know how long it takes. You must be pretty tired.

It's really hot here today. We had our Christmas dinner with the uncles, aunties, and cousins. Granny cooked chicken, gravy, mashed potatoes, and string beans followed by my favourite plum duff with custard. Afterwards, Monica and Peter came over and we listened to records.

I hope I didn't upset you when I asked you to go to confession last night. I could tell you really didn't want to and I wish I hadn't asked. I just always go and I thought you might want to. I'm sorry

"Granny's gone to bed, has she? What are you doing still up? You should get yourself off to bed, too." Mum threw out a barrage of rhetorical questions and statements without expecting a response to any of them. As usual.

I'd put down my pen and folded my arms over the paper when I heard her stumbling around, but it was too late.

"Who's that you're writing to?" she demanded. "Not that Yank, I hope. Do you want a cuppa? I'm going to make one to take to bed."

"No thanks."

"Don't be too long. And don't waste your time on this guy, Catherine. He's gone. You won't see him again. Just like your father. You can't trust him. You can't trust any of them, I tell you. Just wait and see. I bet you won't hear from him. You won't hear from him when he gets back to the States and his girlfriend or wife or whatever he has back there, that's for sure. You're just going to end up getting hurt. And when it happens, don't say I didn't warn you. Are you sure you don't want a cuppa?"

"No thanks. Night, Mum. Have a good sleep." I waited for her to go back to her room, our room, the room that contained a wardrobe, a dressing table, and two single beds. I continued my letter.

Mum just asked what I was doing. When I said I was writing to you she said to say hello. Have you heard from your parents? What did they send you for Christmas?

I already miss you. I'm really looking forward to hearing from you. Please write soon and be good.

Your Friend, Catherine.
PS. Say hi to Billy and tell him I'll be writing soon.

Chapter 5

GONE

January 1968

My enthusiasm for the Concerto Record Bar started to decline immediately after Maureen expressed her doubts about its future. More than that though, every sad love song found its way out of its plastic jacket and onto the turntable over and over again. Reinforcing. Validating. Digging and scraping deeper into the painful pit Tom's absence had drilled. Even the walls seemed to write ballads to him, imploring him to return. But with the same certainty and suddenness as death, he was gone.

One thing my mother's useless cycle of loving, hating, blaming, and longing had taught me was that in order to stop playing the same record over and over for the rest of my life, I would have to move on. Occupy my time and my thoughts with new energies. No matter how hard it was, I had to lift myself up and out of the dark places. So I planned a New Year's Eve party. Nothing big. Just a few friends who'd been around so long it seemed they'd been there forever.

With memories of my father floating dangerously close to the surface, my mother once again visited the bottle, that deceptive cure for pain. My parents' journey of doom had begun its downward spiral when they were introduced at a New Year's Eve dinner dance held at Forest Hill RAAF base. The nineteen-year-old girl and the nineteen-year-old boy welcomed in 1948 and became casualties of the post-war lust for life and living. My mother got violently ill on prawns that night. From then on, every New Year's Eve posed a bittersweet contradiction shaped by memories of meeting the man of her dreams (the one she married), heaving her guts out, and the reality of her abandonment.

She nurtured her resentment by going over it again and again, both out loud and in her mind. Day to day irritations inevitably became issues of betrayal. No matter how many times she replayed the tragedy, she remained stuck in the mire of self-loathing, all of it caused by the disgrace and embarrassment of her husband's abandonment. Replaying the tragedy seemed to comfort my mother. It was something familiar she could grab hold of. Her pain granted her the permission to unleash her pent-up anger. Her anger gave meaning to her life. Or so it seemed.

Tom's letter was waiting on the kitchen table. I could hardly wait to open it.

Dear Catherine,

I was very happy to hear from you. I must say again how much I enjoyed being with you and your family Christmas Eve. You and your folks made my Christmas one that I shall never forget as long as I may live. I would love to return and do it all over again.

Only this time I'd be on time. Besides, I am anxious to sample some more of your cooking.

I think you may have thought I was crazy when we went to Mass, but my mind was filled with all sorts of emotions. I felt sad, glad, good, bad, lonely, and yet I felt that I was with dear, close friends because you were there. You could never imagine all the things that were going through my mind that night.

I had two hours in Saigon the other day and I stopped by the little chapel at the heliport and said a prayer for you and your folks. I am sure a family as nice as yours is well watched over by God but I just thought I would put my two cents worth in.

I hope this letter finds you all happy and healthy, "May God Bless and Keep You All."

Your American Friend, Tom
PS. I'll be going home in four days. I am going to enclose my home address. I am really looking forward to receiving letters from you.

"Well, how is he? Did he make it back okay? Did he have anything to say about the biscuits?" asked Granny, anxious to read the letter herself.

"He's fine. Yes, he seems to be back in the swing of things. He didn't say anything about the biscuits, but I'm sure he enjoyed them. He didn't give me his address in the States and he's going home in four days," I answered, with the hope of satisfying Granny's need for information. "I can't possibly get a letter to him in that short time. Unless he writes to me, I won't be able to write back. Maybe Mum was right. Maybe he does have a girlfriend or a wife, and this is his way of saying goodbye. Not that we were boyfriend and girlfriend," I said, thinking out loud.

"Of course not," she said. "Still, there was something, wasn't there, dearest?"

"He apologises for being late Christmas Eve. And he said a prayer for us in Saigon. I wonder if he noticed the perfume. I sprayed a little of Mum's Chanel No. 5 on my hands and rubbed them on the envelope."

"Why don't you reply straight away and send it to his address in Vietnam?" Granny said with a hint of sadness.

"I don't know. He said the Army wasn't very good at forwarding mail, so he probably wouldn't get it anyway."

Chapter 6

DO WE EVER REALLY KNOW?

Mid-January heat and humidity blanketed the city like layers in a pottery kiln. After closing the Concerto for the day, I called into the Goldfish Bowl for a glass of orange juice and crushed ice before tackling the thirty-minute sweat walk to St James Station. Carol—barely an acquaintance—took my order. We nattered on about the weather and its effect on business.

"Do you mind if I join you?" she said, as she placed the glass on the table. "I've just finished my shift."

"No, of course not." Carol's request took me by surprise.

"I've wanted to talk to you for a while." Her smile was quick and awkward. Oddly, her intensity both intrigued and flattered me. But once she found her feet she wasted no words. "This is about Tom."

My Tom I almost said. "The American," I said instead, "who went back to Vietnam on Christmas Day? Is that who you're talking about?"

She nodded.

"How do you know him?"

"I met him at the Whisky. We went out at night. I saw you walk past with him a couple of times. I know he went to your place Christmas Eve."

She removed a packet of Kools from her pocket and placed it on the table. She slid out a cigarette like a connoisseur about to savour a delicious chocolate and lit up. Her neatly manicured nails blended into the milky softness of her fingers and hands.

I thought of Mum and her Saturday afternoon nail ritual, when she'd scrub the week away with a polish remover that insulted any nostrils within sniffing distance. After removing every hint of the previous week's colour, she'd saw back and forth with a steel nail file to get rid of snags. Then she'd sculpt and refine the rounded shape she preferred. Next, she'd spread out her fingers on the table and conceal the documentation of her health, as recorded in her nails, with brilliant colour. In the final step she'd shake her wrist vigorously and blow a steady stream of smoke breath on them. When she was tired of blowing, she'd place her elbow on the table and shake her hand, more gently this time, like a drooping flag on an almost windy day. From start to finish, the procedure took three cups of tea and three cigarettes.

"Do you like him?" I asked Carol, afraid of the answer.

"Of course I do. It's hard not to like a boy like him," Carol said. "Did you know he's thinking of extending his tour in Vietnam?"

"Why would he do that?" I asked. "He hates Vietnam, and the Army even more," I said, as if I knew all about the person I'd spent a few hours with and fallen in love with that

Christmas Eve—or whatever those feelings of *don't go* and *longing* and *I miss you* were all about.

"Exactly. That's why he's doing it. So he can get out of the Army early. And, so he can get another R&R or a leave, which is a day or two longer." She looked down at the floor. I stared through the window. The icy drink gave me a head rush.

"Why are you telling me this?"

"I'm just trying to be honest. You can't trust a lot of people around here. Everybody's out for what they can get. I thought that if I told you we both liked the same person, well, it would kind of give us something in common. Create a bond between us. Maybe it was a bad idea. Would you like another drink?" She slid her chair backwards to stand.

"No thanks." You think you know someone. Then it hits you square in the gut that you don't know them at all. "I got a letter that said he was going home this month but he didn't include his address in America. Are you writing to him?"

"No."

"Do you want his address in Vietnam? That's the only one I have. There's no guarantee he'll get your letter if you write, though."

Passers-by drooped outside the glass bowl. The odd one wiped the sweat from his forehead or patted her top lip. I'd miss my train if I didn't get out of there in a hurry.

"I've got to go," I said.

I stood and tugged at my skirt where perspiration had crumpled and stuck the flimsy material to the backs of my legs. I fumbled for some change to pay my bill.

"Don't worry about your drink. My shout. And don't worry about his address either. I just wanted you to know, so we could be friends. It's a bit awkward. I hope you're not upset."

"I'm not upset," I lied. "Look, I have to run if I'm going to catch my train. Thanks for the drink." I hustled through the door and into the busy peak hour crowd.

Tom was, as Mum said, here today and gone tomorrow. He had the right to use his time the best way he thought. We weren't engaged. We'd made no commitment to each other, even though for a while it felt like we had with that kiss. We'd done nothing more than create a few moments to remember. And that was all that would remain, a memory to carry around in my brain and try to make sense of…unlike his letter, which I could carry around in my pocket and touch and read and smell and ponder. The words on the paper wouldn't change despite my or anybody else's interpretation. But the images in my brain…well, how static were they really?

Memories were nothing more than expired calling cards left behind on someone else's soul, essential elements in the chain of life that ensured the survival—or extinction—of human connections. This time, the memory that replaced the person threatened extinction. Accepting him as a memory and nothing more required action, not thought. I remembered his first words the day we met in the Concerto: "I like that song. Reminds me of my girl back home." I'd forgotten.

It was easy to fall in love with a memory, or whatever that feeling of longing for another is. If I were to survive, I would need to protect myself from that uncomfortable feeling of abandonment I already knew. The only way was to meet someone else. Fall in love. Hope they'd come back. And when they stopped writing, meet someone else and fall in love. Hope they'd come back. And when they stopped writing, meet someone else, search for my father. And so it went.

Trains serving other lines sped in and fled away while I waited on Platform Three. Carol was not like anyone I'd ever met. She would never be a friend. And yet there seemed to be something innocent about her honesty. I stepped onto the train and left our illusive connection in the bowels of St James Station.

After Carol's revelation, I was surprised to find another letter from Tom.

Dear Catherine,

A lot of things have happened since I saw you. When I returned to my unit in Vietnam, they told me I was going home to train people for Vietnam. It took a week to get out of Vietnam. I never saw Billy again. Also I just received your letter. It went to Vietnam first and then to my home here.

Catherine, I think of you often and wish I had more time to see you. I do hope you'll continue to write to me as I remember you always and think of you often.

It is very nice to be out of Vietnam! I miss you. Please take care and write soon.

Love, Tom
PS Catherine, thanks for holding my hand!

Chapter 7

LA TÊTE-À-TÊTE

February 1968

Most of the time, Paul and I worked the day shift. He cooked, while I waited on tables. Grace moved to nights with Lara. Once in a while Lara asked me to stay into the evening if either she or Grace had another commitment or became ill.

"One of these days I'm gonna tell Lara to shove it," Paul said, thumping his fist on the table hard enough to stamp his annoyance. "She can really get your goat if you let her."

"Why don't you?" I agreed. "You shouldn't have to put up with that." Lara's moodiness and constant complaining caused prickles that were hard to scratch.

"I know, but I like it here. I like working with you." He drummed an obscure code on the table while his thoughts translated. "Bottom line is I'm lazy. I'd have to become more than a take-it-out-of-the-freezer-and-heat-it-up cook. You know? I'd have to think, and most of the time I don't like thinking. Besides, who'd look after you three lovelies? Well, two lovelies."

"I think all the time. Too much, my mother says. She's probably right. So," I said, returning to the point, "how would the three of us, two of us, whoever the lovely amongst us are, survive without you? You are the Tête-à-Tête kitchen god." I bowed up and down like a marionette.

He lifted his arms and swirled his wrists for more.

"Yes! Now fan me with this newspaper and pretend it's made of peacock feathers," he cried with pompous delight.

We pantomimed like bourgeois fools and laughed until his belly flopped.

"Her majesty is due to arrive," I snorted.

"Oooh. And now. We must rehearse our bow before the queen."

"You'd better bow before the queen. Because she'll be mad when she finds us wasting time," I said. "I'm going to clean off the front table and fill the salt and pepper shakers. This place will be jumping when she struts through the door."

"Good idea. She'll be glad to see at least one of us is working. I'm taking a break before the rush. I simply cannot be the kitchen god if I'm exhausted." His eyes closed. The back of his hand drooped on his forehead, mocking remorse.

"It's your funeral," I warned.

"Nah." He shrugged and picked up the paper to resume his daily dose of headlines and eye-catching photos.

Mundane jobs such as filling shakers, dusting, or sweeping emptied my mind of anything important and therefore open to pick up any wandering thought hitchhiking its way through the universe. This time, pouring salt and pepper inspired me to review my job as a waitress. I liked where I was—despite Lara's moodiness and the rushes that sometimes felt like crazy times we'd never survive. Paul's humour really helped to lighten the load. The GIs brought their American tipping custom to Sydney. Aussies welcomed the new gesture of appreciation. I spent my unexpected pocket money on taxi fares to and from home. It was quicker than taking the train. Again, I was fortunate to work in an environment where music connected with the rhythms in my soul. My biggest challenge was to resist walking up and down the aisle, taking and delivering orders, to the beat of whatever played on the jukebox.

"I'm changing the name." Lara roared through her empty coffee shop, blasting the walls with her toxic temper. Straight-legged black pants and long tailored coat gave her the appearance of an undertaker on the loose.

"What name?" Paul asked, snapping out of the newspaper report that had absorbed him for the last few minutes: ANOTHER BABY WRAPPED IN NEWSPAPER FOUND IN HYDE PARK RUBBISH BIN. "What are you talking about?" He folded the paper open to the headline and passed it to me, pointing and frowning at the same time while saying, "Too much of this going on."

"Tête-à-Tête. The name is dull," said Lara. "That stupid Nick next door just settled it. You know what he said? Do you know what that slime ball said? 'The Titty Titty isn't doing good is it?' Can you imagine? The Titty Titty! Anyway, so much for him, I'm not worrying about that little dickhead anymore. Nick the Dick, that's *his* new name. And we're getting one, too."

She locked us into her green eyes, preparing to counter any objection we might dare to utter. "I've already decided what it is. From now on it's the GI's Hut." She flung her head back and reached for a bobby pin to re-attach the few strands that had come loose in response. "*That* will bloody well bring those Americans and their loaded pockets in here. Just look out there. Thousands of them all over the place but not one of them bloody well in here." She thumped the table. "And furthermore, I'm going to meet with Sergeant Peters at the Chevron tomorrow."

Paul kept his mouth shut when Lara pulled out the chair opposite him.

Shakers filled, I ran the tea towel under the tap, squeezed out the extra water, and wiped around the cappuccino machine.

"Maybe the real problem is your lousy bloody cooking, Paul." She pawed closer, a lioness moving in for the kill. "Maybe things are too slow in here because of you," she growled. "Why are you sitting around reading the bloody paper anyway? This is my time, Paul. You are reading on my time."

"Oh for Christ's sake, I'm just taking a break. Check the goddamn kitchen. Take a look for yourself. You'll see it's under control."

"That's exactly what I'm going to do, but you'd better hope it's more than just *under control*. Those fridges and counters better be spotless. The health inspector's coming any day." Lara stood and pushed her chair into the table. She stretched her neck and body to the stained ceiling, pulled in her chin, and glowered at him.

"How do you know when he's coming?" Paul tapped the folded newspaper on the table and ignored her menacing gesture. "I thought they were surprise visits, designed to take you off guard."

"Never mind. All you have to know is that he's coming." She turned and marched towards the kitchen.

"Yes, Your Majesty," Paul muttered.

I'd run out of things to do and hoped, for once, that customers would inundate the coffee shop to diffuse the tension. Lara didn't care what people thought and it never occurred to her to put her disapproval away.

"Do you know how much rent I'm paying here? Do you? And your bloody wages on top of it. You and Grace and Catherine. How much do you think I'm getting out of this joint? Not bloody much!" She stomped up the three narrow, wooden steps to the kitchen and disappeared.

Paul looked at me and broke into a wide smile. "No wonder business is poor, with her yelling like an old banshee."

Every so often drama played itself out as comedy and pushed my laugh buttons. The last time it happened was at a lay teacher's wedding where the school choir had been invited to sing. The director, a soprano crumbling into her eighties, was honoured to prepare us for the event. We sat with due reverence in the gallery as the priest stuttered his words of inspiration. The urge to laugh surpassed the solemnity of the occasion. The more I tried not to, the more I wanted to. And now it was happening again. Despite being sure this would mean the end of life at the "Titty Titty" for me, my response to Lara's words burst out. Paul caught the urge, too. Maybe it was her lisp that did it.

"What the hell is so funny? Both of you get up here now," she bellowed.

Amazingly, we complied like naughty children afraid of Mummy's next move.

She surveyed the wiped counters, the swept floors, the smear-free metal on the fridge and the stove. She swung open both doors of the huge fridge, searching for any hint of spill, mould, or bacteria that would justify her rage.

"Satisfied?" Paul asked, a bit on the smug side.

"Not yet!" She turned again to face the spotless counter. Paul snuck a sly grin from the left side of his face. But the inspection had not yet ended.

Lara ran her right hand under the counter. Within seconds she'd found the perfect excuse to take her fury to the next level.

"What's this shit?" she bellowed, thrusting four fingers into Paul's face.

"Looks like grease. I don't know how that got there. I'll get it."

Lara, lingering in her victory, held the pose as if she were a brass statue.

"Here, move out of the road so I can clean it up," he tried again. "Jeez, Lara, you'd better cool it. You're not going to attract customers if you keep carrying on like this. I bet they can hear you all the way to the fountain."

She lowered her arm, turned on the tap, squirted gooey yellow soap into her hands, and rubbed back and forth.

"I don't give a rat's ass if they can hear me all the way to the Harbour Bridge," she bellowed. "Clean this filthy place up now or you're fired. You, Grace, Catherine, the whole bloody lot of you. You can sit around on somebody else's time. I'm sick and tired of carrying this bugger of a load by myself."

Her rant reminded me of Mum.

* * *

Four customers walked in and seated themselves at a table on the left wall toward the back. Although my shift was finished, I gave them menus, glad of an opportunity to leave the kitchen. Americans stood out—their short hair, their short-sleeved shirts and crisp slacks, their cameras slung over their shoulders during the day, their new suits and Brut aftershave at night. This was a typical evening scene: two guys on R&R and two attractive, well-dressed girls. These girls, however, looked like they had better things to do with their time. Their aloofness suggested they'd been down this road before.

I skipped up to the kitchen and poked my head around the corner.

"Customers," I said in a loud whisper hoping the news would subdue Lara before she scared them off.

The scene to my right was one of relief. Lara, bent over the counter with her head buried in her arms, sobbing. Paul patting her shoulder the way a comforting father might console a distressed child. His face again calm, he nodded to reassure me that Her Majesty was no longer a threat.

"Do you mind taking their order?" he asked.

"Not at all." I turned, and descended one step at a time, feeling light and purposeful.

The shorter American was standing at the jukebox while the other one ran his thumb along the wheel on his silver lighter trying again and again to light the girls' cigarettes.

"Are you ready?" I asked, placing a complimentary package of matches on the red tablecloth.

"I believe we are," he said with confidence. "Four T-bone steaks, please. And could we have four coffees while we're waiting?"

"Sure. Cappuccino, straight black, or flat white?"

"I just want coffee," he said politely enough, but he might as well have added, *what's your problem?*

"I'll have cappuccino," the girl nearest the wall piped up.

"Me too," the other one added.

"Cappuccino is made with steamed milk, a straight black is without milk, and a flat white is a straight black with milk. Not steamed." I remembered the day I introduced Tom to cappuccino and the Australian way of serving coffee. Tom seemed so long ago now.

"Then I guess I'll have straight black. Same for my buddy over there."

"And how would you like your steak done?" I asked, predicting rare and medium rare for the guys, well done for the girls.

"Ladies?" the sitting straight black coffee asked.

"Well done," replied the girl nearest the wall.

"Well done," echoed the other.

"Rare for me. Hey, Pete! How do you want your steak?" the sitting straight black coffee called to the standing straight black coffee heading back to the table after making his selections at the jukebox. The first record had already dropped. The Righteous Brothers, "Unchained Melody."

"Rare is good," he said as he eased around me and slid into the chair beside his friend.

Three out of four wasn't bad.

Lara had moved to the kitchen floor, where she huddled in a pool of loud sobs. She didn't notice when I called out the order.

I returned to the table to set out the cutlery and serviettes. The girls drew long puffs on their cigarettes and made comments to each other that I couldn't hear. The guys, also excluded from the girls' exchanges, began to look like intruders. They thanked me when I placed the last fork on the table before returning to the kitchen.

"I swear I'm going to kick him out. He didn't come home again last night," Lara said as she peered into the mirror by the back door and patted ice cubes on her swollen eyes. "God, this isn't working. I'm going to have to run home for a few minutes. Do you mind staying a little longer, Catherine?" When she turned I saw her red eyes and the mascara running like dirty rainwater down both cheeks.

As insensitive as it may sound, I rather liked Lara's vulnerable side.

"No. Go ahead," I replied, hoping this wouldn't mean I'd be home late.

"Great. I'll be about half an hour."

"How did you get her to calm down?" I asked as Lara disappeared out the door.

"She goes off like this every so often," Paul confided. "Leo, her Greek boyfriend who manages the Pink Pussy Cat, keeps screwing around on her. She finds out somehow. They fight. She shows him the door. He talks his way back into her bed. Things go well for a while. Then it happens all over again."

The tables began to fill with couples, singles, the young, and the middle-aged. The women sparkled with jewellery they'd purchased from Coles in their lower socio-economic effort to match the wealthy ladies from the neighbouring eastern suburbs. The men sported tailored suits and shined shoes. The bored blond girls snuck up the stairs, through the kitchen, and out the back door before I served their steak dinners.

I walked past the table several times, taking and delivering various orders of coffee and BLT's, salads, steaks, chocolate cake, and other decadent desserts. It seemed the two straight black coffees sat alone for a long time. Finally, the one named Pete signalled me over.

"Excuse me, miss," he said in a patient voice, "would you mind seeing if those girls we came in with are still out there?" He checked his Seiko watch. "They went to the restroom, but that was about twenty minutes ago."

The toilets stood just outside the kitchen. There was no sign of the girls either behind the doors or in the darkened laneway.

The two Americans had waited for the girls without raising a fork. They looked a little vacant when I delivered the news that their dates and their mini-skirted long legs had vanished.

"I'm sorry." You could see on their faces that they felt like fools. "Your steaks are cold by now. Would you like them reheated?"

"No, that's okay, just bring the bill," Pete said. He opened his coat jacket and pulled out a black leather wallet.

"I'm sorry," I repeated.

"No sweat," said Pete. "Don't mean nothin'."

Lara walked back through the front door wearing her back-in-charge look just as I was about to tell them to forget the bill.

"Did you notice those two girls who came through here about twenty-five minutes ago?" I asked Paul. "They ditched those poor guys out there. All this steak going to waste." I tipped each plate, allowing chips, tomato slices, lettuce, and steak to slide into the garbage. *Waste not, want not,* I could hear Granny saying.

"Come to think of it, I did catch a glimpse of a couple of hot chicks breezing through. If those guys paid for their services ahead of time, they're screwed," said Paul.

"I've seen those two before," Lara added. "That's exactly how they operate. They're on their way to fleece the next pair of drongos they come across. Probably make ten times as much as I do running this place."

"I feel bad charging those guys," I said.

"Don't feel bad. Serves them right," Paul said. "They've learned a lesson."

I went back to change the tablecloth and collect the money Pete and his friend had left. Their bill came to $24. On the table sat three $10 notes.

On the way home that night, I hoped my quota of drama for the day had been met. I sifted through the letters I carried with me, looking for something that would restore my faith in humanity.

Dear Catherine,

Thanks for your picture and for the tour of Sydney. I got Captain Lefavor to take this picture to show your friends what an American away from home looks like standing in the middle of a rice paddy in jungle greens. I'd rather be in a sport coat and eating Escargot but you know how it is.

I was rash in what I said in my letter yesterday. I may be dissatisfied with what is going on back home but America is my home and even though it may be quite unjust, I've got to stick by it and maybe later in life it will change as I hope others in our world will.

As you can tell, I have gone through a great change. Like a flower who has opened itself to the morning sun and mist. Life is precious and I love it. How can I be sure in a world that's constantly changing? I can be sure with you, can't I? Sit down. I think I love you!

Dennis

Chapter 8

ORIENTATION DAY

March 1968

"One out of every three of you will fail their first year. Look to the person on your right. Look to the person on your left. Who will it be?"

This is how the vice chancellor, Sir Philip Baxter, began his welcome speech to the most recently admitted students at the University of New South Wales in March 1968. The coat of arms stood resolutely behind him, displaying a lion and four stars on the St George Cross and the university's motto: KNOWLEDGE BY HAND AND MIND.

I'm sure mine weren't the only pair of eyes that resisted sliding from side to side that day. We were assembled in the university's newest auditorium's plush red velvet seats, surrounded by earthy terracotta-hued brick walls, and comforted by the sombre filter of faraway ceiling lights. How could a 17-year-old tell who would succeed and who would not?

They might be hard workers, grateful for the opportunity to attend university. They might be slackers who got there by the skin of their teeth and were determined to have a good time. They might be nervous all-girls'—or all-boys'—private school graduates like myself, who finally had the opportunity to sit in classes with the other gender, a major distraction with its own set of hurdles including no uniforms after a lifetime of wearing them. It was impossible, as far as I could tell, to predict just by looking at someone, if they would be success stories or dropouts. I did know, however, that I was only there because of a scholarship—a Teachers' Scholarship. A Commonwealth Scholarship would have given me a choice and allowed me to study where my true passion lay: social work and social justice.

Teaching held little appeal for me. Only a few short months before, I had gone to Saturday afternoon confession and told Father O'Connor that I wanted to enter the Little Sisters of the Poor to work with the elderly. I asked for his help to attain my dream.

"I will make the arrangements for you, my child," he said before blessing me with the sign of the cross.

I left St Joseph's Church, elated that my future had a purpose. The nuns at Domremy had told us at more than one assembly and in several religion classes that the greatest gift we could give our parents was to answer the call. Mum, however, operated outside that expectation and was not one of those parents.

"That's the most ridiculous thing I've ever heard of," she said. "If you want to do something like that, you'll wait until you're twenty-one." She stormed out the door, up the street, and around the corner to St Joseph's presbytery, rehearsing the words that would tell Father O'Connor exactly what she thought of him.

Today, the vice chancellor's message of failure was louder than his words of welcome, so far, which really didn't bother me that much, considering how I felt about my current situation. However, Sir Baxter's reinforcement of my self-resignation took an unexpected turn when he extended a semblance of hope.

"On the other hand, having completed the Higher School Certificate, you are the first students to graduate with six years of high school. Perhaps you'll change this statistic. As you're a year older, we're expecting you to take more responsibility for your learning than those before you. It's up to you."

Sir Philip Baxter's last words concluded Orientation Week. An explosion of applause erupted from the fledgling audience that was soon to prove its academic worth. Anticipating a fun weekend before Monday classes initiated a semester of assignment burdens, the students clambered out of their seats. Among them was a girl that looked remarkably like Carol, but I wasn't sure. She hadn't said anything about going to university. Nothing like that came up in our only conversation about Tom, whom I still hadn't heard from again. I headed to the Student Union to answer one of my letters in peace and quiet before going home.

Dear Catherine,

Things here have been very quiet and I'm very glad for that. The one thing that is foremost on my mind is to make it home safe and sound.

I would like to take a few minutes of your time to comment on something you said: a person shouldn't waste their whole life trying to amass money. I am a strong believer that a person should get a job he enjoys or a job he finds rewarding. My psychology of life is that money is only as good as the enjoyment and pleasure it can bring to a man and his family. I personally hope to be able to provide a good living for my wife and family and still have plenty of time to be with them. I feel that too many men today are spending most of their time at their job and therefore are not devoting enough time to their families. I would like to hear how you feel about this subject.

It is getting close to the time when I will have to take my turn at guarding the perimeter so I will have to bring this to an end.

Phil

I wondered if I would find the job I was preparing for rewarding. I'd registered in a three-year Bachelor of Arts program that would give me the knowledge required to teach high school English and history. This would be followed by one year at Teachers' College where I would learn how to teach and be issued a diploma at the end of it to prove that I could. The scholarship would pay for my tuition and books, as well as provide me with a weekly living allowance. But it wasn't the path I really wanted to follow.

* * *

It didn't take too long to realise that, as far as campus life went, we were on our own. The sheltering and nurturing arms of Domremy were left behind and replaced, now and then, with aggravating insults tailored specifically for girls. While I found the concept that girls "only go to university to get a husband" offensive, Mum hopped right on board and wanted to know why I wasn't going out with one of those nice university boys. Not too long into the first semester, she tightened the screws.

"What's wrong with you? All the other girls have boyfriends."

I didn't bother to tell her that one of those nice university boys introduced himself to me at Central Railway Station while waiting for the bus to Kensington.

"Hi, I'm Chris. I'm president of the Students' Union. If you need help with anything, anything at all, you can find me in my office in the Roundhouse. Drop by for a visit. Where do you live?"

"Lakemba," I replied. "You?"

"Mosman," Chris announced. "I'm a North Shore boy, born and bred. My father's a lawyer. I'm following in his footsteps."

"That's nice," I said, already feeling uncomfortable.

"Are you interested in getting involved on campus?" he asked.

"Not really."

"You should," he insisted. "We have lots of different groups to help first years settle in. That way you get to meet new people, go to parties, join peace marches." After no response he added, "Ever smoke dope?"

"No."

"You've got a lot of growing up to do. I can help you with that." Perhaps he thought he was being suave but all I heard was arrogance. The bus pulled up and he stood aside to let me on first. As I climbed the first two stairs, I heard him say from behind, "It's not hard to see you're a virgin. I can help you with that as well."

Chapter 9

THE QUESTION WITH
NO ANSWER

June 1968

"What happened between Mum and my father?" I asked once more. I'd just read a letter from Billy.

Dear Catherine,

Today's Sunday so we're not doing too much work, more or less just sitting and waiting until someone comes around for supplies.

What's your definition of friendship? For me real friendship cannot exist without the foundation of faith in God, trust, respect, love, selflessness, forgiveness, humility, communication, tolerance, loyalty, admiration, confidence, patience and persever-ance (to name a few), and friendship is a way of life. Catherine, you are my friend.

You know when we were in the Goldfish Bowl we talked about "home" besides other things? I was thinking about this question: is not the personality of a person and the way he feels about this life greatly influenced by the way he was raised? If a person was raised in a broken home, he has one of two ways he could live, either he is going to care, or he might know better but wouldn't care. It works both ways.

Could we blame our parents for giving us a broken home? Or hate the parent who caused it? After my father told me that he didn't have a home anymore, I blamed my poor mother for everything that wasn't right. But after my father was killed in an automobile accident, I felt sorry for her. I have no hard feelings towards her now.

I'll be staying here for 3 more months. That means I can go on another R&R within that time. I'd like to go back to Australia and see you again. I'm waiting to hear from you. I hope you're all right and doing fine with your studies. Take care of yourself.

Your Friend Always, Billy

Granny stuck her right thumbnail into the green pod, slid it along the edge, and pulled it apart to reveal the peas. She placed both arms on the kitchen table and suspended the open pod upside down over the glass bowl. The plump peas fell from their cocoon. She looked over my right shoulder past the sink and over the fence into Johnsons' driveway. She tossed the empty, used pod on the newspaper where it landed amongst others to be wrapped up and thrown away. She ran both hands down the front of her grubby pinny and wiped off the fresh smell of peas. Then she reached for her packet of Viscount cigarettes.

"Granny?" I implored.

The same lighter Mum had dropped outside Coles the day we went to see Maureen slipped from her fingers.

"Just a minute." She stooped to pick it up from the linoleum, worn thin where feet had shuffled their kitchen duties, day after day. The Great Depression had carved three important doctrines into Granny's book of rules. First: If it's broken, fix it. Second: If it can't be fixed, use it until it completely croaks and then put it aside until someone comes along who can fix it. Third: Never throw anything out; you never know when it might come in handy. So, although Mum had discarded the lighter, Granny had resurrected it from the garbage, sticky-taped the crack, and was determined to burn every last drop of fluid in it.

"Your poor mother has had a terrible life." She placed her left elbow on the table and lit her nineteenth cigarette of the day. "Not her fault, really." A cigarette, it seemed, slowed time to a pace where reflection could legitimately replace duty. "She nearly drowned in the Murrumbidgee River, you know. The stupid bloke who was teaching her to swim held her head under the water for way too long. Poor thing was scared to death. She wouldn't go in the river after that. Hates water to this day." Granny took a puff, coughed, and rested her right cheek in her hand. The cigarette burned close to her face and threatened to singe the uncombed hair that stuck out unapologetically like a worn-out broom.

"And of course, there was the time she swallowed the safety pin when she was a year old. Bloody thing was open. That was the first time we almost lost her." She placed her free hand in the bowl, scooped up the peas, and clearly enjoyed the chute of solid green bubbles slipping through her fingers.

"Sickly child from the day she was born. The doctors didn't think she'd make it to her first birthday. But I never gave up on her, by crikey." Granny's stomach grumbled. "Well, enough of that. Got to get this dinner on the go. Your mother will be home soon, and she'll be as hungry as a hunter." She rubbed the end of the cigarette between her fingers, extinguishing the hot glow, and placed it in the ashtray for one more puff later on.

"What about you, dearest? I didn't even ask how your day was. You're home later than usual. Was the train crowded?" She pulled herself out of the cramped booth and got an onion out of the cupboard to spice up the mince for tonight's rissoles.

"Very crowded." Today would offer no answer to my question. There would probably be no answer tomorrow either, or the next day, or the one after that. "I stood all the way, while this lazy boy from Fort Street Boys' sat. He wouldn't even stand up for an old lady who got on at Erskineville. She leaned on her shopping trolley until she got off at Campsie. I thought she was going to topple over."

I herded the discarded pods into the middle of the newspaper where they congregated like cattle at dusk. I folded the paper around them and stuffed the package into the garbage bin by the stove.

"I glared at that boy for being so rude," I added.

"Don't ever do that! You don't do anything that will attract attention to yourself. There's no telling what these buggers might do." Although Granny's outburst had exploded out of nowhere, she just as quickly resumed her calm. "You know, I don't think I've told you, but I'm very proud of you for getting that scholarship. You're the first one in the family to go to university. Are you enjoying your classes?"

"They're okay. I wish I could've gone into social work, though." As indicated by my Little Sisters of the Poor attempt that was promptly aborted, I carried a yearning in my soul to rescue whatever or whoever suffered from the absence of kindness and love. "I really can't imagine myself teaching high school in three and a half years. I won't be that much older than my pupils."

"You'll be just fine," Granny said.

I picked up the ashtray—the first step in setting the table—and put it in its out-of-the-way place on top of the fridge amongst tacky ornaments and power bills.

"Who's this from?" I held up a letter that had been opened and placed on top of the fridge.

"Silly old me. I was going to read it to you when you came in, but we got waylaid on something or other." She said. "Go ahead and read it. It's from Aunty Fran."

Granny and her sister had long ago severed their ties. Aunty Fran lived in Lockhart next door to their mother— Great-Grandmother Catherine, whose name I was given. Granny, afraid to leave me alone with Mum, took me with her when she visited her mother and reconnected with the roots of her country childhood. The journey that began at Sydney's Central Railway Station at eight o'clock was an exciting adventure into the night, just as the first trip from Melbourne had been. As always, the evening turned on its magic when the Spirit of Progress left the city limits, and the recognisable constellations of Orion and the Southern Cross pointed the way. Steam from the engine streamed past the carriage window where I marvelled at the spectacle of stars, shadows, ghost gums lit up by the moon, and the open land.

The last time Granny and I made the eight-hour trip, Fran had estranged herself. With her cup of tea poised on her double-pillowed bosom, she told us that Granny had broken their mother's heart more than once. "Mum's getting older, Flo. She can't stay on her own here much longer, so I'm moving her to my house. You don't need to come out and help anymore. She only remembers that you broke her heart." The first time was when she took up smoking. The second time was when she got drunk while serving as a governess on Macarthur's sheep station in Gunyah. The news had jumped like a blazing bush fire from station to station until it raged out of control. Fran scolded her prodigal sister, who went out into the world and brought shame on the family while she, being much younger, stayed behind, unable to leave.

I wiped off the ashes Granny had dropped on the table, took a freshly ironed cloth out of the drawer, waved it above the table, let it parachute into place, and then smoothed out Mum's stubborn ironing folds.

"Just tell me what the letter says," I said.

"Well, she's okay I suppose, but she's a bit worried about Michael."

My cousin Michael had threatened to humble his mother with his boyish adventures that sometimes got him into trouble and brought attention to the otherwise rule-obeying Catholic family. Michael caused mischief like a blue heeler pup. We'd spent endless days at the sports ground hanging from the monkey bars, whizzing down the slippery dip, making each other sick on the merry-go-round (which we'd challenge ourselves to push faster than the time before), and swinging from the maypole. On summer days, we retreated to the gully, searching for tadpoles and crayfish. At night, he teased me about the Redbacks under the toilet seat of Great-Grandma's dunny.

"Next time you come to Lockhart, I'm gonna shout you to the pictures," he wrote in a letter when he was twelve. But after Great-Grandma moved in with Aunt Fran, there was no reason to visit Lockhart anymore.

"What about Michael?" I asked.

"Well, you know he was called up? He did his recruit training at Kapooka. Now he's doing his specialist driver training at Puckapunyal in Victoria. He finishes up in a couple of weeks." Granny, as usual, spotted some delinquent crumbs by the garbage and reached for the banister brush to sweep them up. "She says she couldn't stand to lose a son as well as a husband. You know Uncle Artie was killed in the war, don't you?" Granny asked. "The one Grandpa used to talk about?"

"Just because he's called up doesn't mean he'll automatically go to Vietnam though, does it?" I rattled through the cutlery drawer for three sets of matching knives and forks.

"Well, apparently he's going." Granny slid the banister brush back in beside the fridge. She turned the hotplate off and reached on top of the fridge to fetch her ashtray and Aunty Fran's letter.

"It says here as soon as he finishes training." She lit the stub that had waited in the ashtray like a needle ready to deliver a fix. She found her spot and read:

He'll be flying out of Sydney. Would you please go and see him off for me? I can't make it to Sydney. I need you to do this for me, Flo.

Also, he has a leave for a few days before he goes over. Do you think you could have him out for a nice meal? I'm sure he'd like to see Catherine. Perhaps she could take him out. I know they were good mates when you used to come down to see Mum, God rest her soul. I can't face seeing him right before he leaves. It brings back too many memories as you can imagine.

Flo, I need your help. If you're busy and you can't, then you can't. It would mean a lot to me, though. And to him. There should be someone there for him.

"What date?" I asked.

"June 18. Look on the calendar. What day is it?" Granny's voice became quiet, wearied by tea preparations, memories of Fran's hurtful words, and the present situation with her nephew.

"It's a Tuesday. Two weeks from tomorrow. Are you going to the airport?"

"I suppose we should," Granny replied. "You'll come, won't you?"

Soldiers in jungle greens and helmets, helicopters, and crying women appeared in front of the rosebush at the louvered window.

"Wasn't he going to Wagga Wagga Agricultural College?" Communication was sparse after Great-Grandma died. Bits and pieces filtered through on the odd Christmas card or via a visiting family member who got along with both sisters.

"Apparently he didn't do too well. Too much fraternising. I think he failed a few of his courses and was unlucky enough to have his number come up in the birthday lottery." She returned Aunty Fran's letter to its envelope and placed it on top of the fridge.

"Of course I'll come with you to the airport," I said. "Someone should be there to see him off, but why can't Aunty Fran get on the train herself?" I asked.

"Poor Fran. She's getting on in years you know. Her hip gives her so much trouble and now she's got diabetes. Besides it'd be bad luck. She saw Uncle Artie off and he never came back from the war. Now Michael. She probably thinks he won't come back, no matter how hard she prays." Her sunken eyes seemed to reach back and recreate a scene from years before, probably the confused anguish she felt when Grandpa went off to war. "And she's got good reason, I might add. It's not that easy to just come down to Sydney, you know."

Granny sat at the table. The rissoles gently simmered in the rich gravy, the mashed potatoes were covered, and the peas drained.

"Where's that mother of yours?" she asked impatiently. "She'll miss the first call at Housie if she doesn't get home soon."

"But Michael's her son. I'm sure he'd rather see his own family than us. And another thing," I added, "just because Aunty Fran saw Uncle Artie off and he didn't come back, it doesn't mean the same thing is going to happen to Michael. This superstition stuff is a bunch of hooey."

"You don't have to raise your voice, Catherine. It's just the way things are. What was that funny little nickname he used to call you?"

"Muffin."

"Oh yes, that's the one."

Granny's superstitions, like the lessons of the Great Depression, had also made their way into her book of rules. She had turned frantic with panic the day I opened the black umbrella in the house just to show her nothing would happen. "Nothing might happen right this minute, but mark my words, by crikey, it's going to if you don't get that bloody brollie out of here," she'd warned.

The screen door opened and slammed shut.

"Smells good in here," Mum called, flinging her red handbag over a dining room chair on the way to the kitchen. After a round of kisses, performed out of a need to touch and connect as much as greet, the three of us crammed into the familiar kitchen booth. This was Mum on a good day—bright, able to lift the air and stir it into a fruity jumble of delightful blossoms just as she did when she sang "Panis Angelicus" at Easter Sunday Mass. She sat down beside me.

What happened to my father and why was it Granny and not he sitting at the table? Would there ever be an answer? For now, it didn't matter.

Chapter 10

My Cousin Michael

"Do you know who put the 'poo' in Kapooka?" Michael asked.

"Probably you," I replied.

"Good one, Muffin, but not this time. The Army did! And a great big, shitty poo at that."

"That's yuk," I said.

"It's a lot worse than yuk. It's fucking ugly."

"Your language has deteriorated I see, Cuz."

"That's what the Army does to ya, Muffin. Turns mere boys into fighting machines with a mongrel's vocabulary to match."

"It's not for me, then."

"Nope. Good thing you're a girl and you can't get called up. You'd hate being a nasho."

"That's for sure," I said. "This is your last Saturday night in good old Aussie for a while. What do you want to do? Pick blackberries?"

"Smart ass," he said. "After going to Canterbury Bankstown Leagues Club every night for the past week, I know *it* and every bloody poker machine in the place better than I know my own house." He paused. "I could go to the Cross but that doesn't interest me either."

"Well aren't you a good boy," I said.

"Nah, I told Donny, Jimmy, Warren, and the boys I'd make up the clues for the car rally tomorrow. I like the idea of figuring out maps, routes, key locations and transferring them to clue sheets. It'll be a while before I get a chance to use my brain again. The Army doesn't encourage you to think much, you know. Follow orders. No questions."

* * *

Five cars screeched to a tyre-shredding halt in front of our house just after six the next morning. Donny and Warren hammered out obnoxious bursts on their horns with no regard for folks needing to sleep in on Sunday mornings.

"Tell those blokes to stop that bloody racket," Mum groaned as I bent down to kiss her goodbye. "I've got a frightful headache." She turned away and dragged the sheet over her head.

"Go back to sleep, Mum. See you tonight," I closed the bedroom door on her torture.

"Don't you be late," she mumbled across the room and through the grey wooden door. "What time are you coming home?"

I pushed the door just enough. "I don't know."

"Where are you going again?" Her voice grated with the gravel of Saturday night's beer and cigarettes. One of the boys pounded his hand on the horn. The blare flung Mum out of her dream state into panic. "Get in here!" I opened the door well beyond a crack this time. She propped herself up on her right elbow. Her hair dribbled down her face, clogged by yesterday's left-over makeup. "Who the hell's out there anyway?" she demanded.

"It's just Donny and the others. They're meeting Michael and me for the car rally today."

I took a quick peep out the window. The boys were standing around doing whatever their adolescent selves told them to do while having to wait: lean on their cars, sit on them, kick the tyres, huddle together in the woollen jumpers their mothers had knitted. Their chatter erupted into boisterous laughter like mischievous magpies lined up on a wire, while the girls stayed warm in the cars and yelled to each other through rolled down windows.

"I'll close the window so they don't bother you, Mum."

"Don't you dare! I'll suffocate." She waved her arms around the way Mrs Gilzean's chooks flapped their wings before their heads were cut off at their Christmas and Easter executions. "Where's Granny?" she growled.

"In the kitchen talking to Michael. She's running a bit late so we're giving her a lift to six o'clock Mass. I'm going now."

Mum flopped back on her bed with a groan and said goodnight and good riddance to the world for the second time in a couple of hours.

The boys greeted Granny with cheeky playfulness. "How are ya this morning, Mrs Schumann? Gonna pray for us sinners, Mrs Schumann?" they said in chorus.

"Go on with ya, you cheeky buggers. You're just a bunch of larrikins." Granny had known most of them from the day they were born. She never missed an opportunity to make them feel important, regardless of their family situation or their marks in school.

We dropped Granny off fifteen minutes late for Mass and headed north. The morning bathed us in its cheery glow as we wound our way through sleepy Sunday-morning city streets.

"This is different than the Hume Highway," said Michael as houses gave way to gum trees. "It's not as narrow or dangerous. I've driven my shaggin' wagon down that road so many times going back and forth to Wagga, and it still pops up with surprises. This is a breeze. No dangerous curves to take you off the road or obstruct your view. Speaking of driving," he said, "I'm leaving my car at your place. Why don't you get your license? You could drive this old girl until you get your own car. She's not the best looker in Sydney, but she's as mechanically sound as they come."

There had been no reason to learn to drive. Buses and trains took me to the university at Kensington and the city. There was always a cab in emergencies. Besides, Mum had made it perfectly clear that the Morris Minor was hers and she was the only one who would ever drive it.

"Thanks for the offer, but I wouldn't feel right driving your prized possession while you're away. One day I'll get my license. Not now, though."

"One of the boys could give you a few lessons. If not, I'll teach you when I get back. It's handy to have your license, even if you don't have a car," he said. "Looks like they're stopping up ahead."

Last in the Sunday morning procession of kids in cars going somewhere other than Mass, we pulled up to see Warren scrambling, no obstacle too great, into the bushes.

"Couldn't wait," commented Michael, stretching out his back with both hands on the steering wheel.

Sunlight beamed from Michael's side through the old grey Holden. My head fell back on the seat and I shut my eyes. Currawongs perched on eucalyptus trees sang a glorious welcome to the morning. Cars sped by. Their whoosh interrupted the concert and left behind the toxic smell of leaded petrol.

"Are you scared?" I asked.

"About what?"

"Going over there. Vietnam."

"Of course not!" he declared, leaving no room for doubt. "Nothing's going to happen to me. Don't worry, I'll be back to keep you on track."

"Promise?" I asked.

"Bloody oath," he replied. "By the way, you never talk about Uni. How's it going?"

"It's okay." As the words came out I realised it was fate and not choice that got me where I was. "I like the tutorials when the discussion is about interesting things like the nature of man and social justice. Otherwise, I'm not really interested." I was sliding closer to the fulfilment of my "one in three of you" failure destination and was anxious to get off the subject. "Do you think man's basically good or evil?" I blurted out as if his answer could give meaning and purpose to my life.

"We're a mixed-up bag of good and evil," he said. It was easy to talk to Michael. He always had an answer. "Sometimes we're good and sometimes we're bad."

"I think we're born with goodness in our hearts. Sometimes, though, I think things happen to distort our sense of right and wrong."

"What do you mean?" he asked.

"Well, abuse can lead a child to operate in manipulation mode without a guiding moral light. Just to survive. Or something can go screwy in a person's brain, causing chemical issues. Both scenarios could carry their legacy into adulthood."

Michael was quiet. I continued. "I think Mum has something wrong with her. Sometimes she's the most beautiful loving person, and other times she's the biggest bitch in the world."

He leaned over and switched on the radio. Normie Rowe crooned "It's Not Easy" in the background.

"About university. I don't know if it's because I went to Domremy and I'm not used to boys in the class, but I keep thinking I shouldn't be there." I looked over to catch his reaction. He stared straight ahead.

"I'm sorry I dropped out of ag college," he admitted. "I wouldn't be in this mess if I'd settled down. But then again, I didn't want to be an aggie, either."

"Mum reckons that sometimes it doesn't matter what we want."

"Well, I reckon it should. It sounds like you don't want to be a teacher."

"I don't. I want to be a social worker."

"Do you know what I want to be?" he asked.

"Probably not a soldier going to Vietnam tomorrow," I replied.

"Absolutely right, Miss Muffin Moreton."

"Well?"

"Guess," he teased.

"Oh, come on, Michael."

"Okay I'll give you a hint." He pressed his foot harder on the accelerator.

"Now I get it." I punched his arm. "You want to be a racing car driver."

He punched my arm back. "And the winner is … in particular, I want to race in the Bathurst One Thousand. I reckon I can drive a Holden and beat the Fords as good as Colin Bond."

"As good as Colin Bond?" I said.

"That's right! As good as Colin Bond," he declared.

"Then why don't you do it?"

"Because, as your Mum says, 'sometimes it doesn't matter what we want.' It just ain't gonna happen."

His words resonated as if this was the first time he'd allowed himself to look critically at his role in becoming a conscripted soldier about to go to war.

"It's not like you'll be in the Army forever," I said. "Conscription's only for two years, isn't it?"

"Yeah," he replied, "but now I'm on this route with no way of knowing how it will change the future." He shook his head. "I don't mind doing my bit, but we're only over there because the Yanks dragged us into it, and our politicians are too bloody weak to say 'No!'" He focused on the road ahead. "I was involved in a couple of peace rallies. A lot of people are against this war, you know." He turned off the radio.

"I write to a few Americans I've met at the Cross. They're nice boys. Just like you and Donny and the rest of the gang,"

I said. "To be honest, I'd rather show them around Sydney than go to my lectures."

"It's not them. It's their government I have a problem with." His forehead tensed. For the first time that morning he turned his head and took his eyes off the road. "You be careful hanging around the Cross. There are some bad buggers up there. Your question about good and evil? Well, some of them would sell their firstborn and not give it a second thought."

I didn't want to admit he might be right, but now and again the same warning was issued in the letters.

Dear Catherine,

I could kick myself in the ass for not asking you out on my last night. All we did was go and get drunk and looked at the girls and then looked at each other and said, WOW, forget it; we'll hate ourselves in the morning.

I sure would like to see you again. It was fun having coffee and getting to know you. I would come to Sydney but I would be eligible for the draft over there, so I can't go. So stay away from the Whiskey a Go Go and all those sex starved GIs and don't do anything foolish, ok.

Love you until the twelfth of never,
Conrad

Chapter 11

LAST WISH

We turned west off the highway at Terrigal onto a secondary road, then headed north on a dirt track until we arrived in a bush clearing somewhere between Bathurst and Newcastle. After everyone had stretched and moaned about the early start, Donny pulled the tab off a can of beer and handed out the clue sheets that Michael had written up the night before.

"Help yourselves, ya drongos," he said.

The boys, who thought they were men, each grabbed a beer and studied the maps while Michael explained the rules and answered questions. The girls stood hugging themselves in the cooler temperatures of June. Now and again, one of them put a hand over her mouth and shared a comment not intended for all to hear. Monica chose me to be the recipient of her private thought.

"Your cousin's nice," she said in a low voice. "He's just the right height."

"For you, you mean?"

"Yes, I do mean for me," she said. "He's a little bit taller than me. His hair colour is about the same as mine, too. Maybe a little browner." She kept her eyes on Michael, who was teasing his friends openly. "Betcha nobody teases him. I hate it when people call me carrot top." She swirled her foot around in the dirt. "I wonder if we have the same coloured eyes."

"He has brown eyes, you dill!"

"Well, how am I supposed to know that with his sunglasses on?" Her spindly legs did well to support her awkward frame as she moved back to the huddle of girls that had begun to form.

Instructions completed and last-minute questions answered, bodies scrambled into cars. Doors banged, horns hooted, Monica hovered.

"Who are you with?" I asked.

"Warren left already." She folded her arms.

"Jump in," shouted Michael, anxiously revving the engine.

Since Michael had compiled the clue sheet, it must have been hard for him to follow Monica's and my commands without giving away hints. But maybe the discipline he learned in the Army had prepared him for that.

Monica screeched hysterically as we screamed around corners, backed up, sped down dirt roads, jumped out of the car, and searched for the next clue. As each carload yelled its determination to win and make a laughing stock out of the other no-hopers, I drifted off to my own inner world.

After a while, winning a car rally seemed unimportant. As Michael and Monica got more familiar by telling each other jokes, I thought about Mum, the Murrumbidgee River, and the open safety pin. I thought about my father. Who was he? I thought about university and why I was willing to skip lectures. Granny's pride, associated with "You're the first one in the family to go to university," evoked some guilt as I thought about why I was late with my assignments and about Michael going to Vietnam and all the others I'd met who were already there. There, Michael had said, because of the American government. There without a legitimate cause, he seemed to say.

Monica likewise grew tired of the game and eventually gave up. We limped back to the starting point without finding a single clue. Donny, Warren, and the others had beaten us. Wired to the hilt, they hugged, teased, and shouted endless variations of congratulatory praises to each other.

"You went off without me," Monica pouted to Warren.

"Sorry, carrot top, but it looked to me like you wanted to go in someone else's car," the boy replied.

Monica turned a brilliant shade of red and huffed off to help the girls spread out the blankets. The boys stood around by the cars and drank from large bottles and smaller tins of beer, goading each other now for mistakes they'd made in the hunt. The girls set out the food for the picnic: Vogel's multi-grained bread, pepperoni sausage, Swiss cheese, boiled eggs, gherkins, potato chips, and crackers.

The wind picked up and played catch with branches in the swaying trees. Leaves shivered at the sight. Paddocks of sticky paspalum bowed their heads when a herd of red kangaroos jumped out of the shrub to graze in comfort on their built-in rocking chairs.

"Look at that!" said Michael. "I'd like to have one of them big bastards for a pet."

We watched like visitors in a foreign land as the locals scratched at the dusty bush floor and sorted out the menu.

"I've never seen a kangaroo up close before," said Monica. Most of us agreed we'd only seen them at the zoo or in reserves and never this many at once. "I'd like to pet one. They look so soft. Look at his paws," she said as a big red munched his salad. "It looks like they've been dipped in tar."

"Wish I could rest on my tail like that," said Donny.

"Your feet are big enough," said Warren.

"'Ow ya goin' mates?" called Jimmy to the assembled macropods as he gulped down his sixth tin of Fosters. "Eh, I said g'day. Care for a tinnie, would ya?"

The wind roared around the shells and into the tunnels of our ears. The tree trunks swayed and kept balance while we guffawed in high and low-pitched outbursts, without regard for the dignity of our hosts. Their boomerang shaped ears straightened. Disgusted with the noise and our bad manners, the herd retreated to a more serene room in their bushland home.

"I've got an idea," Michael said when it was quiet. He jumped up. "Who's game?"

"Yeah, we're in."

With no further announcement, Michael ran to his beloved Holden—now completely covered in red dirt—turned on the ignition, and pumped the accelerator as though he was trampling a funnel-web spider to its death. His muscled arm beckoned through the driver's open window. Donny and Jimmy rumbled and stumbled over each other in their race to be part of the action. Scrambling so as not to be left behind, they wrenched the passenger handle and swung the door open with such force it seemed to come unhinged. In the same bizarre spectacle, Warren dove through the back window and scraped his legs. Michael again pumped the accelerator, forcing the engine to respond with a deafening roar. This was his announcement of the tribal passage about to begin.

"What about the rest of you? Are you coming?" he yelled. A momentary pause provided the opportunity to resist, but the enthusiasm of those already willing to taste the thrill of danger was contagious. Those of us who had hesitated ran screaming to the car, demanding to be part of whatever was about to happen.

"There's no room for me," whined Monica. Despite the improbability and the protests—Get off me! I can't breathe! You're squashing me!—twelve of us crammed into Michael's station wagon that afternoon.

"We're going to hell," roared Michael, like an officer leading his troops into a bloody battlefield. The boys and girls close enough to hear his brazen declaration encouraged him with eager cheers. He didn't need their approval. Wordless and determined, he sped to the dirt trail, a seldom-used bush road, and screeched to a neck-jolting halt. Dust exploded through the windows. We were a roller coaster poised at the top of a terrifying drop. We all wore blinkers padded with ignorance, naivety, and blatant disregard for the looming possibilities that lay ahead.

Michael shoved the car into first gear. Then second. Then top. We flew down the narrow road. The sun shrieked through the gum trees sneering on either side at the fools insulting their dignity with noise and dirt and dust. Faster and faster we went until the speed dislodged stupidity.

"How fast are you taking her?" asked Donny, his voice fragmented by the jarring speed.

"Always wanted to get this baby up to a hundred," Michael responded, his entire body focused on controlling his machine. The muscles and veins in his arms protruded. His blood surged in response to the demands he made. I was about to throw up.

"Stop," I said, too weak to be heard. "Stop," I repeated, desperate for the terror to cease.

The speedometer needle tipped one hundred. The capsule of madness erupted with a primal yell. His goal attained, Michael eased off the accelerator and reduced the speed. I was hopeful that sanity would return, if only to disallow a replay of the horrid recklessness of the past few minutes. As we pulled into a small clearing to turn the car around, I wasn't even sure of that.

"That's it, fun's over," Michael declared. Donny and Warren egged him on and dared him to do it again. Others coughed, their lungs irritated by the red dust or perhaps activated again after holding their breath too long. The reality of what just happened settled on us like melting hailstones. The car was quiet. Michael turned his pride and joy around and crept back down the trail at twenty-five miles an hour.

We arrived at the picnic site tired and exhausted. The day was finished. We'd all had enough. The girls gathered up the paper plates, plastic cups, beer bottles, and cans, and asked the boys to help but got no response. We threw the leftovers into the bush for the birds and animals, made half-hearted attempts to fold the blankets, said good bye, and headed back to Sydney. We decided not to travel in convoy on the return trip, feeling an unexplained need to be independent. Separate and separated. Monica rode with Warren.

"That was stupid!" I yelled at Michael once we were alone. "You're an idiot!" He stared blankly down the road. "You could have killed us, you dipstick. Think about it. What if we'd met a car coming in the opposite direction?" I was shaking.

"What if we'd met a car?" he repeated. "Or we'd skidded and I'd lost control and crashed into a tree? Or the engine had blown? Or the tyres? Or the accelerator pedal had stuck? What if, what if, what if? What if I'd knuckled down at ag college? What if I wasn't going to Vietnam tomorrow? Bloody hell, it's an endless question with endless possibilities, Catherine."

"Not if we'd been killed," I said.

"Not if we'd been killed," he repeated.

There was nothing more to say.

* * *

Dear Catherine,

We've had a bad case of ground and flying accidents so I've had to go out to our sites, visit with the people, investigate the accidents and maybe bring some cheer from our place.

Tomorrow is another dreadful day and maybe I'll go flying just to get away from it all. It's somewhat peaceful up in the clouds. There's quite a bit of hatred and grudges in the outfit so I try to not get involved, but it always ends up that I do. And that's what it's like living in Vietnam.

Please write,
Dean

Chapter 12

GOING TO WAR

June 18, 1968

At 4:50 the alarm blared, pulling me out of dreams where demons in red capes sped down tunnels that ended in fiery pits. Granny sizzled bacon and eggs for Michael. The bubbling fat took the chill off the morning air. Michael, dressed and ready in the precision of his pressed uniform, sipped tea and answered Granny's repetitive questions as patiently as he could. His slouch hat sat on his duffle bag by the door and reminded me of the Dog on the Tuckerbox, waiting for his master's return.

"Do you want to phone your mother again before we leave?" Granny asked.

"Last night was enough, thanks, Aunty Flo."

"Anyone else you want to call?"

"No, I've spoken to everyone I need to. Thanks."

"Do you have everything packed?" Her persistence fell just short of nagging for a soldier trained to be prepared. "Are you sure you haven't forgotten anything?"

"Yes, yes, and yes," Michael replied flatly.

I put my arm around Granny and kissed her quickly on the cheek, careful not to interrupt the transfer of meaty bacon strips from the pan to the plate. I half filled my cup with tea and splashed in some milk. The bitter tartness of a strong cup of Bushells tea summoned the day to begin.

Michael looked up with both hands grasping his cup. A beautiful smile shone through his warm brown eyes. The rest of his face wore the calm of one ready to walk into the future. The tailored experiences that lay within the life and death parameters of war already bore his name.

"Monica likes you, you know," I said.

He nodded. Before he had a chance to speak, Granny was pecking again. "Is your mother up yet, Catherine?"

"I'm up," announced Mum in a bright voice. "We've got to leave just after five thirty. The car needs petrol." Mum's cheeriness jumped into the heaviness of bacon and eggs, Granny's anxiety, and the possibility of Monica and Michael.

"I'll pay for the petrol," offered Michael.

"You don't have to bother, mate. Think of it as my little going away present since I didn't have time to buy you a card," Mum replied in her most generous voice.

She headed for the stove and grabbed the black handle of the metal teapot, snuggled in a tea cosy that Granny had picked up at a school fete years ago. Stains and time had muddied the colours of its brown, pink, and green wool. Mum poured the tea into a mug and drew in its bitterness. Then she wrapped both hands around the mug, overlapped her long fingers, and stationed herself in front of the heater to warm up.

"Ah! Love that first cuppa in the morning," she said.

We all did.

"You're going to have to swig it down or we'll be late," said Granny. "Catherine, go around and make sure everything's turned off, will you, love? Michael, do you have everyone's address?" She had no intention of taking the time to register Michael's silence.

Granny slammed the front door extra hard and pulled on the handle twice to make sure it was locked. Nevertheless, we were already packed into the car when she asked me to run up and check on the door, just in case. Finally, convinced that the last-minute checks securely locked the house, Granny let it go and Mum pulled away from the curb.

To say that seriousness sat with us in the dark green Morris Minor that morning would be an understatement. The only one it escaped was Mum.

"I'm glad we're beating the rush," she announced more than once as we sailed through sections of Canterbury Road that were notorious for knotting early morning traffic.

Mum thrived on the short-term neediness of others. Whether it was the neighbour who suffered a heart attack on the front lawn and required her to phone an ambulance or the cousin who needed a lift to the airport so he could go off to war, she was there.

Granny sat in the bucket seat—the privileged position—remembering the time she saw Grandpa off at Wagga Wagga Railway Station in 1941. "That bloody old bugger had no business going off to the war at forty years of age," she muttered, still harbouring bitterness for the years he made her a single parent and then returned home an invalid.

Michael and I sat in the back, our arms on the duffel bag wedged tightly between us.

* * *

An unregimented maze of emotion—represented by laughter, tears, hand holding, folded arms, serious and frivolous words—filled the spaces and dotted the floor of the departure terminal at Kingsford Smith Airport. In each group, a man in khaki uniform and slouch hat was the focus of attention. The odd soldier stood by himself, sometimes with a cigarette burning between his fingers, his aloneness setting him apart.

Mum had just returned from parking the car when the announcement was made for all military personnel to make their way to Gate 12. Friends and relatives were invited to go to the observation deck to witness the farewell ceremonies and departure of their sons, grandsons, nephews, brothers, uncles, fathers, husbands, lovers, and friends. Nervous tension disguised with laughs and jokes turned to silence, turned to sobs. Women reached into their purses for handkerchiefs. Men grabbed them from their pockets or self-consciously ran their sleeves across their faces. Children burrowed into their mothers' skirts or their fathers' pants, clinging like koalas to their secure branches.

My tears spilled out, despite my effort to hold them back, when Michael leaned over to embrace Granny.

"Thanks for taking me in for the week, Aunty Flo," he said.

She looked so small and fragile. He looked so handsome and strong. The contrast of old and frail with young and brave heightened the unfolding tragedy of forced separation, made worse by the certainty of a hostile destination where innocence would be lost and young would become old before its time.

"You behave yourself now," Mum said, as she pulled him towards her and patted his back. This kind of expression kept the scene light for Mum and enabled her to conceal her own vulnerability, a vulnerability that would have risked exposure had she dared to take her cousin into her arms and bundle him with care. Perhaps such detached contact made it easier for Michael, too.

"Please write," he said, giving me a quick hug. "And study hard." Then he whispered, "I'm really sorry I scared you yesterday. You're right. I was an idiot."

A commotion erupted around us and jerked at the sad and sacred script in which we were engaged, expanding our quiet circle and refocusing our emotions.

"Pile up on Canterbury Road. Held us up for fifteen bloody minutes!" It was Jimmy. His loud, out of breath voice demanded Michael's full attention. "Monica, Warren, and me left a bit early so we could see you off on our way to Uni. Then this stupid bloke changes lanes and causes about six cars to ram into each other."

Monica and Warren nodded.

"Good luck over there, mate." Jimmy grabbed Michael's hand and shook it hard. "And don't do anything I wouldn't do, if you know what I mean." An obscene grin walked across his face.

"I'll try not to," Michael said, claiming back his arm. "Look after yourself," he said to Warren, who stood without words.

Monica, in a bold show of affection, put her arms around Michael's neck and kissed him long and hard on the lips.

"I'll get your address from Catherine," he promised her.

My cousin took a deep breath and braced himself for the inevitable, whatever it was. He smiled and said, "Well! This is it. Bye, everyone. See you when I come home for R&R if I don't decide to go somewhere else." He disappeared through the grieving crowd, leaving us with the weight of our sorrow.

Loved ones stood like statues in the after burn of a significant event. Someone we loved was heading into the uncertainty of his own fate in a vastly more profound way than the rest of us. We stared with grief as the focus of our agony walked through the door.

"Well, we're off, too. See you at Housie on Saturday," Jimmy said, breaking out of the tension before turning towards the terminal doors.

"Yes, we don't want to be late for our classes," said Warren, pulling Monica behind him.

"God, that Jimmy's a loud bloke," said Mum, watching him disappear into the parking lot. "I've got to get going, too; otherwise I'll be late for work." Mum became anxious for the next instalment of her involvement in Michael's departure now that the spotlight was gone. She'd gathered enough information to spin a good yarn later, first to her boss and then to the patients while they sat hostage in the waiting room before their dental appointments.

"Yes, you go, Brenda dear. Catherine and I'll catch a cab after the plane leaves." Things were uncomplicated when Granny gave her permission. "Go on, love. See you tonight." She hugged her daughter. "Careful in the traffic now," she warned.

Granny and I made our way up the stairs to join others on the observation deck. The bright winter sun reflected off the tarmac.

"Another beautiful day," she said.

The troops stood at attention. Families and friends listened in silence as loudspeakers delivered words of encouragement, spoken by dignitaries dressed in garb that represented their particular office. The Governor General and the Lord Mayor, each with his own script, told the soldiers how proud they were of them. How proud their loved ones were. How proud their country was. They delivered their politician speeches of encouragement. They referred to the young men as Australia's sons, and they reminded them of the fine fighting tradition handed down by their Anzac forefathers, the original Diggers. Uniformed policemen faced the crowd and formed a perimeter.

A light wind swirled around the tarmac and distorted the sound. People blew their noses. Sniffled. Explained to little ones, as best they could, what daddy was doing out there. Granny took the lolly pink scarf out of her straw shopping basket and tied it under her chin to cover her ears from the wind.

The brass military band, dressed in bright red coats, black pants, and white safari helmets announced the end of the formalities with a boisterous rendition of "Waltzing Matilda." The men walked single file up the steps of the plane and disappeared. Their families and friends waved, believing the one they loved could see them. Most waited until the Pan Am jet was a speck in the expanse of blue sky and puffy white clouds.

"Why are they flying our boys out on an American plane?" I asked Granny, who held an embroidered hanky over her nose.

"Maybe Qantas can't spare any carriers," replied the man in front of me.

"Bloody Yanks!" said the man to his left.

Granny and I shared a cab to Central Railway Station where the working crowd had left behind the first leg of its efforts to get to where it needed to be in the city. All that remained were the ticket collectors, sweeping up and manning gates in their tired blue uniforms. The magazine and refreshment kiosks recovered and restocked, while university students with later classes queued up at the bus stop. Women—young and old, pushing prams, carrying bags, dressed up, dressed down—emerged from the suburbs for an outing in the city.

"It's cheaper to catch the train," said Granny, conserving her funds until that lucky day when her ship would come in. Housie wasn't the only possibility for her windfall. There was also her Saturday morning bet on the horses and her weekly lottery tickets. Waste not, want not. Gambling was not a waste but an investment for the future as far as she was concerned, a sacrifice for now with dividends to come. One day.

"Think I'll call Fran. She'll be wondering," said Granny. A quick glance at my watch told me the Kensington bus would arrive in five minutes, giving me just enough time to make the history lecture. We hugged. Bye, love.

Chapter 13

MOTIVATIONAL SPEAKER

The Macarthur building housed three barren lecture theatres in a large concrete box to the right of the library on upper campus. Day after day each theatre, dressed in the same shade of grey, greeted students with its lack of imagination and insistence on hard cold fact. Designed for optimum visual and auditory access to the speaker, each one reflected an indoor version of a Greek amphitheatre without the inspiration of sunlight or the freshness of outdoor air.

Professor Arnold had begun his treatise on Lenin's perversion of Marxist doctrine on the stroke of one, three-and-a-half minutes before I arrived. A seat in the bleachers towards the back invited me into its anonymity. The only person in the row pulled his knees to his chest and swivelled to his right to let me by.

Students dotted themselves here and there. Some sat together. Most sat alone and slouched. Some took notes while others, heads resting on their hands, dreamt with open eyes of the latest girl or boy who had seized their passion, rehearsing the words they would use when they saw them next. At least, that was my reading of their posture. I realized that I often imposed my own meaning on the words and actions of others. Right or wrong.

The mini table attached to my chair stuck and unstuck with a low-pitched squeak as my elbow pushed it flat. I rummaged in my briefcase for a note pad and a pen that worked and gave my full attention to Professor Arnold. Michael slipped in as he slept on his way to war. The sadness of his farewell and the uncertainty of danger sat a safe distance away in the clouds. Every minute took him closer to his duty of soldier at war, but for now he was cocooned in the womb of the plane's belly.

My eyes remained, as did everyone else's, on the central figure in the theatre. Funny word, *theatre*. Picture theatre, war theatre, operating theatre, theatre of operations—a theatre being a place for entertainment, for an event, a spectacle, an attack, a surgical procedure. Here now, today, a lecture. A lecture that could incorporate all the other possibilities.

Monica and Michael had possibility. Writing letters could connect them on a deeper level. A yawn pushed at my mouth, but I kept it there and sent it back to where it came from.

Meanwhile, Professor Arnold's words rolled around my ears like drugged drones. Muffled syllables wafted into sounds that soothed. The cement, the bleachers, and the ceiling lights ensured more shelter for my anonymity. The verbal text avoided meaning the way a drunk driver misses road signs. Though my ears admitted his words, my brain refused to process them. It might have been Sunday Mass, the professor delivering his sermon to a congregation of students risking failure if they missed.

The tiny silver weights attached to my lids drew down over my eyes and placed Professor Arnold behind an opaque screen. I tried to pull them up, consciously stretching and raising my eyebrows, even instructing them to open. They refused. I began to float. Without mass. Weightless. Perfect. My head pushed my chin down to my chest. Tom walked by with his girlfriend and said *Merry Christmas*. Carol painted her nails with charcoal. Monica asked Mum how you become a soldier.

A crashing sound jerked me upright, forcing a rod of alertness up my spine. The long-legged student to my left bent over and fumbled for the clipboard he'd knocked off his table. Professor Arnold's mouth continued to open and close as the boy sat up, looked around nervously, and reset his legs.

Exhaustion resumed, sucking me even further into its obscure world of mangled thought. The silver weights on my lids became chains on my legs and on my shoulders, pulling down and setting free every molecule. Sinking and floating at the same time. Floating and sinking. There was no difference. It would have been easy to tumble out of the chair, so my head found an anchor on my arm—on the writing pad—on the mini table—no care—no thought—the transition from one state to another, smooth. Perfect combination of light and heavy, freedom and captivity, surrender and restraint. Michael recited Marx at the annual Australian Communist Party's meeting. Monica and Carol, now Lenin and Stalin, called for an uprising.

"—and if you are so unmotivated that you think you can come to my class and sleep, you need to think again. I'm speaking to you in the back."

I'm in the back. I'm sleeping in the back. I'm not actually sleeping. My eyes are just closed. But my eyes *are* closed in the class and I'm in the back. Now I'm thinking. Am I thinking *again* like the words said? Am I *supposed* to be thinking again? Or am I just in the back? In the back, sleeping?

"Sleep somewhere else! Not here! Not during my time! You are the epitome of ignorance. Raise your head and pay attention or get out!"

His words reverberated off the cold cement walls and into my ears. No longer soporific, they attacked like pins and needles poked savagely into the stuffing of a tribal doll.

But perhaps it wasn't me at all. Maybe the attack was meant for some other person failing to thrive on the professor's words. Maybe it was part of his lecture and I'd just connected with them like in a bad dream. I raised my head to figure out what was actually happening. His awful intensity seared my very soul. How could he have possibly noticed me in this cement morgue?

I pulled back from him—his awful gaze so far away—and pressed my spine straight against the back of the chair. I scanned the student congregation. They looked the same as when I came in. Slumped. Bored. Sleepy. And then the stand-off subsided. Professor Arnold cleared his throat and pointed out how Lenin had completely misunderstood the socialist benefits inherent in Marx's theory.

I wrote furiously, desperate to capture every word. It didn't matter that I didn't understand what he was talking about. The important thing was to record. Comprehension or not, I wrote to show him that I was motivated and that I was not the epitome of ignorance. Writing also helped to channel the nervous trauma that wanted to blast me out of my seat and through the concrete ceiling to some place in the universe far from Kensington and the University of New South Wales. Even into the seat beside Michael on his way to Vietnam.

Finally the sermon ended. The congregation packed up and left. I sought comfort in reading a letter. Unfolding it, I stared at the words.

Dear Catherine,

Your first letter really perked me up and did wonders for ole Dean. It was really great hearing from you, and somehow, while reading your letter, I could picture you right in front of me. My first reaction was to reach out and grab you, but in reality all there was, was just empty space.

It just does wondrous things to me to have a few words of confidence and affection about me. I think it's really something special when we can express ourselves so clearly to each other!

I think I'll always remember "our" water fountain, knowing that it holds so much meaning for both of us.

Dean

I kept my head down and gathered up the humble belongings that defined me as a student and stuffed everything into my briefcase, which clumsily rebounded off the backs and fronts of chairs as I stumbled out of that place.

"Are you going to join us?" a voice called from behind as I hurried past the library, still scorched from my experience in the theatre, which had fulfilled all the possible nuances of its name.

"The marchers are gathering in front of the Students' Union building this afternoon. Here's your chance to do something worthwhile." It was Chris, the president of the Students' Union and just the person to complete the nightmare.

"What marchers?" I asked.

"The peace rally's at three. You are going to join us, aren't you?" he said hurrying past me. "There's a big party afterwards."

Michael's plane would land at Tan Son Nhut Airport in thirty minutes.

Chapter 14

THE GI'S HUT

Sergeant Peters entered the GI's Hut. Something in his stride told me that this American had not just haphazardly wandered into the shop for a cup of coffee. This was confirmed by Lara's behaviour. She put on her most charming self and rose to welcome him.

"Good afternoon," she said. "I'm presuming you are Sergeant Peters."

"Yes, ma'am. And you, I'm presuming, are the beautiful Lara Morgan I've heard so much about." He extended his hand. She ushered him to a table and pointed to a chair. "Please have a seat, Sergeant." I sat at the table behind them on my break. It was hard not to overhear their conversation. "Have you had a chance to look over the proposal I dropped off?" Lara asked.

"Yes ma'am, I have," he said opening the folder. "I see here you want to offer hamburgers, French fries, cokes, and milkshakes."

"That's right," she replied eagerly. "You see, I plan to expand my menu to include the American carte du jour. I want to provide a taste of home for the American boys while they're here. We also have a jukebox with all the top hits, both Australian and American. We're a little behind on the latest tunes from overseas but I figure with your boys out in the jungle and so on, they probably are, too."

Sergeant Peters stared at her with a look that indicated he had something else on his mind.

"Now, the exciting thing is," she continued, "I want to offer exclusive half price nights for your boys who come in between the hours of ten and twelve. The problem is, there are a lot of imposters posing as Americans on R&R as well as—I'm sure you're aware—a number of young fellows who blend in but who deliberately missed their flights back to Vietnam. AWOL, I believe you call it. So I was wondering how the boys on R&R would identify themselves," she said.

"That's easy," he said. "They're required to carry their military ID with them at all times." He continued to sit rigidly straight. He blinked. "Now, exactly what is it you want from us?" he asked.

"I'm told you hand out information packages recommending places to stay, things to do, that sort of thing. I was hoping you'd add the GI's Hut to that list."

I looked up to catch Sergeant Peters fix his eyes on her for a very long time. "Well, Lara, we don't really recommend, but we do strongly suggest appropriate places for our men to visit." He leaned forward.

"So, will you suggest, Sergeant Peters, the GI's Hut as a reputable venue for your troops?"

"I'm afraid I can't do that," he said, sitting back again. "It would be difficult to recommend or rather *suggest* a place offering food I've never tasted."

"Of course!" she said. "How absent minded of me. I'll take lunch to your staff at the Chevron Hotel. No charge. How many men should I cater for?"

"That won't be necessary," he replied. "How about I come back at ten thirty tonight so I can experience exactly what you're proposing?"

"That would be lovely, Sergeant Peters," Lara replied settling back into her chair.

He took her hand. "Please, call me Stan," he said with the relaxed charm of a handsome, experienced man.

Their eyes and hands were still engaged when Leo entered the coffee shop. Neither of them seemed to notice him.

"Hello, Stan, what brings you in here?" asked Leo, ignoring Lara.

"An interesting proposal, Leo," said Stan.

"And what proposal is that?" asked Leo.

"We don't have time to talk about it now, Leo. I'll tell you later," said Lara.

Chapter 15

Equal Opportunity?

In spite of skipping so many classes to spend time with GIs on R&R, the one lecture I never missed was sociology. I even handed in my assignments. And I never missed the sociology tutorial where we discussed issues that were presented in the lecture. Marnie, the grad student running the class, provided a list of topics to be covered during the year. We were each given that list and required to tick off three subjects and to state our preference for debating the affirmative or the negative side. Based on our choices, she assigned the topics and distributed another list with names and dates. Life's experiences had already prepared me for today's discussion: Is There Equal Opportunity in Australia? My opponent on the affirmative side was Chris.

Before we started I reviewed portions of a letter from my friend Billy, who had lived with racial prejudice all his life.

You know, Catherine, I was thinking about you as a white person, me as an Indian, and about our inter-relationships with

*the world, other groups, and each other. Prejudice is something
everyone has in some degree. It has many sources and may be seen
in all areas of life. The fact that a person doesn't violently hate
another race does not mean he is free from prejudice.*

*Some prejudices may be good. It is good to have loyalty towards
the groups and people you're responsible to, but there must be
a balance. Most prejudices seem more harmful than helpful. A
prejudice can cause a person to hate. It can blind him to truth or
cause him to waste time and energy on fear instead of constructive emotions and activities...*

"What we have in Australia is not too far removed from
the caste system in India," I said, empowered by what I'd
seen, rather than by what I'd read. "Society and our government just won't acknowledge it,"

"Are you crazy? It's nothing like the caste system in India.
Everyone in this country has equal opportunity," Chris
insisted.

"That doesn't make any sense," I objected. "You're busy
protesting the war and conscription, and yet you say everyone has equal opportunity?" What began as a discussion on
racism in Friday morning's session, took an unexpected turn.
"The boys who are called up don't have equal opportunity."

"Of course they do," Chris struck back. "They just didn't
work hard enough to get a deferral." That got the attention of
more than one male student sitting around the table.

"Not everyone has the resources available to be a student," I said. "And why would everyone want to be a student,
anyway?" I asked, challenging the assumption that being a

university student had an air of superiority attached to it. "Society needs people in the service and trade industries in order to function efficiently."

"Motivation is everything."

"Are you insinuating that if he's not a student, he's not motivated?" I asked.

"Not exactly. He could be motivated to be a rugby player, or a gardener, or a mechanic."

"Success in those fields doesn't exempt you from being called up though, does it?"

"Of course it doesn't."

"And if you are called up, you don't consider the motivation to serve your country and do the best job you can a worthy one?" I asked.

"We're not talking about motivation in general terms, Catherine. We're talking about motivation to succeed. And the only way to do that is through education so you can make something of yourself," he said.

"I'm sorry, but you're expressing an elitist view that, in itself, reeks of a distinction between the haves and the have-nots," I said. "Success, as defined in your terms, depends largely on opportunity. And not everyone has the same opportunities as you."

"You don't have to worry about finding yourself in a uniform fighting a stupid war," he said.

"No, I don't, but if I did, it would be difficult to deal with the fact that you, the academic elite of my generation, are spitting on me while I'm risking my life for you to have the freedom to say the things you're saying right now," I said.

"It goes deeper than that. It's the whole moral issue about war. War is not the answer, as Marvin Gaye sings and as Martin Luther King has stated," he said.

"I agree, but don't you see you're igniting your own version of war?"

"We're marching for peace," Chris said.

If I didn't know better, I might have thought he was close to tears. I stood back for a moment so that the impact of Chris's statement could reverberate around the room, and out through the open window to the campus consciousness. I glanced down at the letter.

...Catherine, in my opinion, prejudice has many sources and it would be impossible to be insulated from at least some effects of exposure to these sources. We unconsciously pick up attitudes and opinions which we see in those around us, even before we are old enough to understand their significance. Ignorance is another source of prejudice. When we do not understand something we form wrong opinions. People tend to have a fear of the unknown. In order to defend our own sense of security, we may form negative opinions against unknown factors ...

"Fear is at the root of conflict," I said. "Looking at history, who were the spokesmen for the dignity of humanity? Has there ever been a voice capable of understanding both sides? A voice strong enough that it could have avoided war? You and I are involved in a heated discussion right now. Holding onto our truths is fuelling the fire and preventing understanding. Instead of defending our opinions, would we be further along if we cared—or were humble enough—to listen to what the other one is saying?" I asked.

"Unfortunately, mankind hasn't evolved that far yet," he said, as though the thought was meant to say just that.

"We're way off topic, Chris and Catherine," Marnie interjected.

"In the meantime, don't you see that what you're doing demeans our boys in the military regardless of whether they were called up or they signed up?" I persisted.

"That's a different issue altogether," Marnie said in a further attempt to keep us on track.

"Is your issue with those who are called up, those who choose the military as a profession, or with government policy?" I asked, as one topic connected to another—in my mind—in a chain of links that would hopefully lead to a solid anchor of understanding.

"I don't trust that this government won't turn the tables on those of us who are studying and trying to make something of ourselves. The Tet Offensive showed that we're fighting a losing battle over there, but the government isn't withdrawing. As far as I'm concerned, they could keep us there just to prove they're right. The Vietcong have shown how resilient they are," Chris said.

"Poverty and privilege are the real issues on the table, which once more, suggests a class system," I said, in the hope of getting back to the topic. Chris and I were being evaluated this morning and would receive a mark based on our preparation, delivery, and ability to stick to the point.

"Only if you want it to," Chris said.

"Just last year the Aboriginal people were recognised as Australians for the first time. Despite the fact that ninety percent of Australians voted in favour of Aboriginal Rights, we still have a huge problem with discrimination. Don't you think it's odd that Aborigines are exempt from conscription because of the assimilation policy?" I asked. "What does equal opportunity really mean for any of us?"

"Once again, you're a girl. You don't have to worry about it, do you?" Chris had made a choice to answer only one of the two questions asked so I chose to ignore his statement.

"We've stripped the Aboriginal people of their land, their culture, and their dignity. We've taken their children away. Most of them live in inner city areas and are merely surviving. Don't tell me they have the same opportunities as the rest of us. Just look around. How many Aborigines do you see in this room? I haven't seen one since I've been on campus. I've seen lots of them not too far from here, trying to survive in the inner suburbs, though. Our well-meaning programs are so far off the mark. The government provides milk for the Aboriginal children twice a day, but it's making them sick. They can't digest lactose, yet the government refuses to take notice. The government is more concerned with looking good than doing what's right. These Australian children are stuck in hovels with no way out. Often their parents are alcohol dependent, another toxin we introduced them to," I argued.

"The Aborigines drink because that's what they *want* to do," said Chris. "They're not motivated to get a move on. It's pathetic. All they want to do is sit around and bludge off the government. If they wanted to make something of themselves, they would, but they just can't be bothered. Here's a solution to all our problems: get them out of the city and let them go walkabout."

"Really! Just bundle them up and set them on their way. It's not enough that the white man destroyed their culture once. Let's give it back to them now that we've established an alternate path of destruction for them to negotiate against all odds. Let's cancel our plan to integrate them into our woeful ways and send them back to where they came from. It's our interference and insistence on knowing what's good for them and everybody else that's pathetic. Surely it's time to ask the Aboriginal people what they need in order to live fulfilled lives as Australians."

"Good luck on that." Chris seemed to have lost his spark.

"Thank you for an interesting session," interrupted Marnie. "You've touched on a lot of issues, but unfortunately we're out of time. I noticed many of you raised your hands during the discussion and I apologise to you for not having the chance to voice your opinions. This room is free for the next hour if any of you would like to stay behind and add your thoughts."

"I have one more point to make," I said. "My cousin is in Vietnam putting his life on the line for Australia. That includes you, Chris. He is a conscript. He has told me stories about Aborigines he's met who enlisted. In particular, his best friend, Peter. In Vietnam, they don't see themselves as black and white. They are Australians working together for a cause they believe in and keeping each other alive. The enemy is in the field. It's not each other."

"On Thursday we will hear from Dawn and Trevor and their thoughts on the link between poverty and prejudice in our society," concluded Marnie.

The room emptied. Famished teenagers scrambled to get to the Roundhouse and beat the line-up at the cafeteria.

As I packed my briefcase, I lingered over the letter.

...and finally, when a person is not mature enough to try to accept ideas and other people, or when he is insecure, he is an easy victim for prejudice. One way to overcome prejudice is to accept yourself and become sure of your own opinions and abilities. Another way is to accept the fact that new ideas and new people are not necessarily a threat to your security and may enrich your life.

I hope I didn't bore you with my thoughts, but I can't say very much until I hear from you. Do you think you could send me a catalogue of the University of NSW? I'm thinking I'd like to study at your university.

Your Friend Always, Billy

"Want to continue over lunch in my office?" Chris challenged with a wink.

"Sure."

Chapter 16

TOO KOOL!

August 1969

The energy of Kings Cross ignited my spirit more than ideas presented in textbooks and lecture theatres ever could, for the diversity of the human plight was right there—from the underworld with its strip clubs and prostitutes, to the hard workers operating legitimate businesses, to the drug addicts, and then to the stars of the show, the young Americans on R&R.

Because of my humble beginnings I suppose, the plight of the underdog always attracted me. That's why I wanted to be a social worker and not a teacher. And that's why I had been able to speak passionately in a sociology tutorial. My convictions came from what I observed and what I learned in personal conversations. And then of course, from what I dared to venture into and the risks I dared to take. After a year at the university, I had little to show for my efforts, having failed my three other subjects. I managed to transfer to teachers' college, but with a similar lack of enthusiasm. I was, however, the eager recipient of a growing stack of letters and photos from Vietnam and America.

After an hour or two at teachers' college, I'd walk from Paddington down Crown Street past the Women's Hospital to the intersection where William Street handed the city's reins over to Darlinghurst Road and Kings Cross. From there to the El Alamein fountain where the road curved to the left, Kings Cross was, at first glance, like any other Sydney suburb. At least during the day. But unlike other suburbs, the streets had accommodated a look that set the Cross apart. Hotels placed visitors at its epicentre. Predators lay in wait to extract visitors' cash. Glittering entrances drew locals as well as the clean-cut young men, strolling in pairs more often than not.

The GI's Hut was a place to go and take it all in. The double sliding doors opened the street to full view. Across the road, Pinocchio's—a real restaurant with male waiters in black trousers and white shirts, and soft music and lighting that set the tone for a romantic dinner—was a reminder of where business could go if the drive and the cash were there.

The GI's Hut would have been a good name for a soap opera. Whether as a customer or a waitress, my need to be there became an addiction, like the compulsion to tune in to the next episode of a favourite television show: the tragedy of Leo cheating on Lara, which had ended abruptly when she started up with Sergeant Stan Peters, who knew of Leo's unfaithful behaviour through his connection with the Pink Pussy Cat; the on-again off-again uncertainty of Paul and Grace; the developing character of pretty but naïve Carol as one of those sure-to-become tragic characters; the slithering snake named Ron, always lurking in the shadows; the steady comings and goings of Americans on R&R with or without girls by their sides. And then of course there was me; although I didn't realise it at first, I had also become one of the characters. But just what my role was and how I contributed to the plot was as yet unclear.

Carol was sitting at a table near the front of the shop on one of those days I called in just to hang out. It was always obvious what scene Paul and Grace were in. The bliss or the hurt hung in the air until one of them dropped it. This time, through the bunker-like opening that looked down from the kitchen, I saw their heads leaning into each other. I waved to them and decided to sit with Carol.

I admired Carol's elegance as a smoker of Kool cigarettes. Her words flowed around the cigarette and waited while she drew in the smoke. Her chin lifted and turned slightly as she blew it away from my face. Sometimes between puffs she continued her thought. Sometimes she seemed to forget. It didn't matter. The packet called to me with the promise that I would become more confident, more demure, and better equipped to handle my own destiny—like Carol—if I explored what was inside.

"Can I have one of those?" I asked.

She slid the green and white packet towards me. I felt the exhilaration of defiance as one of the expectations that others had established for me—and I had consequently established for myself—was about to shatter. Until this moment it had been an undisputed fact of life that I would never smoke, like confessing my sins and not drinking until I was twenty-one.

"I work at the Whisky now," Carol said between puffs.

Although Mum and Granny smoked and I had seen it, smelled it, and inhaled it every day of my life, I'd failed to notice how they actually did it. How they got the thing going. How they transferred the flame from the lighter to the cigarette was now something I wished I'd observed in more detail.

"The pay isn't as great as the Crest but the tips more than make up for it," she said.

What would the nuns think? I wondered without the slightest regret. I opened the box, pulled out the object that symbolised how common I'd become, and got used to the feel of it between my fingers. The filter wrapper confused the issue with its indiscriminate whiteness. I had no idea which end to put in my mouth.

Carol tapped her cigarette repeatedly with one finger and then rolled it on the edge of the ashtray to remove the grey fuzz not wanting to let go. Finally, I figured it out and placed the filter between my lips.

"Only thing is, I work nights and don't get off 'til three," she said, seemingly unaware of my crisis. "So if I feel like going out, it's a bit of a drag because everything else is closing down at that time, too."

Carol said hello to Graham, a homeless man who entered the coffee shop for his three thirty slice of sheer delight—the signature chocolate cake Lara enjoyed baking. Lara had a soft spot for old Graham. Besides the fact that he would turn up again later to do the dishes and take the load off rush time, there was a special understanding between them. Perhaps Graham reminded her of her father. Or maybe he was just an uncomplicated person who required nothing from her other than the enjoyment of her chocolate cake and the opportunity to feel useful.

"Catherine, what the hell are you doing?"

"It's okay, Paul, I'm just trying it out." I removed the cigarette, held it about half an inch from my lips, and stared straight ahead.

Paul mumbled something under his breath and huffed off to the kitchen.

"I'm thinking of getting a perm," said Carol, pulling her shiny hair up to eye level so she could disapprove of it more closely.

"I think it's beautiful just the way it is," I said. "This is my first cigarette."

She stubbed hers out, flipped the lid on the Zippo lighter she'd obviously been given by an American, and moved it toward my face where the cigarette was poised and ready.

"Just suck the air through the filter and it'll light."

I sucked through the filter like an anemone latching on in an ocean rock pool. And coughed violently.

"Very cool. Very cool indeed," whispered Paul from behind. I doubled over and waved my hand over my mouth. My lungs became stuck, like the summer I was cooling off under the hose and slipped flat on my back, winding myself.

"Learned your lesson yet?" He pounded my back, slapping hard to make a point. "Take a deep breath."

I heaved in a thimble full of air with a desperate shrill. One more strained breath and I straightened, relieved that my lungs were becoming unstuck.

"Thanks," I said to Paul, feeling like a dressed-up circus elephant that had just toppled off her tightrope.

"You won't be fool enough to try that again," he said. "At least I hope you won't."

"Call in to the Whisky some time," Carol said as she stood to leave. She put her arms through the sleeves of her cardigan and adjusted the front and back to drape just the way she wanted. She fastened the top button, then changed her mind. She undid it, opened the front panels, and tugged on the waist of her dress. She looked down to check her cleavage. "There's no cover charge for girls when you join the Madison Ladies Club," she said flicking back her hair.

"What's that?"

"It's a membership to get you into the Whisky. You fill out a form that asks for your name, age, address, phone number, and occupation. Then they give you a card and you're a member."

"Do you pay anything?" I asked.

Paul shook his head in disapproval. I ignored him.

"Nothing," Carol said.

A tall fair-haired American entered the coffee shop, and Carol's manner changed abruptly.

"Hey, baby," he said, snuggling into her hair before a tap on his shoulder interrupted a lengthier embrace. He turned to the GI behind him and said, "What are you doing here, Steve? I thought you were going to buy a wool suit."

"Well, I just thought I'd join you guys for a cup of coffee first, if you don't mind," Steve said, glancing shyly around the shop.

"Catherine," said Carol, "this is Skip and his friend, Steve. Skip and I are going to catch a bite a little later. Why don't you two join us?"

"Nice to meet you." Steve offered his hand. His dark hair complemented the well-proportioned features of his ruggedly handsome face. Dark-rimmed glasses framed his brown eyes. He looked intelligent.

"Well, maybe for a little while," I said. "I've got Housie tonight, so I can't stay too long."

"Well, whatever. You'd have more fun with us." She was right.

"I need to talk to Paul for a bit. I'll see you at the fountain in about fifteen minutes."

"Sure," Carol said as she left with Skip.

"Well, I guess I'll see you at the fountain," said Steve. "By the way. What's Housie?"

"It's like your Bingo."

"Oh."

Chapter 17

VENTURING FURTHER

On my way to the fountain I was tempted, as usual, by Andres. I loved the melt-in-your-mouth comfort of Paddington Chocolates. The extra calories would be shed on my walk to the station and later at Housie, selling tickets. Andres was a tiny specialty shop owned and operated by a family of European origin who had brought with them a recipe for the most sought-after chocolates in Sydney. Mr Armantier, a small round man in his sixties, had a flair for the impeccable that his dress and manner reflected. He infused his chocolates with the same delicious flawless delight.

One foot in the entryway, I anticipated the choices to be made amongst crunchy, creamy, and hard caramel centres. There was no question about the chocolate covering. Milk was much smoother and sweeter than bitter dark. The different foil wrappers flashed their colours through the shiny glass window, describing the sensations they kept fresh and protected from the cockroaches, flies, ants, and other bugs found in Sydney's sub-tropical climate. Six pieces of chocolate in a brown paper bag were enough to make me think I should try to lose weight and save more of my waitressing money, but the taste and the comfort they provided kept me coming back. It was another Kings Cross addiction I cherished.

"Hey, doll!" Images of sweet light-brown comfort melting in my mouth stopped short at the door, as Ron blocked the way. "Haven't seen you for a while. Are you still working up here in the Cross?"

"The GI's Hut," I answered.

"Yeah, I know it! On the other side of the road over there. Not much gets by me. I know everything going on around here," he bragged.

Ron pretended he was an American who'd gone AWOL. He provided options for a price—contacts, safe housing—to those Americans who chose not to turn up at the Chevron on the morning of their scheduled departure. "You don't sound American anymore. Are you still AWOL?" I asked, anticipating the next mountain of lies.

"All in the past," he said. "After a while they forget about things like that. More important things to deal with."

"I find that hard to believe," I said.

"It's not your worry, is it?" His eyes grew wide. His unwashed hair skimmed the top of his black shirt collar and hung in ragged strands. He'd slicked it back with Vaseline at the temples—or perhaps his own body's grease. Unshaven hair poked through his chin and cheeks like stubs left behind in a bushfire.

"Hey," he said with the flick of a lizard tongue, "you busy right now? There's a guy who just arrived this morning, looking for a nice girl to talk to."

"No thanks, I'm busy."

"Your friend, Carol, she's moved up in the world, you know. Works at the Whisky now. I could get you a job there, too. You'd make a whole shitload more money than what you're making at the coffee shop. I swear!"

He turned his back and pointed towards the El Alamein Fountain at the end of the street.

"See him? Look!" He grabbed my shoulder.

"Please don't touch me," I said, pulling away.

"He just wants to have coffee. That's all. They get pretty lonely, you know, these poor guys. Helps to have someone to talk to. They're here all alone without a family or nothing."

Pedestrians and cars attempted to beat the eruption of the pre-evening hubbub as another workday drew to an end. I squinted through the late afternoon street traffic. Carol and the guys hadn't yet arrived.

"I'm busy," I said. He grabbed my arm and pulled me in front of the Lowe's Men's Clothing window.

"Just say hello," he said. "That's all you have to do. Don't be such a snob."

The spray from the fountain, every droplet caught in the sunshine, spilled onto three tiered platforms that never over-flowed. A light coastal wind lifted the spray and distorted the perfect shape of the watery dandelion, now gently caressing passers-by. It added to the chill already biting the air.

I lost my interest in the chocolates and walked towards the fountain behind Ron. He blabbered about the cold and exchanged familiar greetings with both bouncers on guard at the two strip joints we passed between Andres and the ice cream shop on the corner.

"I'll introduce you and then you're on your own," he said as we waited for the traffic light to turn red and the cars to stop.

"Here she is," Ron announced before turning to catch the light. "I'll get back to you."

"Hi, my name is George," the stranger said. "Would you like to come up to my room?"

"I think you may have the wrong idea, George. I'm not that kind of girl."

"I can see that."

"You have to watch out for guys like him."

"Well...I've got nothing else to do. Would you like to grab a coffee anyway? Maybe go for a walk?"

"Sorry, George. I'm actually meeting some people shortly. Maybe another time?"

"Sure. It's cool. See ya!" He left abruptly, crossing the street in Ron's direction as Carol arrived with Skip and Steve.

Skip had kind blue eyes. His long thin body stooped in a gentle arc that made him comfortable to be around. Quiet people sometimes have a way of drawing you in. His hair had already begun to recede from the temples, and he had the air of someone who had learned from his experience. He wore a jacket and tie. He already had his arm around Carol.

"I like your jumper," I said to Steve.

"What, now?"

I like the jumper you're wearing." I pulled on the sleeve.

"Is that what you call it? It's a sweater to us. A jumper is a dress that girls wear over a blouse."

"That's funny," I said.

Even though we spoke the same language I was learning that there were many differences in meanings and spelling.

"I'm kind of hungry," he said. "Anyone else?"

"I've been dreaming of steak for eleven months," Skip said in a near trance.

"Well, I have to go soon, so you guys go ahead," I said, counting myself out. What would it be like to make my own decisions? Wonders floated into questions out of reach, unable to connect to the answers they sought. What would it be like to make a decision and not be concerned about the consequences others would dictate? What must it be like to live free from the fear of the expectations of others?

"Pizza would be faster than steak. Could you manage that?" asked Steve, having tuned into the misfortune of my time restriction.

"Sure."

"Mama Marta's is just down the road. They serve the best pizzas, lots of cheese," Carol said.

An aggravating squeal grew closer and more frantic. It was an ambulance screaming toward the Wayside Chapel. We watched it round the corner, the siren subsiding to a moan. It was either another beating or another overdose.

We headed towards Mama Marta's. On the way, I calculated the departure time of the last train that would enable me to be on time for Housie. I would have to go straight there. I wouldn't be able to call in at home to change. If I stayed for a couple of slices of pizza, I wouldn't need to. I could spend an hour with Carol and these boys before leaving to catch the train. The delicious aroma of pizza spices and meats entwining with tomato and green peppers wafted through the doorway and grabbed our attention. The jukebox played "And When I Die," which we heard well before our eyes could focus on the specials written on the blackboard outside.

"I don't like that song," said Carol.

We blocked the doorway, and waited for the establishment's protocol to tell us what to do. When no directions came, Steve stepped aside and extended his arm.

"After you, ladies."

We chose a table just inside the door by a window that was framed with a curtain of the same material as the red and white chequered cloths covering each of the seven or so tables. Four or five of those tables were occupied by friends exchanging stories and couples in various stages of getting to know each other. Steve pulled out one of the wooden chairs, waited for me to take my place, and glided it effortlessly under the table as I lowered myself onto the seat.

"Thank you," I said, surprised at how the blending of manners and compliance resulted in such a flawless motion.

A heavy man who may have sampled too many of his own pizzas appeared at our table. Red and orange blobs splattered his white T-shirt and the apron that held up his belly. He reminded me of a worn-out version of Paul. Any concern about sanitation, or lack of it, was subdued by the richness of the aroma he produced in his ovens. "A large Mama Marta Deluxe, please," said Carol.

Steve offered his cigarettes. Skip and Carol accepted. I passed.

"You smoke!" Carol said almost accusingly when I declined.

"Of course I do. I just don't feel like one now," I said.

A girl strutted up and down the laneway just outside Mama Marta's. She swung the shortened strap of her shoulder bag around and chomped on her gum. She stopped to take a draw on her cigarette, her other hand posed boldly on her hip. Impatience drew lines on her face and kept her moving while she waited for something to happen, someone to come along. Waiting for her prey. Herself the prey. Her black fishnet stockings were full of holes.

"Gotta have beer with pizza," Steve declared. "Ladies? Skip?"

"Sounds good to me," said Skip.

"Sure," said Carol.

"Not for me, thanks. I have to work tonight."

"So do I. One isn't going to hurt anything," Carol said. Steve and Skip agreed.

I looked out the window to see the ambulance that had earlier done its best to answer an emergency. It waited mournfully at the light, its siren muzzled as it ambled back to the hospital after apparently arriving too late at the scene, a common story in this part of the city.

"Pineapple juice," I said, honouring my pledge not to drink. Although I believed I really was rescuing a tortured soul from Purgatory, I hadn't mentioned it since Tom. Nor would I, realising how ridiculous it must seem to anyone whose religious experiences differed from mine. I was grateful when they let it pass.

At last the heavy man in the grubby apron arrived back at our table and plonked down a pizza generously topped with melting cheese.

"Enjoya youa pizza," he said.

Steve grabbed the largest piece in one hand while waving with the other for us to join in. Skip signalled to Carol and me, before taking his piece. I chose the closest one. Carol reached for the smallest.

The plates had no sooner emptied and the small talk ended when Carol announced she had to go.

Steve and Skip insisted on paying the bill and went to the counter to sort out the details with the waiter, who was also the cook and probably the owner. Carol and I said nothing to each other but watched as Ron appeared on the street outside, speaking to the girl in fishnet stockings. He threw up his arms before charging down the lane.

We headed down Darlinghurst Road towards Whisky A-Go-Go. By the time we turned onto Williams Street we had split into pairs and walked quickly down its steep incline. Steve and I took the lead. Carol and Skip followed.

Retail shops ended sales for the day with the closing of their doors. The flashing lights outside the strip joints shone brighter. The expectant evening throng replaced the tired business community. More girls, standing alone, appeared in doorways and on street corners.

"I'm not dressed," I protested at the entrance to Whisky A-Go-Go when Steve turned in without asking me. The clothes I'd worn all day drooped with tiredness.

"You look dressed to me," said Steve. I checked my watch. Fifteen minutes to catch the train. I could make it. Or I could call in to the Whisky for a short while and catch the next train. Would it really matter if I was a bit late? They always had lots of workers at Housie. I should call Granny. But maybe I could still get there in time without them even noticing.

"Fill out your Madison Ladies Club form now so you can get in for free," urged Carol.

The coat check girl slid the application form along the counter and placed a pen on top of it. I recorded my particulars and was instantly issued a pass.

Dancing with Steve made me forget all about time.

Chapter 18

HOUSIE

"Where the bloody hell have you been?" Mum charged like a jail keeper when she heard the front door unlock. I hadn't yet sorted out my excuse for being late because judgment, though misguided, and wishful thinking were supposed to get me home before the last call. "I've been worried sick about you. When I got to Housie, Granny told me you hadn't come home. And you didn't call."

When I was ten years old I looked forward to Saturday and Monday night outings at Housie. Undisturbed by the coughing and spluttering of old people, I thrived on the unhealthy satisfaction of soft drinks, chips, chocolate, Granny's coloured chalk, and cigarette smoke. The hall above the primary school at St Joseph's opened its doors to welcome the blue, mauve, grey, white haired, and balding generation willing to part with pension cheques rather than miss an opportunity to win some money. They sat wall-to-wall along rows of tables, which were set up before and taken down after each devotional gamble with fate. Now and then, younger people Mum's age showed up. But not too many and not too often.

Sometimes Mum attended Housie and sometimes she didn't, preferring to go dancing, meet friends, work late, or whatever else she did that we weren't informed about.

For the first few years I sat with Granny, sipping bright red Sunset Sip or cloudy Lemon Delight and eating at least two bags of Smith's Crisps. If Granny won, I also got a Cadbury's Crunch. "Pleasantly plump," Granny had corrected, when I told her about Carol Long telling everyone on the playground that I was a "fatty boom breaks."

Between Housie calls, the hall resounded in a boisterous eruption of voices, chip bag rattling, and coughing. At the sound of the caller's voice, amplified through a microphone set at just the right volume, silence descended like a brick. Sneezes, cravings for a salty chip, and the urge to whisper a sliver of juicy gossip were all denied. Missing a number was tantamount to committing a sin. Losing the extra cash that would have allowed a few more pulls on the pokies during the week administered its own penance.

Granny, like most of the players, had a lucky seat. It was two thirds down on the left side by the window that remained open in summer and shut in winter. Her Housie bag contained the essentials: a packet of Viscount cigarettes; a lighter; a wooden box resembling an oversized pencil case, slanted at just the right angle to comfortably mark off the tickets; and paper clips to fasten the tickets onto the board. The last item in her bag of lucky charms was a worn-out bath towel, cut into squares for wiping the chalk off her hands. A panel slid out underneath the box to reveal Granny's tools: purple, orange, green, blue, yellow, brown, and red chalk that left its dust on the table, on our clothes, up our noses, and down our throats, but most of all on our fingers and around the palms of our hands. All of these items she took out of her bag as soon as she sat down and returned them after the last call.

At five cents a ticket, players bought one, two, three, or four from the sellers. Granny reliably chose to increase her chances with four tickets. Sometimes, if she was feeling particularly lucky or particularly desperate, she bought six. Only the truly skilled could handle six tickets at a time as it took superior concentration, a quick eye, fine-tuned hearing, and coordination to successfully mark off every matching number called.

Granny chose her chalk deliberately. Sometimes the colour complemented the ticket. Sometimes it was a mismatch, like a floral scarf that screamed against a tartan dress. She never marked off numbers with chalk the same colour as the card. But if she won with a certain combination, she'd play that colour chalk with that colour card until its luck ran out. In line with her superstitious beliefs, breaking a stick of chalk was bad luck and so was matching colours.

Chain smokers poured clouds of poisonous gases into the already polluted air, invading every cell. Only a bath could release it from our hair and our bodies. Sometimes my clothes had to wait for a week to be freed from the stench. Not that I noticed at first. It wasn't until fifth class, when Sister Rose accused me of smoking, that I became aware of actually wearing the odious and offensive smell. The accusation was humiliating.

As teenagers, we expanded our wallets doing one of four jobs at Housie: distributing cards to the sellers and counting the take, working in the kiosk, walking the floor to give change and call back the numbers on winning cards, or worst of all, selling tickets. This last job required racing up and down the aisles, tearing off the right amount of tickets, collecting the money, and giving change before some lucky person called "Housie!" If a game didn't go off early and there was time, we would run down the wide concrete stairs to breathe in the night air's relief. Sometimes we'd steal a private word with a friend or grab an opportunity to flirt before skipping back up the stairs, mostly two at a time because we'd be late.

I began working in the kiosk when I was twelve years old. Not only did I have something to do but I was paid $1.50 for four hours work. The thrill of putting my own money in my own purse and in my own school bank account was worth every minute it took to earn it.

Eventually, Housie became a social event, a legitimate place for young people to hang out while earning a scrap of pocket money under the dimming supervision of old folk. Donny, Warren, Jimmy, and Monica were among the friends I'd known forever because of Monday and Saturday night Housie.

I knew from Michael's letters that Monica hadn't escaped his attention.

Dear Muffin,

The whole of Vung Tau has been on alert for the last 11 days because of an expected attack. We have doubled the guard and cancelled all leave. Today 21 Australians who were wounded were brought into the hospital by helicopters. The "copters" also brought in two dead. Don't tell anyone we've been in trouble, otherwise Mum might find out and start worrying. Every time I write to Mum I tell her everything is great.

I'm going to come home for my R&R and then when I come back to this Godforsaken place I'll only have about four months before I come home for good. I don't hear much from Jimmy or the others these days but Monica writes all the time.

Please write soon. Michael

Mum's tirade snapped me out of my reflection.

"I even thought about going to the Cross," she bellowed. "You can't do this to your grandmother and me. I almost called the police. Get in there." Her hand struck the middle of my back, pushing me towards the kitchen. I merged myself into the safe place that guarded my soul when Mum entered her rage.

"I'm doing the best I can, raising you on my own, and this is the thanks I get," she screamed.

Granny came through the front door and locked it behind her. She carried her Housie bag in one hand and a cigarette in the other. She stooped lower than usual.

"Where have you been, dearest?" she asked. "I was so worried. I thought something had happened to you. Girls sometimes just disappear into thin air you know. Taken off and thrown into the white slave traffic, never to be seen again. When you didn't call I didn't know what to think," she said, peering at me through grey eyes that retreated behind envelopes of tired and sagging skin.

"I'm sorry." I wanted to tell them that a call would have bound them to remind me of my responsibilities. So I didn't.

"Sorry doesn't cut it, miss!" said Mum. "What about all the people you let down tonight? The Housie workers had to double up since they couldn't find someone to replace you at the last minute."

"Well, as long as you're safe and sound." Granny grasped the black handle of the kettle and took it to the sink to fill with water. "They had enough to cover for you," she said softly, out of Mum's hearing. "Now let's have a lovely cuppa?"

"I need a scotch," said Mum, already pouring from the half empty bottle of Johnnie Walker that Uncle Stu had bought for Granny on her last birthday.

"I'm not finished with you," she snapped, poking her finger into my shoulder. I returned to the safe place deep down inside, the calm place where Mum's words became a muffled string of incomprehensible noise.

"You look at me when I'm talking to you." She poked my shoulder with her long-nailed finger.

"It's getting late, Brenda," said Granny. "How about a nice cuppa, love? That's not going to do you any good," she said, reaching for the bottle of scotch.

"Leave that alone," Mum snarled like a crazed dog protecting its bone. She pushed Granny's arm away.

Granny turned towards the stove and removed the screeching kettle from the burner. She poured three cups of tea before opening the fridge door to get the milk.

"I'm going to have to get into this fridge," Granny muttered to no one in particular. "Hasn't had a good clean out for a while. In fact, Christmas was the last time it had a good going over. Crikey, I'm starting to fall behind on things around here."

She turned the milk bottle up and down several times, pressed her thumb into the silver foil cap, twisted it off, and grasped the bottle with both hands. She opened her mouth wide and drew in as much air as she could.

"Bit short of breath tonight," Granny wheezed.

"What are you nattering on about, you silly old goat? You never make any sense these days," snarled Mum, now turning on Granny. I cried inside.

"Here, love, here's your cuppa," said Granny. "We'll talk about this tomorrow. Things always look brighter in the morning." Some of the hot liquid spilled over the cup into the saucer, as her trembling hands placed it on the table.

"I told you, I don't want a bloody cup of tea." Mum swiped the cup and saucer off the table and sent them careening through the doorway to the dining room where they bounced off a metal chair leg and smashed.

From my safe place, I could see that Granny had slumped even lower. At the same time, I was fascinated by the brown liquid seeping into the light grey sculpted carpet as it spread out in all directions. Steaming and staining.

"I'm sick and tired of everybody trying to run my life. I wouldn't be in this mess if that bastard hadn't left." Mum sloshed back her scotch with a single swig. "I can see I'm not getting anywhere around here. I'm going for a drive." Her words fell out and trailed behind her. With a slam of the front door so forceful it rattled the glass, she was gone.

Granny dragged her tired old body to the sink where she ran the dishcloth under cold water. I sighed too, but with relief that Mum had taken her anger somewhere else.

"Poor thing. She doesn't mean it. She's had such a rough go of it." Granny laboured under another heavy sigh. "Did I tell you she nearly drowned in the Murrumbidgee River and that she swallowed an open safety pin?"

"Many times, Granny."

"Poor thing," she repeated. "She loves you. You know that, don't you?"

"Yes," I said, wondering how it was that someone who loved me could be so cruel.

I took the dishcloth from Granny, got down on my hands and knees, and daubed at the stain. Granny brought the garbage bin over. She eased herself to the floor with the help of the wooden sideboard. Together we collected each scattered shard and chunk of broken crockery. The cup and saucer were pretty once, and delicate. Now their red, blue, and yellow flowers lay destroyed.

"Try and remember that things like this set her off," Granny said. "You should have been at Housie tonight. If you had done the right thing, this wouldn't have happened." Mild irritation leaked into her crackling voice. "At least a phone call."

"I think I'm finished with Housie," I said, standing to freshen the cloth before returning to rub harder at the stain.

"You can't do that," said Granny.

"Yes, I can. I need the time to study. Sometimes I need to go to the library. Housie ties me up too much." The time had come to break away. "And besides I'd like to go out on Saturday nights."

"Who would you go out with?" Granny looked astonished. "All your friends work at Housie."

"No they don't." It had become too difficult to share the meaningful episodes of my day, even with Granny. "I have other friends."

"Not from the Cross I hope," she said as if reading my thoughts. "I'm a bit worried about you up there."

As she hauled herself unsteadily up from the dining room floor, I grabbed her arm just above the elbow and took her weight.

"Don't worry about me, Granny." I gently pulled her shrinking body closer. She drew back, opened her mouth, inhaled as much air as she could for the third time that I'd noticed, and rested her chin on my shoulder. "I'm not dumb, you know," I said, patting her hair. "What happened to your blue rinse?"

"Can't be bothered lately." She put her hand to her mouth and heaved a gurgling cough.

So much about Granny I took for granted.

"Do you think you should give up the smokes?" I dared to ask. She felt like a worn teddy bear as I held her—one that had been so loved its ears were half chewed, its button eyes loose, and its fur patchy. Just like the one she gave me for my first birthday.

"Never!" she said.

Before going to bed, I searched through my letters so I could reread the one about love.

Catherine, I was thinking or wondering about a word you used to close your letter. Maybe you know more about it than I do, but I think I need to share my ideas about "love" with you. To be frank, I don't know what it means to really love someone.

You know I come from a broken home. I don't think I know much about loving someone else but since I started believing in Jesus, I felt like I can, maybe, express myself a little about "love."

I have asked myself many times, "What makes a home a home?" In my life, I've lived with the rich and the poor. I've seen many broken homes and broken hearts. No matter where I've been, I've seen homeless children, unmarried mothers, illegitimate children, wedlock brutality, delinquent kids, alcoholism and tragic, sad stories of families.

I asked myself why there are broken homes, or why some houses are just houses, not homes. I realized that a family living in a house doesn't necessarily make a house a home. Love makes a home because each member of the family truly loves each other. Then I asked myself, "What is love?"

Personally I realized that love is not just emotional feeling. It is more than feeling. It is not only feeling but love is also patient, kind, understanding, tender, unselfish, does not demand too much, does not expect too much, is not too critical, is not too sharp in words or unfair in judgment, or unkind in deeds, and it is never envious, not arrogant, or proud, or self seeking, or touchy, or resentful.

This is a description of love not a definition of love. Even though we can talk about love and read about it, we really can't define love by words, for words are too crude for the highly refined characteristics of the true love — but one can express love by words and deeds.

My hope for my own love may be too idealistic to ever be too practical or true, but that's what love means to me.

I asked one friend who is married and happy with it, what his love meant to him before he was married. He said, "It was an itching sensation in my heart that I didn't know how to scratch."

I hope you're all right. Take care.
With love as a friend, Billy

Chapter 19

NOWHERE TO GO

In my dream, I ran down a narrow, one-way road. The tricky landscape twisted and turned, making it impossible to see around the next bend. The terrain was so barren, rocky, and brown that nothing grew. The bare hint of even a blade of green was nowhere to be found. Tigers came running at me and passed me by. Relieved, I carried on. Snakes, bigger than I'd ever seen, slid over me and passed. Around the next bend, two ferocious lions charged at me and passed. Out of nowhere, one of the lions attacked. Salvation had teased me only to abandon me again. I would not survive the terror of this wasteland.

"It's all your fault!" Was it God? Was he punishing me for not going to Housie?

"If it wasn't for you, I'd have been a famous singer like Shirley. I wouldn't be in this lousy mess of a life." Had one of the lions pulled the blankets off my bed and clawed my shoulders?

"I didn't ask to be born," I uttered, speeding into a consciousness worse than the dangers of my dream.

"And I didn't ask you to be born. You were the result of your father's pleasure."

The slap across my head struck me like a bolt of lightning. My tormentor wasn't God after all. It was my mother.

"Mum," I pleaded as she dragged me into her ride through the flames of hell. Beautiful once, she was now ugly. Alcohol and cigarettes had weathered her skin, yellowed her perfect teeth and fingers. But it was her smell that repulsed me. Her breath and perfume reeked neglect.

"You're just like your father. You look like your father. You act like your father." The wire coat hanger stung my arms as she struck to the rhythm of her hatred. Then it was over.

"I'm sorry." She began to weep. "I do love you. Wait here, I'll be back in a minute." She stumbled to the bathroom, bumping into doors and walls that got in her way.

"What in the world is going on in here?" Granny appeared at the door. Squinting. She hadn't taken the time to put on her glasses.

"No more," I said calmly, buttoning my skirt while slipping the cotton jumper over my head in one miraculous motion. I was already half dressed.

"Where are you going?" Granny asked.

"I don't know yet." I gave her a quick kiss on the cheek. I opened the front door, turned towards her, and put my finger to my lips before gently pulling the front door closed.

Leaving Granny on the other side of the door, I stepped into the fog that constricted Sydney's inner western suburbs that morning. Images of thick London fogs and sinister events lurked behind every decaying bush, every prowling hedge, and every insidious brick fence veiled and out of view. A steel teasing comb became my weapon of defence. Its long-pointed handle offered the vague reassurance that I was armed for any Jack the Ripper mimic who dared to be skulking around the streets or loitering in darkened shop entryways—or anywhere else for that matter.

Focused fear can suspend time, and that's exactly what it did that morning. My arrival at Belmore Railway Station was seamless. The fog's ominous charade had dissolved any sense of a beginning and an end.

The station's iron gate guarded the kiosk, ticket office, and platform from after-hour thieves and vandals. Somewhere behind its bars dozed the stationmaster, I imagined, his feet plunked high on his disorganised desk like a pair of leaning bookends. In contrast, the ticket booth was well ordered with mini shelves that accommodated various coloured tickets denoting both the day of the week and the destination. I knew this from many train trips to the city. All of it, the order and the disorder, waited behind the brown, rusted gate.

My mother's violence and her love for me twisted into tight cords of rope around my thumping heart. I pressed my back against the sandstone wall beside the gate. Every breath warned the consequences of a sudden attack out of the darkness. The fog reached its fingers to the stationmaster's door, taunting him to turn on the lights and unlock the gate. I craved the flow of normal life and ached for the day to begin. Even after it did, safety would be an illusion. I had no plan and no knowledge of what the rest of the day would bring.

Commuters began to emerge from cars that pulled up and drove off. They milled around in the relaxation of their good night's sleep and the predictability of their brand-new day.

Finally, keys jangled from a large metal hoop and released the gate so it could crunch and rattle to the other side, at the same time slackening the rope of fear around my neck.

A shockwave of pain shot straight to my heel. There'd been no time for stockings to protect against the rubbing of the new shoes I'd paraded around the house for Granny's approval the day before. Perched on top of their shoebox by the dressing table, they were there to assist my escape when the time came.

"Next!" yelled the ticket clerk behind the counter, annoyed at the monotony of the first commuter rush that caused him to rally far too early after a heavy night. My foot dragged its shoe to the window.

"Single to the city, please."

Predictably on time, the carriages of the 5:30 train rattled along the track from Lakemba Station to stop at Belmore. Commuters had less than a minute to board. An on-time delivery depended on a strict order of business with no time for lollygagging. Commuters had spread themselves along the platform, lining up with the carriage that would open its door close to or right at the stairs of their destinations. Scrambling down the stairs to catch the train that would leave without me if it could, I tripped on a step. The conductor noticed and delayed his signal until I got through the door. Passengers flung their seat backs forwards or backwards, depending on which way they preferred to travel—facing the forward direction with control and purpose or turning their backs on the repetitiveness of a five-day work week.

A few men sank their faces into the quick snippets and teasing captions of the *Daily Mirror* or the *Sun* newspapers. The more serious folded their attention into the *Sydney Morning Herald*. Older ladies clicked steel or plastic knitting needles, weaving pale pink, blue, white, and yellow wool into jumpers for daughters, granddaughters, and grandsons. Friends dumped complaints on each other with the hope of lightening their loads. An ageless man and woman held hands. Their contentment raised them above the obscurity of a foggy morning. I chose the window seat across from them and settled into the green leather, reassured that the next half hour demanded nothing as the train sprinted to the city, catching its breath at each stop.

Dear Catherine,

I was lying here in bed spraying bug spray at mosquitoes when the bus driver handed me your letter. I was the only one to get any mail tonight. I've read your letter over six times and the more I read it, the more I think about what a mess I'm in. You told me a lot about yourself, so I am going to try and explain my background and tell you what I really believe and how I act.

I am moody as hell; I'm selfish and I have always had a playboy attitude and treated girls as toys. When I met you, though, I saw myself as I really was. I felt rotten inside because you are so young and innocent and as you said, religious. I can't stand religion as it is based solely on money nowadays (Christianity in particular). But I needed something to believe in and to lean on, so I turned to marijuana and acid when I was 16. I don't believe I've ever really had any love in me – only selfish interests, whether sexual or to better my own position in society.

To put it all in a nutshell I am a mixed up guy. Vietnam has straightened out most of my juvenile tendencies but now, one question remains to be solved. Should I commit myself to trying to find love or should I go on playing this pseudo game of the hardened punk, cheating myself and believing all the lies I tell myself?

I hope you write, Dennis

As heavy air outside turned to water, a light drizzle dotted the window with tiny bubbles that stretched into streaks with the train's speed. Track scenery blurred, left behind in a flash of muddied colours.

I pictured Mum propped up in bed, a cigarette in one hand and a cup of tea in the other, staring at the large wardrobe that ran the length of the wall at the foot of her bed. The cheap wooden crate—housing boxes of photos, underwear and nighties given as gifts, jumpers, shoes, and a rack full of dresses and skirts that might come back in fashion one day—also served as the wailing wall. She'd be sipping tea from the cup with one hand and flicking off ash with the other. Then she'd inhale the smoke and repeat the pattern. If she put the cup down it would settle into the saucer on the dresser to the left of her bed. If the cigarette left her hand, it would be placed in the ashtray on the window seat.

I closed my eyes and hoped Granny had gone back to bed. The rattle of steel wheels on steel rails over wooden sleepers and rocks changed rapidly once the train left Central Station and entered the constricted blackness of the city loop. The wind-tunnel shriek announced it was time for a decision. I hoped to find clues for my next step, like Michael had prepared for the car rally, but none came so I got off at Town Hall, the first underground station.

Commuters joined the flow from the opposite platform to stream up the stairs and out the ticket gate. While others continued up the last flight of stairs to the city, I sought refuge. The entrance to the ladies' room offered a place to hide.

I sat on a wooden bench that shook with the thunderous arrival and departure of trains on various levels of concrete above and below. Concrete again. Whether a concrete lecture theatre or a concrete ladies' room in a concrete station, it was cold.

Worn and dishevelled women, without homes to showcase the fabric of their lives, passed in and out. Most of them were plagued by a cough. Their rough skin repelled the gentlest gaze. Their coarse or stringy hair hung like overgrown weeds. Their clothes—Granny would call them rags—simply performed a function. The ladies' room offered them shelter as it did me. With purpose, they did what they had to do and grunted at the lot life's playing cards had dealt them.

Commuters, in stark contrast, dropped in to do what *they* had to do—fix their hair, put finishing touches on their lips, cheeks, eyebrows and eyes, and adjust their clothing. With a destination and a purpose, they checked in the mirror one more time before they left, making sure that what they were about to present to the world was acceptable and that it would last until they arrived at the job, the interview, the meeting, or perhaps the breakfast date.

It could have been ten minutes, an hour, or even a day that I stared through the cement wall as if it were a chiffon scarf. No thought. No tears. No blame—until the chiffon scarf lifted and billowed with taunting laughter at the sight of a Catholic girl with nowhere to go but the ladies' room at

Town Hall Railway Station. *See, you're no better than anyone else*, it mocked. In the strangest way, it felt like I'd joined Jesus in the desert.

I climbed the stairs out of Sydney's bowels. My chafed heel was relieved by a dampened wad of toilet paper, positioned as a buffer between my skin and the white shoe. The top stair opened onto a morning offering hope. The sun played on George Street, peeking around sandstone buildings and coursing blades of light here and there. Caught in one of its streams, I lingered and basked while city life bustled and unlocked the day.

Cars and buses released their carbon fumes. Traffic lights dictated the rhythmic ebb and flow of cars and pedestrians, like the moon does for the tides. A frightful screech of brakes signalled the avoidance of a shattering crash. The footpaths teemed with shoppers, men in suits, office workers, and mothers pushing strollers or dragging toddlers too little to keep up the pace. A jackhammer punctuated the crisp morning air and pounded my ears.

The Black Cat, a coffee shop located a short way from the railway entrance, provided a retreat of a different kind. Bizarre in its contrast to the ladies' room, it was a circus of cat play in black and white. Mirrors ran the length of the wall behind the counter and greeted patrons. Two waitresses laughed with high spirits as they furtively caught their reflections. A third waitress, enduring a morning not so bright, prepared a pot of steamed milk for a cappuccino. I opened my purse and found the torn off cigarette package flap where Steve had written his hotel and room number twelve hours before. Seemed like weeks. I ran my thumb over his name.

"And what would you like?" asked one of the bubbly waitresses. Her presence startled me. Her get-up looked silly—white blouse, frilly black apron, and matching cap. My mind had crammed itself with such chaotic blabber that it buried my reason for being there, and I couldn't answer the question.

"Would you like me to come back later?" she asked. I nodded, relieved not to have to make a decision. She returned to her spot behind the counter and leaned with her back to the tables so she could keep an eye on herself as well as the customers. I stared out on the morning glare of George Street and wondered how it could look so bright. No sooner had she left than she was back, repeating her waitress question.

"You can't just sit here without ordering," she said, ushering me out of the coffee shop. Did I look like a bag lady? I couldn't be sure.

Back on George Street I headed in the direction of Circular Quay towards the harbour, stopping every block or so to adjust the crumbling paper serving as a Band-Aid. I turned right at the GPO in Martin Place—where friends and relatives made overseas calls to loved ones—and headed towards the Cross. A passing thought fluttered by on a phantom breeze: Would my father know me if I called him on the phone?

The elms in Hyde Park provided beauty, majesty, shade, and relief. The Archibald Fountain, bigger and bolder than the El Alamein Fountain, drew people of all ages to its statues and the comfort of its hypnotic spray. On the other side of the park, St Mary's Cathedral, where Sydney's most important Catholic events acted themselves out in appropriate pomp and ceremony, stood like a sanctuary. It provided refuge for the weak and feeble as well as the strong and righteous.

I pulled on the brass handle of the heavy, leather-padded door, welcoming the chill inside the dark sandstone building. I limped down the aisle towards the main altar, adorned with a display of large stemmed flowers arranged in a show of August's best floral colours and designs.

On either side of the centrepiece altar, smaller altars paid homage to Our Lady and St Joseph. Candles lit by the faithful in need of comfort and fortitude flickered brightly in the dimness. Their wax dripped deliberately into the copper holders.

I knelt down, separated from the statue of Our Lady and her sanctuary by a rail. I took five cents out of my purse and dropped the shiny, silver coin into the padlocked offering box. It jingled as it fell amongst other coins. I lit my candle from one already representing the suffering, gratitude, wants, and needs of others who had made their offerings earlier that day. The wax dripped like lava, so I pushed the candle into the nearest space and made the sign of the cross. In the name of the Father, the Son, and the Holy Ghost.

The gentle face of Mary looked down as I knelt in prayer. Compassionate mother. Hail, Mary, full of grace, the Lord is with thee. Blessed art thou amongst women and blessed is the fruit of thy womb. Please, dear Lady, help me. I don't know what to do.

Her plaster eyes looked at me without judgment. Her outstretched hands invited me into her serenity. Although I waited for a sign, none came, apart from the sense that it was time to leave the Cathedral's marble grandeur and sanctity and, most of all, the stillness that had offered a few moments of peace.

Outside, a bowling green shimmered with ladies and gentlemen dressed in white, rolling black balls down greens. White hats with green brims protected them from the glare of the Australian sun. I left their exuberance behind and turned left onto Williams Street.

Chapter 20

SAFE HARBOUR

Whisky A-Go-Go looked different in the daytime, without the glitter of flashing lights. Lifeless. Hung over, sort of.

I hobbled into the GI's Hut. Carol, who hadn't been a customer there for a while, sat alone for the second day in a row. Smoking. She looked distant and barely acknowledged me as I passed her table. Paul was on his break, sitting in his usual spot at the back table.

"You look terrible. What's wrong?" he asked.

I collapsed into the chair across from him. Even Grace softened and allowed a brief sympathetic look to sweep over her face.

"Do you have a Band-Aid?" I asked.

Grace grabbed the first aid box from under the counter.

"Don't you think you should wash it first?" she said, as I figured out how to cover the wound and avoid placing the sticky part over the snarling flesh. "Just wait. I'll get a wet cloth." She pulled out a chair. "Rest your foot on this so I can get at it."

She knelt on the floor. For the first time I noticed how badly stained the red carpet was, despite daily vacuuming. She carefully daubed and wiped where the skin had torn away.

"There's just a bit of Dettol on the cloth. It'll get rid of any infection. And just to make extra sure, I'm applying some Mercurochrome."

"My grandmother is a firm believer in that," I said. Mercurochrome was the killer of all germs according to Granny, who was always careful to cover more than just the wound. "I wore the red stuff proudly as a child."

Grace arranged cotton wool over my heel and secured it with three Band-Aids. Satisfied with her effort, she rose from the floor.

"Grace wants to become a nurse someday, don't ya, babe?" Paul said.

"Someday," she confirmed. A wide grin softened her face as she rolled the cotton wool securely back into the purple packing. "When I get enough money to go to The Women's College on Carillon Avenue," she proudly added.

"You'll make a good nurse," I said, grateful for her attention.

"Thanks. You should stay off it as much as possible. Get your feet into some thongs for a few days. Give it a chance to heal." She packed up the medical supplies and returned the box to its place under the counter.

The tables began to fill. Paul sauntered back to the kitchen to fill steel baskets with raw potato strips for frying. Grace prepared the coffee machine. I took my shoes off and walked over to Carol.

"So, what happened with Skip last night?" I asked.

"He left just after you and Steve." Her tone was distant. She'd been crying.

"Are you okay?" I asked, setting my own worries aside.

"I'm pregnant." The smoke from her cigarette curled around her. She looked directly at me, waiting for a reaction.

"Carol?" was all I could say.

"I swore I wouldn't have another abortion," she said, beginning to tremble.

"You had an abortion?"

"Yes, I had an abortion." Her eyes looked into the distance beyond the bustle of Darlinghurst Road. "My father said he wouldn't stand for another embarrassment to the family. My brother is a spastic. He had a hard time being born. Dad always said if I ever brought a kid like that into the world, he'd kill it. So I saved him the trouble. Even if the baby had been okay, he would have done something bad to punish me for getting pregnant."

"What about the baby's father?" I asked.

"He was my first boyfriend. We started going out when I was fifteen. When I told him about the baby, he said it probably wasn't his anyway and started going out with my best friend. We'd been together for a year. I hadn't been with anyone else. After that I left home and moved to Sydney. When I got pregnant the second time, I was determined to keep the baby."

"What happened?" I asked.

"I was alone. I didn't know what to do when the baby came. It was a girl, but she died when she was born. I wrapped her..." Carol's face became sad and long. "And..." She choked back the words and blew her nose, rolled up the used serviette and put it in her purse.

"That's really sad." I remembered the *Sydney Morning Herald* article eighteen months earlier about the Hyde Park baby wrapped in newspaper.

She buried her swollen face in more serviettes. Carol, who only the day before had epitomised the essence of cool on the outside, wore the painful wounds of a treacherous life on the inside.

I placed my hand on hers. "Do your parents know about this one?"

"Not on your life! I haven't seen them since I came here. They didn't know about my little girl, either. I gave her a name, you know."

"What did you call her?"

"Mary," she said in almost a whisper. "If everything's okay after this baby's born, I might tell them. But probably not. I'm scared. I'm not going to lose this baby. Nobody's going to take it away from me," she said with determination.

"What about your Mum?" I asked.

"I phone her once in a while. I tell her I'm doing well and making lots of money. I don't say too much about what's really going on. She's got enough on her plate. She's afraid of my father, too."

"What about this baby's father?"

"He's an American I met when he was on R&R." No longer capable of shielding her pain, the serviettes began to shred. Black rivers pooled beneath red puffy eyes and meandered to her chin, turning grey along the way. Half on and half off, her eye shadow resembled the efforts of a little girl who'd got into her mother's make-up for the first time. The image of Carol as a little girl, despite the things that had happened to her, was dominant in the scheme of things.

"Does he know?" I asked.

She closed her eyes and lowered her head. "No."

"Are you going to tell him?"

"I don't know."

"Why wouldn't you?"

"Because the last one was American. He said he was coming back, but he went home and I never heard from him again." She rolled the used serviettes into a ball, tore it apart, and clenched each half tightly in her fists.

"It doesn't mean this one will, too," I said. "Is he a nice guy?"

"Of course he's a nice guy. They're all nice guys. Only problem is they leave. And they don't come back. Remember Tom?" she asked. Compassion snapped to suspicion as I realised the kind of relationship Carol and Tom may have had. "I'm moving in with two of the dancers from the Whisky who have a flat in Coogee. Just until the baby's born. I don't know what I'll do then."

I wanted more than anything to be the angel of mercy and tell her everything would be okay, but at the same time I was agitated by what I didn't know about Carol's personal life. I asked if she was hungry.

"Food would make me sick right now," she said. "I really don't feel very good."

"You and me both," I said.

"I'm sorry. You must be pretty shocked. I didn't mean to tell you about my horrible life. No one else knows this stuff. It just tumbled out. You must think I'm an awful person."

Carol wiped her nose with the back of her hand and retreated to the mirror out the back. Someone pulled out the chair and sat beside me.

"How would you like to be a model?" It was Ron.

"What do you mean?" I asked, thoughtlessly responding to a stupid question.

"Photo shoots. Have your photo taken in a bikini," he said.

My self-consciousness in a bathing suit was painful enough. A bikini was as unlikely as a hailstorm in the desert. As far as allowing people to take pictures and why they'd even want to was unfathomable. I didn't even own a pair of shorts. *For the love of Pete, get inside and take those off. Your legs are too big and fat to wear shorts*, Granny had said one scorching December day when I was ten years old. Her remark was potent enough to burn through my skin, much deeper than if she'd branded me with a poker. That's why I skipped physical education classes—to avoid the humiliation of wearing the white bloomers with elastic in the legs that Granny had sewn so I could be modest and not waste money.

"I don't have a bikini," I said.

"No sweat, I can get you one. I can get you lots of them."

I shook my head.

"It's a paying job with good money," he said.

For a moment I thought it might have been too bad I was overweight and self-conscious. "No thanks."

"What are you afraid of?" he goaded. "Losing your cherry? Don't tell me a girl that looks like you still has her cherry."

I pictured a missile landing on Ron and sending him to the middle of the earth where he would disperse into tiny, useless particles.

"How's the heel?" Grace appeared at the table, pen poised and smiling. I looked up at her and pulled a face that told her of my wish for the parasite sitting beside me.

"What will you have?" Her voice dared him to order.

"I'll have you, bitch!"

Grace slammed her docket book shut, shoved it into her pocket, and pointed her outstretched arm to the door. "Get out and don't come back," she shouted.

"You don't have to be rude," he said, getting out of his chair.

"And neither do you," I said.

"You'll learn some day," he sneered.

"I hate that asshole," said Grace. "If he dares to come in here again I'm calling the police. He's just a bloody gutter-snipe. His mother was a prostitute who threw him out on the street to raise himself. He's bad news. Don't get mixed up with him."

Carol walked slowly back to the table, her arms folded protectively across her belly just as Ron skulked through the doorway.

"What did he want?" she asked.

"I don't know," I replied. His proposition wasn't worth the breath required to repeat it.

"I have to get ready for work," she said. "See you later?"

Chapter 21

LONG DISTANCE

In the storm of her worry, Granny would be imagining the worst. I borrowed fifty cents from Paul and thanked Grace once more. The coffee shop now full, she scurried about, carrying out her duties with the unruffled efficiency that was her trademark.

What Paul loved about Grace was clear to me now. As I left, she marched an order to the kitchen and caught every beat on the jukebox. "Venus" by Shocking Blue.

Instead of heading to the platform at St James Station, I took a sharp turn left in the direction of the Hyatt Hotel. I caught the elevator to the sixth floor and knocked on the door of Room 607. My heart thumped loudly, even skipping a beat now and then. Relief overcame disappointment when no one answered. I waited for the elevator so I could escape the scene of a foolish mistake without being caught. As I pushed on the flat glass door to leave the hotel, they stood before me.

"Hello," said Steve, almost no space between us.

"I just called up to your room," I confessed, "but you weren't there so I'm going home. I mean to the station. To catch the train. Home. I don't know what time it comes. So I'd better leave now." Once again I felt handicapped by the legacy of growing up without males.

"Have you got time for a cup of coffee?" he asked. I reconsidered. After all, I wouldn't have gone to his hotel room if I didn't want to see him.

"I'll catch you later," said Skip, taking the opportunity to leave.

Suddenly things felt somehow right.

As Steve and I walked around the city streets, we drew each other into the material of our lives. He talked about his family in Nebraska, the farm where he grew up, his brothers, the malaria he caught the month before while out in the weeds, and his plans to go to college when he got back to what the GIs called The World. He wanted to know about my family. I told him my father left when I was six and my mother moved in with her parents. I told him she worked and that Granny was more like my mother, and that Mum was actually like an older sister.

"She works hard and gets tired a lot. She often gets migraines." I tried to explain the facts without judgment, to provide information without detail.

And there we were, standing outside the GPO waiting for the light to change. I backed away from the curb.

"What's wrong?" asked Steve.

"I want to phone my father," I surprised myself by saying.

"Okay."

"I don't know his number though."

"Look it up in the book."

"I can't. He lives in Canada."

"Do you know where in Canada?"

"Alberta."

"What about the town?"

"I don't know."

"It's a long shot but the overseas operator might be able to find it for you."

"Do you think so?"

As with every other sandstone building in Sydney, as soon as I stepped inside the GPO I felt insignificant. The marble and tiled floors as well as the high ceilings created an echo chamber that allowed the clamour of voices and footsteps to rebound in chaotic anonymity. We stood like children in a maze and read the signs on each of the counters, searching for the one marked OVERSEAS PHONE CALLS.

The high and officious counters in the GPO separated the common folk from the government representatives, the same way court benches separated the observers, lawyers, witnesses, and the accused (guilty and innocent alike) from the judge. Workers stood behind high wooden barriers. When they bobbed down to locate a form, they completely disappeared. Secure and proud in their positions as public servants, they were the facilitators of people's desire for communication.

"It will cost you ten dollars for a five-minute phone call to Canada. Pay here, then you can use one of the phones over there." The clerk, Sally Johnson—her name displayed both on her copper lapel tag and the counter—pointed to five booths in the far corner, the middle one occupied by a young man stooped over in a chair too small to properly accommodate his long lanky frame. He studied the floor as he spoke into the receiver and cupped the other ear with his spare hand. His bony elbows stuck into his knees.

Sally Johnson studied us. Girl. American on R&R. Phone call to Canada. Possible scenarios.

"You need the number," Steve said. His voice was surprisingly clear in the din of a high and hollow space.

"I don't know his number."

"Give me his name," said Sally Johnson.

"Robert Thomas Moreton. Alberta, Canada."

"City?"

"I don't know."

"I'll check the overseas directory. You can take a seat over there, if you like." She pointed to a row of backless leather benches on an island in the middle of the oversized room.

"I have no idea what to say," I said to Steve. "I don't even know him."

"Until yesterday, you didn't know me either, but here we are."

"That's different."

"How?" he asked.

"Well, for a start you're not my father. But he is. Technically, he's part of who I am and I'm supposed to have always known him. You and I, on the other hand, have met in a collision of events."

"Collision of events or a planned series of events?"

"Who knows?"

"Maybe I'm your guardian angel sent to guide you through this experience."

"Maybe you are, but you know what, I'm starting to think this is a really dumb idea. I hope she can't find the number. Let's go. Really, I mean it, Steve. Let's go."

I stood and turned to see Sally Johnson motioning us over.

"How do you want to pay for the call?" My blank stare revealed more than just the fear of speaking to the stranger who was my father. I had not factored a cost for this undertaking as one of the conditions. I had three cents and a borrowed train fare. Sally looked and waited. Wrote something on paper. Looked at me again. Glanced at Steve. "I can reverse the charges and see if he'll accept," she offered.

What if he won't? I asked myself, while nodding in agreement.

"Your name and your relationship?"

"Catherine Moreton. He's my father."

"Take a seat while I make the connection."

The brown bench was a welcome retreat. Adrenalin on an empty stomach had turned into nausea and self-doubt. Perhaps I'd try another time. Mum was right. I did have some crazy ideas, and this was one of them. To think that someone—that *someone* being my father—would accept a call that he'd have to pay for from a child he hadn't bothered to contact since she was six years old was wishful thinking. Pathetic thinking.

"Nine years ago Mum took me for a holiday after I had my appendix taken out," I told Steve. "We caught the train to Albury and stayed with Aunty Nancy and Uncle Bill on their dairy farm. Aunty Nancy is a cousin of Mum's. Two things happened that I'll never forget. The first was on an icy morning when I went with Uncle Bill on his milk run.

I dropped off two bottles of full cream milk at the gate of a farmhouse and was charged by a growling, barking Alsatian. Sometimes, in the middle of the night, I see him snarling at me through saliva-dripping teeth. I don't know why he didn't bite me."

"Smart dogs, German Shepherds. That's what we call them. We have three. Mitzy, Ranger, and plain old Dog."

"I'm glad I'm not delivering milk to your place at five in the morning. One was enough for me. The next part of the story is what I really want to tell you," I continued. "After Albury we went to Melbourne to visit my father's parents. Grandma and Grandpa Moreton gave me their Christmas cards to look at in the lounge room while they spoke to Mum in the kitchen. The prettiest one was from 'Bob, Pamela, and the kids.' I knew from Mum that the woman my father ran off with was named Pamela. Mum had wanted to name me Pamela but my father refused, saying he knew someone by that name who wasn't a very nice person."

"I like your name. Catherine sounds classy. It's got style." This stranger was more familiar to me than my own flesh and blood. "Would you mind if I hold your hand?" he asked.

I slipped my hand into his, grateful for the contact, and continued the story.

"I knew this awful card was written by him. The realisation that my father was someone else's father—someone who actually knew him as a father—crushed my ten-year-old spirit. My father had gone from an idea to someone who was real through a Christmas card I wasn't meant to see. He'd turned his back on me and not even once acknowledged that I existed. How could he do that?"

Steve squeezed my hand and nodded, as if he recognised my story.

"His father, my Grandpa Moreton, had a job with the GPO in Melbourne," I continued. "He was chauffeured to and from work."

"That's impressive. What did he do?"

"No idea. All I know is he was an engineer. Do you think there could have been some sort of energy transfer from him that led me to make this call at the Sydney GPO? I mean, when we were at the traffic light and I pulled back from the curb, do you think that maybe my grandfather set this call up?"

"I don't know," he said. "It's an interesting thought, though. I do think there's something to energies, whether they're actual physical entities like you and me or thoughts that initiate energy waves and cause things to happen just by thinking about them."

A smile and a beckoning from Sally Johnson indicated she'd made the connection. "Second phone on your left facing the wall."

"He accepted?" I asked.

"Pick up the receiver and he'll be on the other end," she replied.

"I'll wait here," said Steve. "Go for it."

I sat beside Steve in complete safety as someone else's body floated to the phone and lifted the receiver.

"Hi, this is Catherine." Although I wanted to address him more personally, it was inappropriate to call him Bob. And Dad? That was a word I'd never used. Daddy, maybe, probably once, but the memory was long gone. It was an uncomfortable word. I thought of him as my father but never as Dad.

"How are you?" a clear male voice with an American sounding accent asked.

"I'm fine. How are you?" Surely there was more to say.

He took the lead with questions. I awkwardly followed. He asked what I was doing and if I ever planned to travel. He asked how the weather was. I remembered to thank him for accepting the charges and apologised for bothering him. He hoped we would see each other one day. Then it was over. I'd snatched a verbal glimpse of my father, but the time had run out, just like it did with Tom and the others I'd met who went away and never returned.

Unable to distinguish between feelings of euphoria, disappointment, regret, betrayal, and longing, I said to Steve, who was still seated on the brown bench, "Wow, that was neat."

What I really felt, though, surfaced as a priority above all other sensations. Restlessness was that feeling. By speaking to him I'd found out my father was real and that he was willing to talk to me—even though our conversation was more like two strangers conversing on a train ride home than what I imagined a real father would say to his real daughter.

"Thanks for encouraging me to phone. He's so far away but it was like he was here."

I waved to Sally Johnson before we left the bench. Once outside, I grabbed Steve's hand and reached up to kiss his cheek. His arm folded around my shoulder and we walked towards the station.

"Maybe you really are my guardian angel," I said.

"I am," he replied, as natural as could be. "Do you know a good place to eat in this part of town?"

My heart sank as the awareness I was feeling of Granny's worry was about to interrupt, but hopefully not sever, the connection Steve and I felt. The possible scenarios she would imagine I'd got myself into would be driving her to panic, and I didn't have enough money to call her. I hoped Mum had regained her sanity. By walking out that morning, I had shown myself—and maybe her—that I would deal with her ranting in the future and not just take it. In stark contrast to the uncertainty of the morning, I felt strong. How could Steve understand the complexity in these layers of events that had compacted and pressurised over lifetimes?

"I have to go home," I said. "It has been an incredible day."

"Why do you have to go?" Steve was in Sydney with no context. He had no one to answer to. His only agenda was to leave the jungles of Vietnam behind for five days and enjoy what pleasures were offered, pleasures that the rest of us took for granted. "How old did you say you were?" he asked.

"Nineteen."

"Old enough to do what you want, I'd say."

"And that's exactly what I'm doing. Right now it's important that I go home and let Granny know I'm okay." For me it was more important than staying out with this person I barely knew but also knew.

"Can I see you tomorrow?" he persisted.

"I've got classes. I'm trying to improve my attendance this year. I don't have a very good track record," I confessed. Physical education, the one class I deliberately missed, mostly because of the humiliation of the bloomers, was unfortunately scheduled on Wednesdays and Fridays.

"What about tomorrow night? Would you like to go to a club?"

I knew he would think I didn't care and had just used him to accompany me while I made the telephone call, but it would not be easy to get out of the house after my abrupt departure. Not only because they would not approve, but also because I needed uncomplicated space. We all—Granny, Mum and I—needed healing. We could do that just by sitting in the living room watching television together, Mum knitting while I sat on the floor and rubbed her feet, Granny dozing off in the old rocker that belonged to Great-Grandma before she passed away in her sleep.

Steve and I stood on the top step that led down to Town Hall Station.

"Tomorrow morning. Right here. Nine," I said.

"What about your classes?" he asked.

"I'd rather spend the day with you."

Chapter 22

PAIN RELIEF

My arrival home late the night before had created an explosion of anger and frustration over the unfair life Mum could neither correct nor control. The care of Grace and Steve—and even the sound of my father's voice confirming that he was a real person—had all helped to rescue me from the hurt and pain I'd felt that morning. So did the letter from Michael I had reread on the way home. It had an air of normalcy, despite being written from a war zone.

Muffin! How are things with you? Everything is all right over here with me. I'm now back from the bush (thank God!). We came back to our nice huts at Vung Tau army camp a few days sooner than they said we would.

They put me on a bus run. All I do is drive people that have leave into town and back again. Also I drive the Vietnamese people that work in our camp to work and home again.

I stop at the R&C which is the rest centre at Vung Tau for about fifteen minutes every hour. The R&C was built in 1964

*for the Australian army when they get leave which is two leave
days a month. It's like a big hotel/motel kind of thing. It has 92
rooms and a 52-foot Bar. I sometimes come down here when I'm
on a rest day as I can go up to the flat top roof and sunbake with
a nice cold beer and there is always a cool wind blowing up on
the roof as it is three stories high. It is just great down here when
you are on leave.*

Michael

"Dearest," called Granny, in a rush to give me one of her
welcome-home-glad-to-see-you-safe-and-sound-I've-been-
worried-sick-about-you hugs.

There was no need to tell her about the call to my father.
She'd only worry where it might lead. When acquaintances
had cared enough to inquire about my wellbeing after Mum's
marriage broke up, Granny would say, "She's fine. She's just
a kid. Kids bounce back." So no one ever explained to me
what really happened, as if by not talking about it, the shame-
ful event would go away. The only information came from
Mum's outbursts, a one-sided view tainted with bitterness so
toxic it stained her life. And was leaving its mark on mine.

"Where's Mum?" I wanted to see her, let her know I'd put
everything in perspective and that I'd forgiven her. I wouldn't
tell her about the call, either. That would just trigger another
rage.

"She's got one of her migraines," Granny said. "She's been
sleeping most of the day."

I opened the bedroom door. Mum lay flat on her back
on top of the sheet, the covers rolled back. She wore a white

singlet. Her bra cut in around her ribs. The over-stretched straps hung loosely on her upper arms. Her belly arched under her faded nylon pants. A pillow of skin draped above the elastic.

"Mum," I whispered, aware of how the slightest movement irritated her migraine's revenge. "Mum," I repeated, rocking her shoulder lightly.

Granny appeared at the door.

"What's wrong with her?" I asked.

"She's just tired; that's all."

"Has she been drinking?"

"A couple of scotches earlier. Nothing much."

An empty pill bottle labelled Valium stood on the dresser. The white lid lay upside down on the linoleum floor. Another bottle, the lid still on, sprawled amongst Mum's white bras and worn out underwear in the half-open top drawer.

"What are these for?" I asked.

"She takes the Valium for her nerves. Mogadon helps her sleep. Dr Morrison prescribed them a couple of months ago when she had trouble getting to sleep." Granny tucked the undergarments back into the drawer and slammed it into the dresser. "She's fine. She'll wake up rested in the morning."

"Mum," I called. No response. I grabbed her wrist and felt her pulse. It echoed the languishing of a tired heart. I shook her hard this time. "Something's wrong, Granny. We've got to call an ambulance."

"Don't be silly," she pooh-poohed. "Your mother doesn't need an ambulance. The last thing we need right now is the bloody neighbours gawking at us."

"It doesn't matter about the neighbours, Granny. Mum's in trouble," I said. "With alcohol, sedatives, and sleeping pills in her system, she could be in a coma."

"Oh for heaven's sake, Catherine. What utter rot and nonsense. Why do you have to exaggerate things all the time and get so bloody dramatic?" She flung out her hands in disgust. "Dr Morrison wouldn't have prescribed them if they weren't safe. And your mother trusts him. She'd let him cut her head off if he said it was necessary."

"It's the amount and the combination that's the problem," I said.

"Where have you been all day, anyway?"

Perhaps she thought by changing the subject I'd forget about the ambulance. Her question was neither easily answered nor appropriate. I bumped her accidentally on my way to the telephone in the hallway and ignored her question. She grabbed the dresser for balance.

The phone number for Canterbury Hospital, together with the numbers for the police and fire departments, had been taped beside the telephone since the beginning of time. Cigarette smoke had turned the paper yellow, the numbers barely legible. I dialled and waited for what seemed an eternity, stuck there by the coiled black cord that didn't reach far from the phone.

"We'll send an ambulance straight away. The doctor on call will be there shortly," a voice assured me through the earpiece.

I pictured that voice sitting at her ordered desk in her starched, white uniform. I was glad she'd taken my concern seriously. Granny had tuned herself out enough to make me wonder what pills Dr Morrison had prescribed for her. Within minutes, we heard the siren screaming down Canterbury Road.

"I can stabilise her," the young doctor said after checking Mum's vitals, "but I'm treating this as an attempted suicide. I suggest admitting her to Broughton Hall."

"What's Broughton Hall?" I asked.

"A psychiatric hospital," he replied matter of factly.

"What utter rubbish and nonsense," Granny declared, indignant at the suggestion that her forty-year-old daughter would even remotely entertain the idea of taking her own life.

"She's lucky she's still alive," the doctor said. "She's going to make it, but only just. When someone does this, it's a cry that something is wrong. If she doesn't get a diagnosis of her condition and some help, she's going to do it again. We might not be able to save her next time."

Granny was right. Mum was, in fact, my "poor mother," her temper tantrums came from pent up cries from deep down inside. Perhaps she really did mean it when she said she loved me—loved me, that is, in the best way she could.

"Who will sign the admitting papers? Will you?" he asked Granny.

"Of course not!" Granny yelled.

"I will," I said.

"She'll never forgive you," Granny said. "And neither will I."

"Can I go in the ambulance with her?" I asked.

Despite Mum's ferocious rages I felt a strong urge to protect her, as if the tables had turned and I was now in the role of mother. Images of straitjackets, shock treatment, lobotomies, and zombies paraded through the bedroom. Handing her over to the mercy of the institution, though necessary, seemed oddly like an act of cruelty.

Granny backed away and retreated to the kitchen. Perhaps she accepted she was wrong.

"Better if you let us get her settled," said the doctor. "You can go over later tonight. She's not aware of what's going on around her anyway. I'll stay with her and get her checked in." He placed the stethoscope once more over Mum's heart.

"She'll be frightened when she wakes up." I reached for her limp hand.

"Excuse me," said the doctor, pushing past. "The staff is well qualified to handle cases like this. She'll be perfectly fine." His professional manner displayed competence in a field I had no experience to comprehend.

The ambulance drove off. Neighbours, milling around in front of their houses with arms folded, sauntered back inside, having gathered all the information they needed for the day. They would draw their own unique conclusions. After all, they would have heard Mum's frequent outbursts gunning down the neighbourhood, particularly in spring and autumn when the windows were flung open to welcome the fresh air.

"Jesus Christ...what's going to happen next?" Granny sighed, near breaking point. She took a juice glass out of the cupboard and emptied the scotch bottle with a single pour. She shuffled over to the kitchen nook, fumbled for her cigarettes, and lit up. Her shaky hands dealt out the cards for a game of Patience.

"Do you want one?" she asked.

"One what?" I replied, wondering if she was offering me a drink.

"A fag." She plonked the packet of cigarettes in front of me.

"I haven't eaten much today," I said. "It might make me sick."

"Don't inhale, then."

It felt strange to take one of Granny's Viscounts out of the packet and light it while she sat there. With one eye on the cards and one eye on me, she seemed to be estimating how many times I'd already smoked.

"We'll catch a cab over to see your mother tomorrow night. Give her a chance to settle in," she said.

"Okay."

"She should never have gone back to him."

I agreed. I was disgusted at how easy it was for the local drug peddler to dole out prescriptions, with little or no thought for the potential of misuse.

"She broke off the engagement, you know." Granny wasn't talking about Dr Morrison.

She turned up the jack of spades and slapped it on the queen. "He went crying to my mother. The bastard convinced her to talk to Brenda so she'd take him back." She turned up her last three cards and checked to see she hadn't missed a move. "It worked."

"I wouldn't be here if she hadn't," I said.

"That's right. You wouldn't be here." Granny was displaying the Nazi side of her German heritage, the same one that gave her permission to strap me when I was late home after helping the nuns clean the floors after school one day.

"That's a bit cruel," I said.

"Not really. It's just a statement of fact.

* * *

Catherine, I've watched so many people die over here and the more I think about it, the sadder I get. It's hard to be an infantryman in a combat zone, not just physically but mentally. I'm tired of running around the jungles and mountains looking for more people to kill. I hope that when my judgment day rolls around, I'll have a lenient judge. I've killed 9 people in the last 10 months. My squad killed 17 in one afternoon. Seventeen people, 17 human beings.

When I got to Sydney it was like being born again. When I was with you it was just great to be alive. Please don't think me too forward for saying these things and please don't think that I'm looking for a shoulder to cry on. It's just the way I feel right now. I shouldn't even be writing this. I'll write again when I'm in a better mood.

Until then…Love, Jim

Chapter 23

TRUST

Dear Catherine,

The past few days have really been full of pain and misery. I have the flu plus a nice little case of strep throat. I had the same thing last year so it's nothing new to me. Guess I'm truly in "The Valley of the Dolls," with all these pills I'm taking. It's really been miserable, but sickness is all part of the tour in Vietnam. And believe me I've had my share!

As soon as I returned from Sydney I started going to church every day, something I enjoy doing but haven't done since I left the States. But I lasted for only 2 days until I got sick, so tomorrow I'll try again.

One little extra note, everyone was asking me why I was going to church so often and I said "it's amazing what a woman can do to you when you find out you share the same religion." Not only have you helped me spiritually but in so many other ways that only a man can feel himself. It will be hard not having you with me!

Till next time, Dean

* * *

My mother's overdose was a cry for help that spiked my shame and guilt. Questions hung on doorknobs, like clothes to be worn. Would she have done it if I'd been on time for Housie instead of dancing with Steve? Would she have done it if I'd been a better daughter and attended classes instead of hanging around the Cross and causing her to worry? The call to Broughton Hall the next morning almost felt like a betrayal. The Judas who caused her pain was her own daughter.

"She has settled, had breakfast, and is now resting," said officiousness on the other end of the telephone. "Anything else?"

In contrast to the compassionate receptionist at Canterbury Hospital, the Broughton Hall voice was cold. I imagined her to have long nails painted bright red.

"Please tell her I love her and that we'll see her tonight." I hung up.

Granny was still in bed when I left. Waking someone whose world was falling apart seemed an unnecessary torment for both of us.

Rather than wait for late or missed trains, I decided to catch a cab. A vacant taxi soon appeared in the stream of vehicles flowing down Canterbury Road towards the city.

"Where to, love?" the cabbie asked.

"Town Hall, thanks."

These were the only words that passed between us. From then on the cabbie and I kept out of each other's business for the next thirty minutes. Wordless space enabled a cocoon to wrap itself around me in the back seat. Sleep crept in and locked out the sticky confusion of an absent father, a deserted mother, and a grandmother's generosity turned to resentment.

Whether it was the mind's programming, or coincidence, I opened my eyes as we approached Town Hall.

"You can drop me at the lights," I said, as they turned yellow. A glance at my watch indicated I was ten minutes late. The train would have set me back at least forty minutes.

Steve had his camera perched on the ledge that enclosed the stairs to the station. He was bent over, focusing on the statue of Queen Victoria rising up in the middle of the Y where George Street veered right and Kent began—or ended. I waited for the tethered rush of the shutter before tapping him on the shoulder.

He turned and invited me to his side with a smile as wide as the ocean. How could you recognise someone with your heart even though you had just met him? And on the other hand, how could you be born of someone, with his blood flowing through your veins, and be a total stranger? The loneliness of a soul unrecognised, misunderstood, and unloved can be so easily transformed into something more beautiful with the simple recognition of another soul.

"What are you doing with that?" He pointed to the briefcase clutched in my left hand.

"It's habit. I just brought it along."

"You going to take me to classes? I wouldn't mind seeing what Australian colleges are like."

"It would be a huge waste of your time." The teachers' college in Paddington was a former inner city public school. An old brick building with a small cement courtyard, it was a vulgar third cousin to the city's two universities with their prestigious buildings and well-groomed grounds. Students crammed into the rooms and corners of Alexander Mackie like big, clumsy inmates with briefcases. Wire protected the windows from intruders. "It feels more like a prison than a place of higher learning. It's not the place to sacrifice precious hours of your R&R."

"I'll take your word for it. Wildlife management is my major in college. I have two more years to finish when I get back to the States." He went quiet. His face betrayed a worry about the reality of seeing home again.

"When will that be?"

"Not long. I start processing out as soon as I go back to Nam. Yeah, not long at all 'til it's my turn to get on that old freedom bird and fly out of that sorry place, back to The World."

"You're in the world no matter where you are," I said.

"Not when you're in the Nam you're not. That's a godforsaken hellhole on the other side of the earth from where I live. I don't mind doing my duty. And I want you to understand we're doing a good job." He slung the camera over his shoulder, put both hands in his pockets, and started walking. "Do you mind if we talk about something else?"

"Would you like to hear about what a slacko I am?" I asked.

"Well, I might, if I knew what a slacko was," Steve said with a huge smile.

"Slacko is an Australian slang term for someone who shirks their responsibilities."

"You don't seem like a slacko to me."

"Oh trust me, I'm a slacko."

"Tell me more."

"I was at university last year. This year I'm at teachers' college, all because I was a slacko. I skipped classes and I didn't do my assignments. I basically failed but did well enough to transfer and still have my tuition paid for."

"So what you're telling me is that you're a badass."

"No, I'm telling you I'm a slacko, but I'm trying to do better. Nevertheless, here I am skipping classes again."

"Then I'd say you're a hard-core badass slacko."—I almost fell over laughing.—"Will it make you feel better if you carry your briefcase around all day, or do you want to drop it off?"

"Okay."

"Okay what?"

"Okay drop it off."

"Let me carry that beast of burden for you so you can drop your guilt and we can enjoy the day." He grabbed the briefcase in one hand and wrapped his other hand around mine. Our grip firm and purposeful, we headed to his hotel.

"I'd really like to visit Taronga Park Zoo," he said.

"That's a good idea."

"Wait here while I run it up to the room. Or—do you want to come up, too?"

"I'll wait."

We arrived at Circular Quay just as the *Waratah Lady*'s plank was hauled back to the wharf and the ropes were wound around the ferry's cleats. With an hour before the next departure, we bought our tickets and strolled around the other side of the quay where the Opera House had begun to reveal its unique design.

Steve's thick brown hair defied the clipped precision of the typical military cut. The bronze skin on his arms glistened with a hint of sweat.

"They're mighty big shells," he said, as we got closer to the Opera House.

"Well actually, they're sails," I said.

"Whatever they are, they're spectacular."

"Some people don't like them. They think they're an eyesore and spoil the look of the harbour."

"Is that right?" He focused his camera. "New things, new ideas, and new people often meet with disapproval until folks get used to them." He spoke like a realtor armed with a degree in psychology. "People like to resist change. The people of Sydney will get used to it one day. And they'll be proud of it. You'll see." He searched through his lens for just the right angle. "I like it." His affirmation helped me to see the structure in a new light. "It's different. Just like the Harbour Bridge." Shutter click. "And you."

"I suppose," I said, pretending not to have heard the last part. The page was blank when it came to responding to a compliment.

Strolling back to the wharves, we met other couples heading off to get a closer look at the unique architectural design taking its place on Sydney Harbour. One girl, attached to the guy she was with like a second skin, had been in the GI's Hut the day before, displaying the same degree of adhesiveness to someone else, who more than likely had returned to Vietnam that morning.

"You're right," I finally admitted. "It is a magnificent structure, and it's about time we had a decent place for our cultural events. I don't care for opera, though. I used to go to the Royal Theatre in Hurstville to watch my mother rehearse with the local opera company. She was a full bottle of scotch ticked off when she was passed over for the lead role in *Madame Butterfly*. That was enough to put me off opera."

"What kind of music do you like?" Steve asked.

"Classical. I started piano when I was six."

"I took piano lessons for a while but I hated practicing, which drove my mother nuts. Finally she gave up and let me drop it," he said.

"I didn't mind practicing. It was nothing for me to sit at the piano for three hours. Sometimes I imagined I was a famous concert pianist playing for a hall full of long gowns, sparkling jewels, and black tuxedos."

"Do you still play?"

"Not much. I'm far too busy being a slacko."—He smiled.—"My favourite composer is Beethoven," I continued. "Did you know he went deaf and continued to compose even though he couldn't hear? My piano teacher used to call me her little Beethoven."

A horn blast announced the ferry's approach.

"Syphilis," Steve said.

"I beg your pardon?"

He'd quietly and without emotion said one of those words the nuns warned about.

"Syphilis. That's why he went deaf."

Sister Isadore hadn't mentioned that detail when she prepared me for the history part of my music exam.

"How do you know that?" I could not imagine how this could happen to the man who had so accurately written my emotions into his melodies, harmonies, and rhythms two hundred years before I was born.

"It's well documented that he visited the brothels in Berlin and Prague. And that's how he got it."

"The nuns never said anything about that."

"I suppose not."

"Not that they avoided the subject," I said. "In fact, they used it as a warning. Sister Stanislaus told us that if we had sexual relationships before marriage, there was a good chance we'd get venereal disease. She said it was God's punishment for those who disrespect the sanctity of marriage."

"Is that right? And is that what you believe?"

"I don't know about the VD part of it, but I think it's a good idea to wait—at least until the right person comes along, the one you plan to marry."

Circular Quay sighed like an unoccupied house. In the middle of a weekday morning, it lacked the excited anticipation of weekend crowds headed for Manly Beach. Boarding the ferry without being jostled was luxury, the feeling of velvet. The plank's rope slid under the palm of my left hand. Reflections of the nuns' warnings sat just beneath the dark green water below.

"The nuns told us that some of us would be like honey pots, attracting bees. But it was our duty to keep them at a distance. If we encouraged them or gave in they'd sting us and move on to the next one."

"What about the ones who aren't honey pots?" he asked, humouring me.

"I suppose they don't have to worry. But they got included in the other image the nuns used. Butterflies and hunters."

"And how does that one go?"

"Well, if we wanted to ensure our happiness, we needed to remember that we were the butterflies and they—meaning boys—were the hunters. Delicate butterflies fluttering in a field on a sunny, spring day, flitting carefree and avoiding the hunters' nets."

"It's too bad they branded males as predators. We're not all like that, you know."

"I know. It's all a bit silly. It's kind of amusing to me now, thinking about the tactics the nuns used to ensure our abstinence from just about everything."

Chapter 24

AFTER THE STORM

A few light clouds whispered their loveliness on the harbour. The sun's happy glow bounced off the water, making it sparkle and shimmer as the ferry pulled away from Circular Quay and steered towards Taronga Park Zoo. I faced the cabin and leaned against the rail where harbour travellers before me had left behind their land-dwelling shackles.

"I spoke to one of your guys on the radio last week." Steve leaned into the rail and clasped his hands above the water. "Good guys, the Aussies."

"My cousin's over there. Vung Tau."

"He's pretty safe then. Vung Tau is an in-country R&R location. It has a nice beach. Kind of like a resort town in the middle of a warzone."

"He's only got a few more months. He seems okay. He writes daily to a friend of ours. I wouldn't be surprised if he asks her to marry him when he gets back." I turned to look over the rail. "He also has a nickname for me."

"It couldn't beat slacko."

"I wouldn't say that."

"What is it?"

"Muffin." I knew Michael would approve of Steve if he met him. And I hoped he wouldn't mind me showing Steve his letter.

Dear Muffin,

On Thursday I drove the gun jeep, which is a land rover with an M60 machine gun mounted on top of it. The best part of the trip was when we came to a hill about ¾ of the way there. The road down the hill was much the same as that road we all drove down in the Holden, the only difference was that I was doing 55 mph down it in the jeep and hanging on for dear life. To make things harder on our rear ends, the road we took had not been used for some time.

When we got back, the gunner said he would never go with me again. He also put in a report to our captain. So it looks as though I'll be in for it because we're not to go over 30 mph on any open road. But who gives a hoot about it after all. At least I got them back in one piece.

Please don't forget to write because I'm dying to hear from you. Also tell me how everyone is at home, OK.

Later, Michael

"He started calling me Muffin when we were kids. And it just stuck."

"Hmm…muffin or slacko?" He tilted his head and smiled. "Slacko works better for me."

The possibility of romance bobbed up and down on tiny crests with no hope of tomorrow. "I get an uneasy feeling when I look down into the water."

"Are you scared of it?" Steve asked, focusing his camera on the sandstone structure of Fort Denison standing proudly in the middle of the harbour.

"What's *it*?" I asked.

"Water," he said.

"Sort of. When I try to look through it, my stomach sinks because I can't see the bottom. I imagine what it would be like to fall overboard, unable to feel solid ground beneath my feet and to realise that the water is so deep, so full of secrets, I never would. Then I imagine a shark heading for my floundering legs with his jaws ready to snap. I see the blood rushing out of my severed limbs, and it makes me sick."

"That's gruesome. This ferry makes me think of the *Titanic*, its majesty and what it must have been like as it went down. Being a Midwestern boy from Nebraska, though, my ocean experiences are somewhat limited. My only ocean cruise was on the troop ship to Vietnam." His eyes and camera continued to record the angle of the sandstone island rapidly changing in shape but not overall appearance. The ferry, now at top speed, chugged towards the zoo.

"Fort Denison is also known as Pinchgut Island. The worst convicts—the murderers and violent types—were imprisoned there when Sydney began as a penal settlement about a hundred and eighty years ago. They didn't have a hope of escaping. The harbour is full of sharks. Maybe that's what inspired my fear of falling overboard."

"Quite possibly." Steve captured the sandstone structure—a reminder of Sydney's questionable beginnings—through his camera lens. "So you're descended from the convicts," he teased.

"Not on my mother's side. They're German, Scottish, and Irish. I don't know about my father's side...although I wouldn't put it past them. Particularly with a name like Moreton."

Steve hummed the Simon and Garfunkel tune "At the Zoo," while we wandered hand in hand from cage to cage, gawking, sympathising, and admiring the animals. His admiration for snakes kept us at the glass cages while they slept, slithered, and flicked their tongues. He told me, sparing no details, about the rattlers back in the States and his near miss with a green tree snake in Vietnam. The monkeys, remarkably human-like, amused us with their antics. He snapped more than enough pictures of the koalas and the kangaroos, occasionally sneaking one of me. A young mother pushing a stroller obliged when he asked if she'd take a picture of us together.

Bigger clouds rolled in from the southeast. The wind swirled dust, dirt, and animal smells around as we trod the beaten tracks in a happiness that needed no words. The animals, more attuned to the warning signs of nature, disappeared and sought refuge in their man-made shelters, anticipating the storm blowing in from the ocean.

On the way back to Circular Quay, the ferry swayed from side to side as the white-capped waves scooped it up and dumped it like a bobbing cork. The rocking made me regret the Cadbury's chocolate and bottle of lemonade we'd shared earlier. I placed my head on Steve's shoulder and closed my eyes. He put his arm around me and drew me closer. His jumper felt warm against my face. That familiar smell of Brut once again drew me into its promise of protection. His head rested gently on mine.

"I like your aftershave," I said.

"Thank you."

"It seems like all you guys wear it."

"It helps get rid of the jungle stink."

The approaching storm left no time to find balance on the wharf. Two or three taxis ignored Steve's signal, leaving us no choice but to try to out step the storm.

We hurried along George Street, our arms weaving us together. The odd lightning bolt zigzagged through the sky. Thunder tumbled in from the east and rolled around like barrels of boulders. As we waited for the lights to change so we could cross to the GPO side of George Street, Steve bent down and placed a kiss on my forehead.

The wind counselled the crowds to clear the city streets. A few drops of rain found us in the maelstrom and landed on our faces. Lightning cracked and lit up the darkening streets. More thunder rumbled across the sky, threatening to topple the buildings off their very supports.

"These have to go," Steve said and reached under his jumper to tuck his glasses into the pocket of his shirt.

The light and sound show erupted. Too late to out step it, we were drenched. Raindrops turned to splatters that turned to a downpour. Steve pulled the jumper over his head where it hovered like a kite above his shoulders. Then he wrapped it around me and sheltered me as best he could.

"Do you want to go up and dry off before you head home?" he asked as we arrived, surprisingly soon, at the Hyatt.

"I have to get my briefcase anyway." I was glad to have a reason to be alone with him.

For a moment, we stood like orphans lost on a city street, trapped in the place between last chance and last call—the choice to go where the unknown beckoned or retreat to the certainty of our separate ways.

We bustled to the elevator, shivering and hanging on to each other. Once inside the refuge of Steve's room, we threw back the curtains and marvelled at nature's spectacle. The rain hammered against the windowpane as if it wanted to get inside, but it could not touch us on our harboured observation deck. Steve had grabbed the cover off the bed. He drew it around himself, stood behind me, and enveloped us both in the melting warmth of human touch.

Still wrapped, I twisted to face him and snuggled into his chest. His sopping shirt squelched against my cheek. I looked up. We fell into each other's gaze, so deep I felt sure I saw into his soul and was equally convinced he saw into mine. Our lips quivered as they met, pressed, and danced together, moving forward while holding back.

"I'll get some towels before we get chilled," he said, breaking away.

I trembled and froze. Trembled and could not speak. He returned with two fluffy white towels. He unbuttoned his shirt and hung it by the door. The triangular shape of his muscular back was more beautiful than anything I'd ever seen.

"You're probably going to take this as a line, but we really should get out of these wet clothes," he said.

He pulled a dry shirt out of the drawer. "This should fit you. Think of it as a mini skirt," he said. "If you're worried, don't be. I'm not going to take advantage of you." I had mixed feelings about his comment and continued to stand frozen. "Unless, of course, you want me to." He smiled. "Really, you'll catch a cold if you don't get out of that wet dress. I'll look the other way."

He turned towards the door. I reached behind and unzipped my dress. I let it drop to the floor and draped the bedspread around me. Steve scooped my soaked dress off the floor and fetched a pair of neatly folded slacks. He grabbed a hanger from behind the door, and went to the bathroom to change. On the way back, he turned on the radio by the bed. The volume was low, the music soft, the lyrics suggestive, sculpting the essence of a perfect love song.

"Wanna watch TV?" he asked.

"You just turned on the radio."

"I did?" He looked oddly surprised. "Are you hungry? We could order room service." He crossed the room to where I stood huddled in the cover. "To tell you the truth," he said, searching for my hand, "I'm not hungry at all. I'd just be happy to sit and look at you."

For the first time in my life I felt fully present. Without concern for what had happened the minute, the day before. Without wonder for what lay waiting in the future.

The cover dropped as I reached for him. He embraced my face with his strong but gentle hands and dotted my forehead, my eyes, and my cheeks with tender kisses.

We lay in each other's arms. The sheet draped us in a cover of weightless purity. The heartbeat of the world had found us, recalling a familiar sensation of being held and soothed. Time forgotten, we drifted in and out of sleep. That I should feel this contentment took me by surprise, while bliss rendered me delirious. Neither of us aggressive hunters, we soared on the flutter of butterfly wings.

Somewhere in a chamber of my otherwise hypnotised brain a message sought my attention, all too soon. Visit Mum. Granny. Broughton Hall. Agonised torment best describes the level of mental and physical strength it took to pull myself out of what I wanted—more than anything in that moment—to last forever.

Steve insisted on seeing me home. We sat in the back seat of the cab, his arm around me and my head on his shoulder. I asked the cabbie to drop me off on Canterbury Road. There would be too much to explain, and it would take too much energy to try if Granny saw us pull up out front.

"It's better this way, Steve," I said, persuading him to get back in the cab.

"Thanks for skipping classes today, slacko."

"You mean hard-core badass slacko."

"Yes, ma'am, I most certainly do."

He pulled me close. "Seriously, I will never forget this day."

I put my hand over his mouth and said the words I didn't need to hear back. "I love you." I turned away and ran down the street to my house, Granny's house.

In a few more hours Steve would pack his bag, put on his uniform, and make his way to the Chevron Hotel to be processed out. He would be one of those guys on one of those buses heading to the airport for his flight back to Vietnam. And just like Tom, he would be gone. The chance of seeing my guardian angel again despite all the best intentions in the world—well, probably not.

* * *

Dear Catherine,

Writing to a girl I just met recently but falling head over heels for is an occurrence strange but beautiful to me. It's hard to believe I have only known you for a few days yet it feels we have been together for ages.

On the way back I kept asking myself was I dreaming or was my stay in Sydney for real. The past six days in Sydney will probably be the most wonderful days of my life. Even though we have only known each other for a short time I feel I know the real Catherine.

Being twenty two I sometimes wonder if I know what love truly is. I either fell in love with you or got one hell of a bird's eye view of love. It just amazed me how we could converse with one another and get along. If I honestly believed I was ready and prepared for marriage I would put a ring on your finger quicker than you could blink an eye. I guess only time will tell.

I wish I could promise you I'll be back soon but that would be one big lie. All I can say is just wait and let time decide the outcome. Right now I have a lot of things running in my mind but let's just wait. I'm still in hopes of being back in the States in about a week.

Also this morning I enquired about the GI Bill. It's possible to receive benefits in a school outside the U.S. If I were to carry a full load I could receive $130 a month. How about that!

It's getting late and I have to catch a flight tomorrow, so must close. I will see you again!

Do write!
Love You, Steve

Chapter 25

MISS MORETON

January 1970

Mum resented me for signing the papers that admitted her to Broughton Hall. It wasn't long, though, before her resentment turned into gratitude, although I don't ever remember her saying thank you. It wasn't anything I did to change her outlook; participating in group sessions made the difference. Listening to others tell their stories of trying to keep afloat on the turbulent ocean of life's roller coaster, she realised that her situation wasn't all that bad. And contrary to what Granny had threatened, Mum forgave me.

The staff at Broughton Hall did a thorough investigation into her physical and mental condition during her month-long stay. She learned that she had allergies to tomatoes, oranges, and nuts; they triggered a chemical imbalance. She also learned that Valium and Mogadon were dangerous cocktails, let alone in combination with alcohol. The family doctor hadn't mentioned this when he wrote the prescriptions. Perhaps now she'd think differently about letting him "chop her head off." She learned to take notice of triggers that sent her body into the panic state she previously couldn't control. She was given strategies to deal with the extreme ups and downs of her moods and her anger. And she gave up drinking. For a while.

The normal structure of life, whatever normal means, resumed. The normal pattern of annual change since graduating from high school remained the same. So after a year at university and a year at teachers' college with neither degree nor diploma, I took a job at St Joan of Arc Primary School. My high school Modern and Ancient History teacher, Sister Bridget, had just taken on her first principal position and was desperate to hire someone—anyone— to fill the empty first class teaching position. When she offered me the job for $25 a fortnight, I accepted.

Strolling around the asphalt playground on supervision before school were a random cacophony of my far away daydreams, the demanding attention of little voices, and the odd minor accident or disagreement.

The children jockeyed for position, hoping to get hold of at least a finger. If unsuccessful, they'd slide in as close as they could, often grabbing my skirt or scrunching my pants leg, spontaneously reaching for a hug from time to time.

"Miss Moreton, Miss Moreton." It was Angela who had pushed her way through the mini crowd. Chattering and daydreaming stopped abruptly, as we all anticipated something more interesting. We focused our attention on six-year-old Angela as if she were the goddess of all knowledge.

"This morning I heard the butterflies talking to the flowers," she said.

The bell rang.

"That's nice, Angela," I said, recalling the ugly butterfly brooch I hadn't worn since the day Mum took me to meet Maureen. Come to think of it, I hadn't even seen it. It was probably lost, conveniently or otherwise, in the house clutter.

Children scurried to line up for morning announcements. Teachers appeared, cradling coffee cups like security blankets, to march their students into classrooms where they would sit in scratched wooden desks lined up on gouged wooden floors surrounded by bare whitewashed walls.

Sister Bridget led the assembly of children and teachers in prayer before announcing that there would be no more tittle-tattling on the playground. "No one has time for that, and no one wants to hear it," she said.

"Now…" She drew her clasped hands to her chest and declared the news of the day, restraining her obvious excitement as best she could. "Our school has been chosen to go to the showground to see and hear Pope Paul in November. Just imagine! Being in the same place as Christ's representative on earth."

She clasped her hands tighter and enjoyed the synchronised gasp of children responding to the enthusiasm of adults. She ran her eyes over the heads of children lined up in rows who were, nevertheless, anxious to get out of the sun. It must have been disappointing for Sister Bridget. She signalled with a stern nod for the marching music to begin.

The playground became lifeless as the little ones walked in single file, without speaking, to their classrooms. The occasional mother straggled back home, likely wondering how she'd fill her day.

"Where are those hands?" bellowed Gloria, the other grade one teacher, as she walloped the yardstick on a desk. Our rooms were separated by a thin partition. "Keep your hands folded on the desk and don't touch anything," she scolded. "We'll sit perfectly still for the next ten minutes. Look at the clock on the wall. That's when the big hand reaches the twelve." She seized the moment to teach more than intimidation.

Gloria was a childless former nun who had married a former priest three years earlier. She was pleasant enough in the staff room. In contrast to the eager chatter and oft-times chaos in my classroom, hers was like a house of horrors. The children spent long days sitting and standing like garden gnomes. Not surprisingly, it was her children who got into scraps on the playground. Their anger spilled over when she was not around, and their behaviour often resulted in a caning. Defensive explanations invited more of the cane, reminding voiceless children of their place. If Gloria was this wicked as a married woman, she must have been a hell raiser as a nun, which put an end to Hilda Hogle's theory as far as I was concerned.

Hilda Hogle was a brilliant but off-the-wall genius who attended Domremy for one year before she was expelled. Her large frame, pimply moon face, and frizzy hair—which she twisted between rolling fingers when explaining an idea—put her on the fringe. Her outspoken opinions were spiced up and flavoured by a unique view of the world. Her comments in class, her responses to Yates and Chaucer, never failed to challenge our brains, distorting and moving them to strange new ways of looking at things. Most of us were incapable of such mental contortions. Her bizarre habit of going to the Domain every Sunday afternoon, where she confidently stood on a soapbox and talked about whatever was bothering her, caused further dismay. The most disturbing idea, however, and the one that got her expelled was the one she shared while at the house of her only friend. Unfortunately for Hilda Hogle, the friend's mother overheard and reported to the nuns the blasphemous kernel of her thought, which was that Sister Martha, our shy English teacher whose beauty could not be concealed behind a veil, was repressing sexual desires for Father Matthews, the handsome curate who visited our class now and again for religious instruction. In Hilda Hogle's opinion, both of them should have left their respective orders and married.

The scandalous rumour spread like wildfire despite efforts to keep it contained. The concept, one I would never have considered by myself, had possibilities. But neither the nun nor the priest did anything to satisfy the sensational rumour Hilda Hogle had started. Sister Martha maintained her role as a kind and caring teacher and at the end of the year was transferred to Wagga Wagga. Father Matthews stayed on as the curate and continued his compassionate work in the parish. Both apparently were content to repress their desires for each other, if indeed they ever had any.

I had nothing in common with Gloria or the other three lay teachers at St Joan of Arc. The nuns ate lunch together in their own private room. I designated a few moments of uninterrupted time to be with the letters people had taken the time to write.

Dear Muffin,

I have been having a ball all this week with the bus run. I have even got used to the drunks that get on the late bus which runs from Vung Tau to our camp at 9:45 every night. Just about everyone on the bus are drunk and sing and rave on or try to tell me how to drive the bus.

I think the best run of all is the Cat-lo run which is driving the South Vietnamese people that work in our camp, from Cat-lo to work and home again. I have got to know the Vietnamese people quite well on this run.

The hardest part about driving the Vietnamese around is working out what they are saying. They try to tell me what is going on in town or what they have been doing. Some of them ask about Australia and I think it is just great to get to know the people of Vietnam.

How are things going with teaching? I think I mentioned I heard from Monica the other day. By the way, I've just been to Vung Tau and I can get some leather to make your shoes. So as soon as you let me know what kind of shoe you want I will make them up for you.

Love, Michael

Chapter 26

IT'S A BOY!

Carol had progressed from being a waitress to being a dancer at the Whisky A-Go-Go until her condition became obvious. These days she supported herself by playing wife or pregnant girlfriend to whoever took her up on the deal for the few days they spent on R&R in Sydney.

She displayed an oval bulge beneath her mini sundress on the lazy Sunday she made a surprise visit to the GI's Hut. I hadn't talked to her since she told me about the baby, but I knew she wasn't working. I was glad to see her and greeted her with a hug as she braced herself in the entrance.

"Are you okay?" I always seemed to be asking her that question.

"Just a bit of a cramp. It's nothing." She walked to a nearby table like a hen aware of a fox in the chook house. She fumbled in her shoulder bag and took out her cigarettes and lighter. She stiffened and clasped them in her fists, her knuckles pressing into the cloth-covered table. Her eyes shut tight.

"Are you sure you're okay, Carol?" I asked again.

"It's nothing to worry about. The baby's not due for another six weeks. I think." She began to relax. "At least, that's the date marked on the calendar." She lit her cigarette as if it contained the potion that would end her discomfort.

"Are you seeing a doctor?" I asked.

"Crown Street Women's Hospital. I go once a month for check-ups. Well, I've missed a couple. You know how it is." She scanned the menu, which she probably knew by heart by now.

"Sure." I nodded.

"I've been through it before. I know what's going on," she said.

Carol seemed oddly young and oddly old at the same time.

"Can I have a black coffee and a salad sandwich, please?" She took out her purse and placed it on the table.

A smattering of customers munched on sandwiches and nattered away between coffee slurps.

"Shit," said Carol as I placed the cup of coffee on the table. "I think I'm in labour."

"What happens now?" I asked, unprepared for her reply, though eager to be included in the mystery about to unfold.

"The hospital. But first I have to get my things." She stood. "Would you come with me to the flat in Coogee while I collect them?"

I ran to the kitchen and explained to Paul that Carol's baby was coming and that she needed help.

"Go," he said. "I'll cover here."

Carol had already hailed down a Black & White taxi by the time I grabbed my purse from under the counter. The strap thoughtlessly latched onto a stack of cups and threw them on the floor.

"Darn!" I yelled loud enough for customers to turn around.

"Go. Go! I'll get it," called Paul.

Carol eased herself into the back seat of the taxi like a porcelain doll that would crack if bumped the wrong way. I clambered in beside her and slammed the door. The cabbie waited for a lull in the traffic, spun the wheel around, and made an illegal U-turn. Carol grabbed my hand and squeezed hard, releasing it only after the pain had run its course. In a bizarre way, I basked in her discomfort and enjoyed the feeling of being needed. I began to understand Mum's elation when others required her help.

Carol was unusually calm as if she'd rehearsed every move, playing out the scenario in her mind so there'd be no surprises.

"Just be a tick," she told the cabbie as he pulled up at the top of the hill on Brighton Street. The elegant brick building in Coogee, one of Sydney's better beach suburbs, stood proud as it surveyed the ocean below.

"I'll be right here, love," replied the driver, leaning across the front seat to the open passenger window. "You take your time."

"I don't have much of that," she said, swaying up the paved path. She paused and I gave her my arm. Stopping every couple of steps, we eventually climbed our way to the door of her flat.

To say I was surprised with the condition of things inside the flat would be an understatement. Considering the girls she lived with, I expected it to be untidy and dirty. Sue and Sandy were hard-core streetwise girls. Nothing seemed to scare them, and I couldn't remember seeing either of them smile. I was never really sure if they were the blondes who ditched the Americans in the coffee shop or not. Between them they owned and flaunted a series of long, short, straight, curly, red, black, and yellow wigs which dramatically altered their looks as often as they needed.

Drawn blinds kept the flat cool while its occupants went about their business elsewhere. The dark wood panelling in the lounge room added a sombre serenity. The hardwood floors were bare except for a sculptured green square of carpet under the coffee table in the lounge room. TV tables with scenes of people of all ages skating somewhere in Europe stood at either end of the couch. A red geranium graced the kitchen counter beside the sink.

Carol neither opened the blinds nor switched on the lights until she got to her room. There she reached under the fringe and pulled down the tassel to turn on her tiffany lamp. With meticulous care, she had assembled the appropriate greetings for her baby. The Americans she entertained had provided for her and her unborn child and together had become the collective father. The navy-blue pram was filled with shawl, pillow, stuffed koala, an assortment of different coloured baby clothes, and a yellow dummy. A cot under the window awaited the new arrival. A row of brightly coloured plastic balls was strung from side to side.

She grabbed her hospital bag out of an elegant wardrobe with ornate knobs and double-checked that her nightie and baby clothes were all there.

"I think that's it," she said after a final scan of the room. She straightened out a wave of the bedspread with her hand and pulled the ends so they were exactly even. It was obvious she was pleased with her preparations and that she was looking forward to the birth of her baby. I wondered if her lifestyle would change or if she had become so dependent on the support of the collective father that it couldn't.

The emergency waiting room at Crown Street Women's Hospital was crowded with sad and tired women either sick themselves or waiting for a friend or family member's diagnosis. A little girl, maybe two years old, told her own private tale. Any zest she once had was sapped long ago. Her drained eyes spoke of abuse and hopelessness. I hadn't seen her before but I recognised her.

Carol was whisked away by a nurse she knew. With no member of the collective fatherhood present, who else supported her at this important time? Without family or friends, she was alone. Except for me. And in that moment, I was proud of her for carrying through with this baby— not giving up, as she had twice before. I also felt privileged that she'd invited my help, even though it was just a matter of serendipitous timing that I was there when she needed someone.

I made a nuisance of myself asking the nursing staff if anything had happened yet and realised that I didn't even know Carol's last name. Eventually I closed my eyes and dozed off, strangely lulled by the sober swoosh of the overhead ceiling fans and the silent misery of those around me. I had just shuffled into the Town Hall ladies' room carrying a paper shopping bag in each hand when a voice snapped me out of my dream.

"Carol's out of the delivery room." My thoughts ricocheted from confusion to joy to confusion again. And finally, to disappointment. "She's been heavily sedated and is sleeping.

I suggest you come back tomorrow." The nurse who'd kept me updated on the progress of her delivery turned to walk away.

"Is it a boy or a girl?" I called after her.

"Boy," she replied.

"Can I see him?" I asked.

She waited before answering. Maybe she thought someone should admire and welcome the new baby. Maybe she thought shock therapy would steer me away from the same predicament.

"Come with me," she said and led me down the long corridor to the nursery.

A hand-scribbled card at the foot of his incubator said BABY MARTIN. I wondered if Martin was the name Carol had chosen or if it was her last name. The baby was long and dark. He didn't move except for the occasional jerks that triggered a feeble high-pitched squeal. I didn't know why he lay there naked for the world to see, while the other babies on the far side of the nursery lay wrapped in blue and pink blankets.

"Is there something wrong with him?" I asked, noticing the lesions all over his skin.

"He's got a few problems. We'll have to wait and see." She offered no further explanation.

"Does Carol know?" I asked.

"Not yet," she replied. "Right now she needs to rest."

"Is he spastic?" I asked, remembering Carol's father's threat.

"Not exactly. His condition could have been prevented. You must be a good friend."

"Kind of," I stuttered. We'd shared maybe five conversations together and she'd taught me to smoke. Did the number of conversations really matter? At that moment, I was her best friend and she was mine. "Are you sure I can't see her?"

"Come back tomorrow. She's pretty groggy and may not recognise you."

"If I get some flowers will you see she gets them?" I asked.

"Don't be long then," she said. "Visiting finishes in an hour when the doors will be locked."

I sprinted down Darlinghurst Road and ran straight into the florist shop next door to the coffee shop. I chose a bunch of carnations with white baby's breath.

"It's a boy," I exclaimed to Paul when I rushed into the GI's Hut while the bouquet was being arranged and wrapped.

"How are they?" he asked, lowering the basket of chips into bubbling fat.

"Okay," I answered. "He has all his fingers and toes."

"Okay? Is there a problem?" he asked, shaking the chips around to stop them from sticking.

"I'm not sure. Carol was sleeping, but they said she was fine. Gotta go."

Cradling the flowers under my chin, I darted across busy roads and stumbled on uneven footpaths back to the hospital. The janitor was locking the doors.

"Will you give these to Carol Martin in maternity?" I asked, barely able to catch my breath.

"I'll give them to the nurse," he grunted.

In the rhythmic rock of the train ride home, Carol's aloneness struck me like a dissonant chord. She hadn't asked me to phone anyone to announce the birth of her baby. Family mattered.

Dear Muffin,

By the way, I had my first accident in an army vehicle the other day. I had stopped just outside of the gate to give some ice to the guard. Then an MP signalled me on so I drove forward about five feet. I hit a car or he hit me. Seeing that he had come from behind me, I could not see him. So as you can see I'm in the right and the other driver and the MP are in the wrong. But the MPs say that I'm in the wrong.

But not to worry. I will find a way out. I have already talked my way out of four speeding fines since I got over here so I think I can get out of this one, or at least I hope I can.

Have you got your shoes yet? I hope you like them. I chose the colour of leather I thought you'd like. I was told by a few of my mates that some of the things they sent home in the last few weeks have gone on a walkabout somewhere. When you get them will you please let me know you have them so I can stop worrying about them.

Love, Michael

Despite Granny's recent crabbiness and Mum's upside-down view of the world, I was glad they would be there when I got home. Carol's story would either distress or delight them, but their possible reactions weren't worth the risk. This would be another story I would keep to myself. Regardless, I was glad they'd be there, with the predictable permanence of their random and sometimes heinous instability.

Chapter 27

WINDOW TO THE WORLD

June 1970

I continued working at the GI's Hut on weekends and holidays. Oddly enough, it was where I found a comfortable balance of stability and variation. The unpredictability of people coming and going added its own dimension of interest.

Writing letters to soldiers who had come in and out of my life served both as a way to reflect on the world around me and to tap into theirs. A new friend's first letter was always full of promise, but the correspondence eventually stopped. Even Steve got on with his life and forgot to write. Or was too busy. Or chose not to. I came to expect the letter writing to stop and to accept the way things were. Except for Michael. He wrote regularly about things he thought we'd find interesting back home, but nothing about the reality of his world while there. So when he arrived home unannounced, there was an immediate distance. He had changed. He was quieter and more serious. He also drank a lot, much more than before he went away. He went to the club a couple of times with Jimmy and the boys, but they had nothing in common anymore.

Jimmy wanted to know what it was like over there. "Fucking moron," was all Michael had to say. "What do you know about anything?" Despite his regular letter writing, he'd been disappointed not to receive more mail back. The shoes he finally finished were two sizes too small but I didn't have the heart to tell him.

He made a quick visit to Wagga Wagga to show his mother he was still alive then returned to Sydney where he collected Monica in his brand new racing-green MGB and headed down the south coast.

Chapter 28

A REGULAR PEYTON PLACE

Dear Catherine,

    How are things going? Are you still loving your jobs? I hope so.

    My sister had a baby a couple months ago and every letter I get from my mom is concentrated on telling me about the baby. It's almost like she wanted the baby more than my sister did.

Be good and stay sweet.
Love, Burt

*   *   *

"I'll let them know when I'm ready," Carol replied to my offer to call her family.

"It's your baby's feeding time," announced the nurse. She turned to me. "You'll have to leave."

"Are you feeding him yourself?" I asked Carol.

"I'm not breast-feeding, if that's what you mean. I don't want to be tied down to that. And besides, I can't afford my boobs to get all saggy."

"Have you decided on a name?" I asked.

"Jefferson Nathaniel."

"What a handsome name," I said. "It sounds dignified."

Carol stayed in the hospital an extra week while Jefferson gained strength and was treated for a variety of conditions that his mother didn't seem to understand. By that time news had spread and a steady stream of admirers flowed in and out of the ward to congratulate her. Wrapped in a blue blanket, Jefferson Nathaniel looked just like the other new arrivals. Carol resumed her former glow under the care and attention of the medical staff, particularly the nurses. Her skin resumed its radiance. Her eyes cleared. And her hair shone again.

It wasn't long, though, before she was pushing the pram along the streets of Kings Cross, wearing one of her tight miniskirts and matching skimpy tops. Uncomfortable and inappropriate though they looked in her new role as mother, her high platform shoes showed off her bare, shapely legs.

"I don't know about Carol. She doesn't seem herself," said Paul when I called into the GI's Hut. "She's been in here with three or four different guys this week, all over them like a rash."

"What about the baby?" I asked.

"No sign of him. I've seen her talking to that Ron loser on the street, though. Apparently she's back dancing at the Whisky."

"I haven't seen her for a while," I said. We'd drifted back to life as we knew it before the night Jefferson was born. Somehow we managed to avoid each other.

"She's changed from the sweet country girl she was when she first came to the Cross," Paul said. "Drugs have a lot to do with it. I'll bet my money on that one." He scratched at a blob of dried tomato sauce stuck to the tablecloth. "What about you?"

"What about me?" I asked.

"Where do you see yourself headed?"

I pulled out a serviette from the canister and offered it to Paul.

"I don't know. After this year, I'll go back to teachers' college for two more years. And then I think I'll travel."

"Don't you have a bond or something you have to pay back for getting a free education?"

"Okay. I'll work for two years and then I'll travel."

"Where to?" he asked.

"I don't know. Anywhere. I haven't given it that much thought to tell you the truth. But I'm thinking I'd like to teach in different countries and cultures for about ten years. When were the tablecloths last changed?" I asked, lifting the corner of the cloth, unable to stand his picking any longer.

"Grace changed them at closing last night, but she obviously forgot this one." His picking expanded to other, left-behind food droppings. "Maybe because I was sitting here admiring her while she worked."

"Didn't Lara cook last night?"

"Yeah, I just came in to walk Grace home." Paul was protective towards Grace but it was easier for me to imagine her guarding him.

I went behind the counter and picked up the garbage of used coffee grounds. I shoved the bin towards his face. He got the hint, aimed and sank a basket with the scrunched serviette.

Two tablecloths sat folded on the shelf in the kitchen. I grabbed one, snatched the disgusting one off the offending table, and smoothed out the fresh cover. Paul sat back with his arms folded behind his head. I returned to the kitchen and threw the soiled one into the laundry bag.

"How come they haven't picked the laundry up yet?

"The wife or the son is sick or something, so they're running behind. Lara will be in later to take them over herself," Paul replied.

I'd hoped to leave before she arrived since Lara managed to find something for me to do even when it wasn't my shift.

"Do you think you and Grace will get married soon?" This was not the type of question a person looking for an opportunity to leave would ask.

"I would have married her a year ago, but she keeps saying there's no rush. She still wants to get her nursing diploma before we get married."

"Sounds like you're going to have a long wait," I said.

"It's just the way she is. Girls these days want their own pay check. You know that."

Independence was important.

"How do you see Carol then?" I asked.

"What do you mean? I already told you she doesn't seem herself."

"Besides that. She dances at the Whisky, but she also lives off the guys she's with. Do you think she's independent?"

"She's got the best of both worlds, I guess."

"But you're worried about her."

"I wouldn't say I'm worried about her. It's just that something's going on with her that's not quite right." He thought for a moment. "Actually, come to think of it, she's probably got the worst of both worlds."

He put his hand on mine. "This place can eat people alive, Catherine," he said, echoing Michael's words. "Why don't you get out of the Cross?"

"I need a job," I insisted.

"Get a job in the suburbs."

"It's dull in the suburbs. Everything's predictable and the same. Monica had a weekend job in a delicatessen in Belmore that specialises in chicken parts. Roasted whole, halves and quarters, raw breasts, legs, backs, necks, hearts, and gizzards. Just before closing she bagged up the leftovers and bleached the trays and counters. No thanks. Do you think a place like that would attract interesting customers? Well it doesn't. Just housewives."

"Why do you need a weekend job anyway? You've already got a full-time job."

"I love my job, Paul, but the pay is lousy. Even though I have my own class and the same responsibilities as a qualified teacher, I take home under forty-five dollars a month, after taxes and other fees."

"That's not much."

"You know, Paul, you're a good friend. As my grandmother would say, you're worth your weight in shivery grass." It was a huge compliment to a man who carried around at least an extra fifty pounds.

"Well, isn't this lovely." Lara stood over us as though she'd caught her slaves in an act of passion. Leo had been more subtle when he walked in on her flirtatious beginning with Sergeant Stan Peters.

"It's not what you're thinking, Lara." Paul was already on his way to the kitchen.

"What do you think Grace is going to say about this when I tell her?" she snapped.

Paul stopped in his tracks. "We were having a harmless conversation; that's all. Drop it, Lara."

"And if I don't?"

"Then I'll quit."

"And where the hell do you think you'll go?"

"As far away from you as I can get."

"Now is not the time to argue. I'll tell you when it is. There are carrots that need peeling." She dismissed people as easily as swatting dopey flies on a hot summer day. Paul turned and headed towards his carrots.

"How dare you!" she said, turning on me.

"How dare I what?"

"Try to take Paul away from Grace."

"I'm not trying to take Paul away from Grace," I said almost yelling. "That's ridiculous! I love Paul, but not the way he loves Grace."

"You can get any guy you want. I've seen the way you flirt with the customers in here. Enough of this. The salt and pepper shakers need filling."

"I don't work on Friday nights, Lara. I just called in to see Paul."

"Well isn't that cosy. You're not even scheduled to work. Just came in to see the cook."

"What's wrong with that?"

"When the cook is Paul," she said, slowing down her pace, "and Paul is Grace's—my friend by the way—there's a lot wrong with that."

Her absurd reasoning triggered one of those belly tickling bursts of laughter I had difficulty controlling. So I walked out of the GI's Hut, wondering how things were going between her and Sergeant Stan Peters now that he'd been sent back to Vietnam, and if Leo had known what was really going on between those two. There was a twister everyone knew about, but no one other than Leo would dare accuse Lara of inappropriate behaviour.

Chapter 29

THE DEVIL

I wandered around until my feet took me to the Whisky A-Go-Go. The Whisky had become a place to satisfy my compulsion for emotional abandonment. The Americans continued to leave as surely as they arrived. But the whole experience began to feel that it was winding down.

Dear Catherine,

I thought I'd write once more before leaving Vietnam. In 15 days I should be back in the United States. I really don't know what to expect when I get back. I'm kind of apprehensive right now about going home.

With only a few days left in my battery, things seem to be going smoother. Soon this period of my life will come to an abrupt and long awaited end. There is one memory however, that I shall carry with me forever. That memory is of you and Australia.

Thanks for being you.
Andy

Regardless, I still hoped I'd meet the love of my life and that he'd come back. I seemed to have forgotten that my father left and didn't come back. Sometimes it takes a lifetime to learn what has always stared you in the face. The feeling of loss was as constant as the appearance of yet another possible soul connection. The absence of context established normally by job, friends, home, and parents enabled such encounters. With so little time to explore a relationship, the formality of meeting friends and family was usually not a priority.

The people I wrote to often shared stories of buddies who'd met a special girl. Sometimes I'd meet the girl, the stories remarkably the same. Guy coming back. Guy gone home. Guy not coming back.

Nevertheless, I burrowed deeper into the Kings Cross culture.

Inside the Whisky, girls danced in cages. Bright lights blinded them from the crowd. The detachment they wore on their faces masked the innocence they may have once had. Their hips moved in slow downward circles, supported by feet planted wide in high-heeled shoes. From time to time their arms waved loosely above their heads. Now and again they squatted then twisted their way back up, careful not to turn their ankles. Tonight, Carol was one of those girls.

Bartenders with collar-length hair wore white shirts and black ties. They dispensed drinks to the packed crowd with amazing speed. The waitresses, although a little daggy, looked comfortable in their long muumuus. They were a dull but wholesome contrast to the spectacle of young womanhood on display in the glittering cages.

Carol almost fell through the beaded bars at the end of her set.

It wasn't long after she'd left to change that Ron appeared in the dim light. Everything about him was rancid, even more so in the smoky haze as he worked the males in the crowd— serious head-down snatched conversation here, flamboyant back-patting laughter there. He turned to a thin girl hanging nervously behind him and summoned her with a snap of his neck.

Ron cornered Carol when she reappeared from behind the black curtain where go-go girls entered the stage to meet men who wanted to get to know them better. I moved toward her, hoping that whatever Ron had to say would be over soon. After all, his business was the quick and dirty exploitation of another human being, male or female.

"You can stick it up your ass, you bloody pimp. I'm finished," yelled Carol through eyes so light they'd almost lost their colour.

"You owe me, you fuckin' bitch." He swiped her face with the back of his hand but no one else seemed to notice. "You've got 'til tomorrow to pay up."

The timid girl who accompanied Ron stood off to the side and watched. Her calf-like eyes reflected neither shock nor fear.

Carol uncurled from the slap that had wheeled her into a spin. Visibly dazed, she regained her balance as Ron roughly grabbed the dark-haired girl by the arm and turned to bulldoze his way through the crowd. Only a few who happened to be close by had witnessed Carol's assault. They did nothing but turn away when the action was over. Carol staggered to the bar.

"Well, if it isn't little miss-cherry-too-good. What are you doing hanging around here?" Ron demanded, as if it was any of his business.

"I'm here to see Carol," I said, once again giving him an explanation he didn't deserve, because Granny had told me to tell the truth at all costs, I could never find the words to put someone like Ron in his place no matter how many times he crossed the line.

"Well isn't that nice," he sneered.

Ron turned back to look at Carol as one of the bartenders handed her an ice cube wrapped in a small cloth. As swift as a piranha he turned around and was again in my face.

"Ready to earn some real money yet?" he asked.

"I've got a job," I said. Obviously I'd learned nothing from Grace, the day she banned him from the coffee shop, other than to admire her style.

"Your loss." He shook his head. "Hey, we're on our way to a party," he said without even looking at the girl who now stood with her head down. "Come with us. You'll have a great time; I guarantee it."

Ron was the closest thing to evil I'd ever encountered. He even looked like the devil. It wasn't hard to picture him with a pitchfork and flowing cape, wallowing in the flames that destroyed everything around him.

"One day I'm gonna get you. Oh, go on, get outta here." He said as if talking to a stray dog.

I worked my way through the throng of tightly packed bodies to get to the bar where Carol was already gulping down her second vodka. She showed little recognition when I put my hand on her shoulder.

PLEASE WRITE • 237

"What are you doing with Ron?" I asked.

"I work for the bastard."

"Doing what?"

"One day he asked me to go to a hotel room to meet a guy he said was lonely. You know, like he did with those two guys we met at the Rex. Was that you? Maybe it was Sandy. Or someone else. Shit, I don't know. Doesn't matter." Her words oozed out in incoherent spasms. She ensured it stayed that way with another guzzle of her drink.

"Did you go to the hotel room?" I asked.

"Yeah. His name was Chuck."

"What happened?"

"He'd already paid for me. What do you think happened?"

I imagined her baby screaming in the corner while a crime was committed on his mother, too weak and too diminished to protect herself let alone her son.

"Where's Jefferson?"

Carol's eyes were vacant. I wasn't sure she even recognised me.

"Gone." Her voice was devoid of emotion. She sucked on her cigarette and surveyed men who paid no attention to her on their way to the bar.

Suits and miniskirts continued to pack into a more than usually crowded Whisky A-Go-Go. Some stood their ground while others shoved and jostled around them. The thirsty crowd bumped each other and added to the nightclub's boisterous din. I suggested we go to a booth downstairs where it would be more private. The only one available was at the back by the men's room.

"Where's he gone?" I asked, knowing that Jefferson was her hope of redemption.

"Sue and Sandy complained about his crying." She reached back and pulled up the yellow, straggly strands that had begun to look more like straw than hair again. Her breasts disappeared against her chest and her bra puckered as she stretched even further and extended her arms. Her hands grabbed a passing bottom. The alarmed GI flung himself around, ready to strike.

"Sorry," she said without a hint of remorse. "Whatsa matter, baby? Never had your ass squeezed before?"

Even though she was old and withered, Granny was eye catching in comparison to Carol that night. Carol's youthful joy, wonder, and innocence had spent itself long before it had time to transform into at least a semblance of wisdom.

"Neighbours in the flat below complained, too. Reckoned he was left alone at night. I gotta get out of here." Her thoughts wandered like a stray cat looking for a handout. "A few hours wouldn't have hurt anything. But the little bugger started his squealing and kept everybody in the bloody building awake."

"Do you know where he is?" I asked, so close to tears I didn't dare blink.

"Nope, he's a ward of the state. They won't tell me where he is or who has him. He's better off without me. I was never meant to be a mother anyway." She stood as if she was about to leave and fell back into the seat. "What's your name again?"

"Catherine."

"Can you lend me some money, Catherine? Bit low on cash, if you know what I mean." She put her hands on her hips as if resurrecting an evasive spot of pride. "It's only a loan I'm asking you for. I'll pay you back," she pleaded.

"I'm truly sorry, Carol but I've only got my fare home."

"Forget it then." She scraped herself out of the booth and stumbled towards the foyer.

Whatever I wanted to say was stuck in my throat. I followed her until she faded into the front seat of a waiting taxicab.

Chapter 30

THE DOWNHILL SLIDE

Dear Catherine,

So good to hear from you. And yes, please tell me everything that you've been concerned with about your religion problem. My brother in the seminary is the only full-fledged Catholic in our family. Due to medical reasons he quit for a semester and doesn't know if he's going back. He has a real good job, so I'm sure he'll know by September when school begins again. Right now he says he's free. Myself I have to practice on the side. It seems everyone holds that against me. After my mother died, dad took us out of the Catholic Church. This is really a sore subject in the family and I'm doing my best.

Sorry, but I have to go, Dean

* * *

The fabric of my Catholic upbringing had begun to tear and fray at the edges. This particular Friday had chipped away at my disintegrating tolerance. The nuns had been excited about the Pope's visit in November. Like young girls with crushes, they tittered about details and the inevitability of seeing him in the flesh. In preparation, they would spend the first of three weekends at the Retreat House, cleansing themselves. Although chaste, they were still human which made them also prone to lies, gossip, and impure thoughts.

Banners, posters, news articles, and Sunday sermons vied to match the frenzy of a pop star's visit. I pictured the nuns crying when the Pope's plane landed in Sydney in 1970, just as I had when the Beatles arrived in 1964.

Souvenirs promoted and commemorated the first papal visit to Australia. Decals, fixed either to the outside or inside of windows, displayed the Pope's connection to our country. Every Catholic family was encouraged to buy at least two, but preferably one for each family member. Granny bought one for five cents that featured Paulus VI Pontifex Maximus superimposed on a red map of Australia. The kangaroo and emu, our national symbols—chosen because neither of them can walk backwards—faced him on either side. A red waratah, its spindly petals able to defy the harsh Australian climate, mustered behind a yellow boomerang in the middle of the Great Australian Bight. Pope Paul's blessing hand was raised while the other crossed his stomach. A compassionate balding figure, his expression spoke austerity through kind eyes set in deep hollows, inspiring humility or subservience, reverence or awe, depending on what Catholicism meant to each person. The flash and extravagance of the red and yellow transfers, however, contradicted the image of purity and a simple life. The Pope's regal garb and the bejewelled ring—that some would have the opportunity to kiss—flashed wealth and abundance.

As I watched Carol's cab disappear, the glitter and flash of Kings Cross continued to beckon.

Holy hell! What are they doing here? I was snapped out of my concern about Carol and the Pope's visit by three veiled faces peering out from the back seat of a taxi headed towards Rushcutter's Bay. Sister Bridget and the others must have been on their way to the weekend retreat to purify themselves. And they'd seen me standing outside Whisky A-Go-Go in Kings Cross. The lights flashed in my head, forcing me to justify myself. But to whom? The nuns? Myself? God?

For some fateful reason I could not name, my place was there. And *there* was important in the grand picture, despite what it meant to outsiders or the nuns and even Paul's well-intentioned advice to get out of the Cross.

Images of butterflies quivered timidly around me. Taunting me. Inviting me to flutter with them. Hunters waited in the bushes swirling their nets. I wished I'd taken the time to ask Angela what the butterflies said to the flowers that morning on the playground instead of listening without even hearing. I'd lost an opportunity to learn something important. Monday was too late. She'd already forgotten the strange and beautiful words had even spilled out of her curious mind. Moments lost, I realised, entombed opportunities that may never return.

I walked to the Texas Tavern where whisky barrels overflowed with peanuts. Their discarded shells crunched beneath male and female shoes hoping to meet the love of their lives, or if that wasn't a consideration, someone to pass the evening with. A tall dark guy with a moustache and dark brown eyes, perhaps of Italian or Middle Eastern descent, sidled up and yelled something I couldn't hear. The jukebox belted out Creedence Clearwater's raunchy delivery of "Suzie Q." I smiled and nodded, pretending to have comprehended his words. It was a waste of time to say, "Pardon?"

"Would you like to join me for an Irish coffee?" he repeated. This time I heard and thought, *Why not?*

Drinking out of an elegant glass coffee cup sedated me into the self-deceiving belief that I wasn't really ingesting alcohol. A generous dollop of whipped cream filtered and mellowed the causticity of the whisky. The warm sensation that flowed from the tip of my toes to the top of my head made the world right and my brain fuzzy.

Rick, the stranger, listened while I told him about Lara's absurd estimation of my relationship with Paul. I prattled on about other ridiculous matters of no interest to him. Giggles bubbled into laughter. Laughter exploded into hysteria. Hysteria roared into a raging river, opening the floodgates and freeing the tears I thought would never stop.

Five cups of Irish Coffee later, I could barely stand. The room spun into a whirlwind even more so when I realised I'd blown the pledge. With only a few months to go I'd given up and trapped the poor soul it was my job to get out of Purgatory. Guilt ridden for a brief moment and horribly disoriented, I struggled to figure out how to get home. And didn't remember how I did. Or even…if I did.

The next morning Paul found Carol slumped in the entry of the GI's Hut when he arrived to open up at six.

"She is not!" I yelled.

"She sure as hell is!" he said. "Needle marks all up and down her arms." Palms up, he thrust out his own arms so

I could visualise where Carol's heroin addiction had left its trail.

"It was just lucky I came along when I did," he said, still shaking.

Victims of addiction often draped the doorways of Kings Cross. How many times had I just passed by and left it to someone else to be the Good Samaritan? Now that one of them had a name they all flashed before me.

"She's gone down the tubes, Catherine. The way she looked this morning, it'll be a miracle if she pulls through. The ambulance blokes couldn't even bring her around."

The letter that came in the post that day made me realise how fragile life is. I hoped Carol got a miracle whether she deserved one or not. And I hoped Buddy made it home safely.

Dear Catherine,

It's Saturday and I'm wondering what you're doing. You're probably getting ready to go out and I'm sitting here in the Nam bored to death.

Just think, Catherine. I came into the Army with about 730 days and now I'm down around 90! Now that I think of it I haven't heard from you for some time now. I hope your all right and everything is going well for you.

Watch those GI's over there and don't take any of them down walking along the shore!

Take care and please write soon.
All My Love, Buddy

Chapter 31

VISITATION

November 1970

The most important day of the year arrived. We were the chosen ones, blessed with the opportunity to see the Pope on his first and possibly last visit to Australia. The nuns had thoroughly cleaned house with meticulous mental and spiritual preparations. For months the priests had led their congregations in praying for the forgiveness of our sins so that our souls would be pure.

Growing up, everything was a sin. Not anymore. Gone were the days when I confessed to the priest every little nuance of divergence from complete purity, including chewing the insides of my mouth until they bled. As a habit I had trouble resisting, it was considered a form of bodily harm and therefore a sin. Regardless, nothing felt quite as good as pulling my cheek between my teeth and biting off the surface flesh. Chances were, as I thought about the Pope and his visit, I'd be doing it again and risking my soul being stained by a venial sin. But I wouldn't be telling Father O'Connor about it.

The showgrounds were groomed, the food and souvenir stands were strategically placed, the rostrum was constructed, and the transportation was arranged. We were ready to meet the Holy Father.

On the big day, every girl and boy was checked for cleanliness and conformity. The girls wore blue checked dresses and straw hats that displayed the school colours of blue and gold under the brim. The boys wore navy blue shorts, light blue shirts, blue and gold ties, and no hats. The teachers were ordered by Sister Bridget to inspect hair and nails, shoes and socks. Anyone not meeting requirements would be left behind and would have to go home. The Pope didn't want to see grubby children who didn't care about their appearance.

The nuns usually did their own check, suspicious of what the lay teachers might miss. But having earned a place almost comparable in status to the dignitaries, the chosen nuns were assigned chairs towards the front of the stage and instructed to arrive early. So it was Gloria, in her unhappiness, who noticed Angela's scruffy patent leather shoes that had already been worn out by two older sisters. Not only that, Angela had forgotten or deliberately not worn her white socks.

"You won't be seeing the Pope today, which means you've missed your opportunity of ever seeing him," Gloria scolded.

Angela stood with her arms dangling and her head bowed. Straggly locks of fine auburn hair concealed the shame on her face. I stood by while Gloria carried out Angela's thorough humiliation. The other girls and boys stood like soldiers at attention, relieved they'd passed the appearance test that measured their worth.

I stepped in, just as Gloria grabbed Angela's arm to pack the little girl on her way back home.

"Angela is coming with us." I put my arm around shoulders that were as delicate as a bird's and drew Angela into our flock.

"Sister Bridget would not allow her to see the Pope looking like that." Gloria's hand ran a vertical line up and down Angela's tiny height, her pointer finger protruding like a witch to reinforce her contempt.

"Sister Bridget has already left with the other officials in the area. She won't even see us."

"It's disrespectful to see the Pope looking like that," said Gloria. "Her shoes are a mess."

"What sort of man is the Pope," I asked, "if he scorns a little child because her parents are too poor to buy her proper shoes?"

"It's not the Pope," she insisted. "It's about her not having enough respect to dress herself appropriately. It's like she's spitting on him."

"Didn't Christ say, 'Suffer the little children to come unto me and forbid them not'?" I reminded her. "Did he mean only the clean, well dressed ones, Gloria?"

"You're a fine one to quote the scriptures, dressed in your miniskirt." Until this moment I hadn't detected any personal resentment from her. Strangely, I didn't take offense. The calf-length floral skirt and green blouse that buttoned to the neck not only covered her bulk but also disguised her sadness and confusion over who she really was. Nun? Wife? Lesbian perhaps?

"She's a child," I explained. "She has no concept of being disrespectful because she's wearing the only pair of shoes she owns."

"Then how is she going to learn?" Gloria asked.

"Same way as you, I suppose." I pointed to her open-toed sandals. "Where are your socks and lace-up shoes?"

"I'm not required to wear a uniform. But they are," she said, nodding to the children who waited in the hot sun. "And, as representatives of St Joan of Arc they will do it appropriately."

"They most certainly will, Gloria."

The procession of children began to leave the playground. Angela looked up, her little face wearing a veil of fatigue. She took my hand and together we led our class and fell in with the others. We walked to the end of Boomerang Street where green and yellow double-decker government buses left every fifteen minutes for the showground. Every grade, from kindergarten to grade six, walked hand-in-hand in silence.

Hundreds of rows of school children were already queued up when we arrived at the enormous brick fence that enclosed the showgrounds. Numerous stalls selling last chance mementos decorated the fence. It was November and it was hot. We were already drenched in sweat by the time we got off the bus.

As the children were herded onto the paddock that seemed to stretch without end, cries of thirst and heat exhaustion emitted intermittently from little bodies unfamiliar with the stories of Auschwitz and other concentration camps. That's what the occasion made me think of.

Our designated spot was about as far back as it could be without losing sight of the podium. There in plenty of time, we stood on the parched dirt and waited for Pope Paul's arrival.

Eventually the Bishop of Sydney appeared and stood, a purple speck in the distance. His voice cut through the heat as the loud speakers delivered his message of welcome. The anticipation was stirring. Reverence fell on the crowd with the relief of a heavy rain cloud. We knelt on the dry dirt, which pocked our knees, and made the Sign of the Cross. His Holiness led us in solemn prayer, invoking God to make this day meaningful for us all. And while we weren't watching, the Pope arrived.

The air was charged. Spontaneous prayer erupted as Pope Paul walked onto the platform. Hearts beat a little faster. Perhaps we anticipated a miracle. At the very least, even the cynics amongst us hoped to walk away somehow changed.

Eventually the Holy Father spoke. I waited for something, anything, to come over me. I wanted to be touched, moved, now that I was there and prepared to recognise that this was a spectacular event. But he was so far away and his Italian accent sounded like he was speaking in a different language.

The words *Holy Father* began to play tricks. No wonder I couldn't feel anything. How could he touch my soul when he was so far away? Like the lecturers at university, he didn't even know I existed. Fathers, it seemed, were destined to keep their distance.

Suddenly I felt weak and started to tremble.

I woke up on a stretcher in the first aid tent where the attendants spoke softly and gave me water. I returned to my fledglings in time to leave. Angela said she'd get me a beer because that's what she did when her Mummy got sick.

"Did you like seeing the Pope?" I asked her on the way back to the bus.

"The girl in front of me was too big and I don't know what he said." She squeezed my hand and looked up as we flowed along with the crowd. "I was scared when you fell over and wouldn't wake up, miss."

"It was too hot for me," I explained. "I'm sorry I scared you."

"That's okay."

Angela, in her complete and utter innocence, had given meaning to my day and made it worthwhile.

* * *

Dear Catherine,

I imagine by now you're preparing for the Pope's visit to Sydney, or rather by the time you receive this, it will all be over. I imagine the place was really crowded. I do hope it was an interesting and fulfilling experience for you.

I've been back in the states about a week now. It really was good to see my parents again. I'd almost forgotten what home was like. I plan on travelling quite a bit with my parents. They really are wonderful to be with. I see them in such a different light now as I do most things around here. My experience overseas has truly had a greater affect on my attitudes than I ever expected.

I'm out of the Army for good now and I have the good Lord to thank for keeping me safe and showing me what to do with my life.

I have the Beatles Let it Be *album on the stereo and the song "A Long and Winding Road" is playing. Just remember that on a clear day you truly can see forever.*

I hope all is well with your family.
Take Care, Terry

Chapter 32

MAKE THE TIME

Catherine, I don't like to wait for a convenient time to do what I believe or feel is important, because if I wait for that time that time will never come. If I feel that I don't have the time, I will never have the time. So I have to make time for what I feel is important and do it within that time.

Each day I like to get away so I can be alone with myself and be alone with my thoughts and write a few paragraphs on what I feel, what I think about, what I'd like to share with you and what you might enjoy reading about, because you mean that much to me.

Your friend, Billy

* * *

There was a time when I thought Granny was immune from the fate of mere mortals and that she would live forever, partly because I couldn't imagine life without her and partly because she was born in a caul. Her grandmother, Biddie Walsh, was a midwife who delivered her own grandchildren. She told her daughter, Catherine, that Flo was special and would be protected from all harm.

Despite Granny's good fortune, though, a recent regression peeled away her lusty energy and replaced it with a lethargy that seemed to creep up on her with a predator's stealth. She hadn't been herself since the day Mum went to Broughton Hall. Scared of death, she scheduled weekly appointments with Dr Morrison, who prescribed enough pills to stock a chemist's shelf. She still refused to acknowledge that the pills he'd prescribed for Mum might have contributed to her overdose.

Subtle signs revealed my grandmother's deterioration. She retired to bed earlier and earlier without even bothering to put on her lipstick. Sleeping pills enabled her to fall asleep and stay that way until morning. She took frequent and longer snoozes through the day as well, aided by other medications that built up in her system, inevitably undoing and confusing her body's ability to sort itself out. Nicotine didn't help. Her joints began to stiffen. Veins knotted in her legs and made walking painful.

Dr Morrison prescribed painkillers to deal with the arthritis and thrombosis. Other medications dealt with her blood pressure and underactive thyroid. When Granny started losing track of what she'd taken and what she hadn't from her survival stockpile of twelve mainlines a day, Mum bought two seven-day pillboxes and assumed the responsibility of keeping them supplied.

My grandmother's trips to Belmore shopping centre, mostly social in nature, were reduced to once a week when she caught a cab there and back to pick up "a few odds and ends." She didn't even bother with the shopping trolley after a while. It was too cumbersome to load in and out of the taxi. Besides, she had neither the strength nor the breath to drag out the ordeal that shopping had become.

The once vibrant woman who chatted with Miss Hill in the cake shop when she'd call in for half a dozen neenish tarts, now went about her business in a turtle's shell. She no longer craved the jam and cream-filled pastries she'd enjoyed twice a week for morning tea. The days when my grandmother shared irreverent comments with the boys in the butcher shop, got the lowdown from Mavis at the barrow, talked about the government with the workers in the Post Office, or engaged in intellectual chatter with Mr Archibald the chemist gradually drifted away. Formerly an anticipated social event, shopping became a chore. She even passed by her old bowling cronies and the women from St Joseph's, most of them funeral ladies who knew the details of every death in Belmore.

The loudest testimony to her decline was when she stopped going to Housie. This meant that Mondays and Saturdays were drawn out like accordions to include the evenings, just like every other day of the week. With Mum and me working through the day and "finding" ourselves at night, Granny spent most of the time alone. So I joined her whenever I found her sitting at the kitchen table where a cigarette burned continuously in the ashtray as she peeled potatoes or carrots, trimmed the beans, chopped pumpkin, or shelled peas… snatching moments that one day would be gone forever.

Her hacking cough begged her to give up the habit she never would. I sometimes joined her in smoking, which brought comfort, regardless of its promise of ill health. Taking a puff allowed for pause and reflection. Smoking brought Mum, Granny, and me together, giving us a reason to pass the time. Like sitting by the ocean with a best friend or a pet dog during the last days of its life, time lingered as we drew the toxins into our lungs, and the cigarettes burned inevitably to their end. Unless one of us had to leave the house, we'd make the choice to light up another so we could stay right where we were until, once again, the grey ashes reached the filter. Stubbing it out left us with a choice to light up another or change the activity. Perhaps Granny's cigarette burned continuously like a beacon, in the hope someone would stay.

Granny seemed to have figured most things out. "If I was younger I'd try it," she said one day during a discussion about marijuana being a good or a bad thing.

"What would Aunty Fran say about that?" I asked, remembering how her sister had never forgotten—or forgiven—the shame Granny's drinking and smoking had brought on the family fifty years earlier.

"None of her business, is it?" she snorted.

I liked my grandmother's broadminded thinking. Sometimes it was as if she'd been stuck in a time warp all her life, never able to truly express herself the way she would have liked. Trapped by what the neighbours and the rest of the world either thought or would think.

"Maybe she should try it. Might help to get her finger out of her bottom."

That was another thing I loved about Granny. She could be shocking without sounding like a crusty old banshee.

"Naughty grandmother," I gasped.

She tossed me a cheeky glance that triggered a snicker neither of us could resist.

As Granny withdrew, however, she became less hinged to what was proper and grew increasingly attached to the stories that were her life. I hungered for those stories when I realised one day that I'd only half-heard them over the years. Listening to her was like tuning the dial to her version of *Blue Hills*, the radio serial that the ABC aired for fifteen minutes, Monday to Friday, before television came along. Each telling delivered something new and recaptured my attention.

I was curious as to why she told her stories over and over. Was she entertaining me or was there something in the stories she thought I needed to learn? Was she holding onto the important historical events of her life and sorting out their meaning? Her meaning? Was she trying to show me how stories can stretch and distort us, mould and change us? Was she showing me that we not only learn from our stories, but also teach others? Had she ever asked herself these questions or sorted out their answers? I never thought to ask.

"Have you spoken to Aunty Fran lately?" I asked.

"No. Why?"

"I was just thinking that I haven't heard from Michael since he came back from Vietnam and thought she might have some news." We sat in silence for a few moments and stared down at the table. "He might be cross with me for not writing much when he was over there."

"I wouldn't worry about it if I were you. Besides, apparently he's pretty taken up with that Monica girl."

"Well that's good. She liked him from the first moment they met at the car rally. And she wrote to him regularly, too." I felt an unexpected wave of guilt.

"Fran told me Monica's family stopped talking to her when she decided to drop out of university and run off with him," said Granny.

"That's pretty mean," I said.

"Well you can't just run off like that. They were paying her tuition and that's not cheap, you know."

"No, I didn't know," I said. And I didn't really care. After all, I had dropped out of university myself. Time to change the subject. There was always tomorrow to find out where he was and what he was up to. I would give him a ring then. Or even drop him a line if I felt like it. Right now Granny had a story to tell.

"Now, tell me about Gunda Singh," I said, wanting to finally understand the evasive part of the story.

"Well," she began, "Old Gunda Singh was one of the Indian gypsy hawkers that peddled their wares to the farmers. He travelled all over the countryside and came to our district two or three times a year selling all kinds of goods and shackles."

"What goods and shackles?" This telling would fill in the blanks once and for all.

"Oh, you know." She lifted up the aluminium saucepan that would boil the water to cook the potatoes. "These things." She tapped a fingernail on the metal. "He also peddled blankets, table cloths, cleaners, medicines, and salves that cured anything and everything from spider bites to foot rot. And he had quite a collection of treasures from all over the world."

Her eyes sparkled as she remembered the brass, copper, silver, and golden trinkets.

"Ah yes, it was a day to look forward to when Old Gunda Singh came around," she said.

"So, it was like a travelling Grace Brothers or David Jones?" I asked.

"More like a travelling market," she corrected.

Every bit of information turned the key to unlocking the next morsel.

"Old Gunda Singh even told fortunes for a small fee." She enjoyed baiting her audience with enticing titbits that kept us on the edge of our seats and anxious for the latest version.

"Did he tell yours?" I asked.

"Not exactly," she said. "My mother told him I was born with a veil over my head, so he said I'd have riches and fame." She looked disappointed. "It could have happened," she reflected, memory drawing her back to another treasured story. It was as unique and valuable as Gunda Singh's trinkets, judging by the look on her face.

"Go on," I said.

"Well, one day at Manly Beach a stranger commented on my legs and said I should have entered the Miss Australia contest. He said I was better looking than Beryl Mills, who won the first one in 1926."

"What were you wearing?" I asked conjuring up vintage magazine images of bathing beauties.

"My lovely black and white neck-to-knee swimming costume that had a grey stripe running through it. That's what the women wore in those days. Not all the same colour of course. I sewed it myself." She was young again, walking down that promenade and showing off her legs from the knees down.

"But I never pursued it. Married your grandfather instead. Besides, I wouldn't have known where to start."

Although she never said it, Granny probably married the wrong man—just like her daughter, my mother. Grandpa was never much of a provider. She felt deserted when he went off to war at the age of forty. Left to her own resources, she fed her family by sewing for others who could afford to pay. It was not enough to make her wealthy but she did earn herself the reputation of being a fine dressmaker. I remembered the day we sat at the table after Mum went to Broughton Hall and only now understood why Granny was so sure Mum should never have married my father. She was shedding tears for her own decision to marry the wrong man.

There were always more levels to her stories, which would only be revealed if her audience made the effort to participate. Grasping the depth of each story required activating my brain, my heart, and my imagination. Not just my ears.

"At twenty-five, I was well on the way to eternal spinsterhood," she said. "If I hadn't married your grandfather I might have been left on the shelf."

I could see in her eyes that being "left on the shelf" might not have been so bad in the end. Little diversions in her stories provided new insights into the woman who was my grandmother and whose blood also flowed through my veins.

"Well anyway," Granny said, "Old Gunda Singh was from India, and before he died he told everyone he wanted to be cremated and have his ashes scattered on the Ganges." She took a puff.

"How were they supposed to get the ashes to India?" I asked.

"They didn't have airplanes back in 1915, so they would have had to send them by ship, I suppose," she said.

"And who would have scattered them?"

"I don't know. Lots of people were fond of the old bloke, but nobody had enough money to go to India; that's for sure. So they decided on the next best thing: scatter his ashes on the Murrumbidgee River." Forgotten faces re-emerged. She was fourteen, a flaxen-haired girl with curls the envy of the entire Riverina. This detail often appeared in her stories, so I came to see it even though she hadn't said it this time.

She went to the sink, placed the potatoes that had been draining there into her apron, and folded the corners so they wouldn't slip out on the way back to the table. She had a couple of draws out of the blue inhaler Dr Morrison had recently prescribed for her short-of-breath episodes. It didn't venture far from her red and gold cigarette packet. Her habit had crept to two packets of twenty a day. Carefully, she set each clean moist potato on the newspaper then placed both hands on the table to get back into the bench. She took a puff of her cigarette— without bothering to flick off the grey ash that hung onto the orange embers—and grabbed hold of the thread of her story.

"The people around Lockhart wanted to do the right thing by him so they got together and built a bier."

"What's a bier?" I asked through her gurgling cough.

"Stick things that raised him off the ground. We'd never seen anything like it." She took a handkerchief out of her pocket and wiped gluey strings of mucus from the corners of her mouth. "Lots of people turned up to have a gander."

"What do you mean, 'stick things'?"

She sighed. The effort to recall details made her tired.

"They wrapped him up in a white sheet thing like a mummy. Then they placed him on a board that they lifted and placed on the stick things. That's the best way I can describe it."

I caught the image, or at least my version of it. The image, the one that only she knew, gave her a second wind and she chuckled to herself. She took another puff. She hadn't peeled a single potato, although she held one in her left hand. She placed the cigarette into the ashtray and took up the paring knife. Recalling Gunda Singh in this particular telling seemed to require more energy and focus than any of the other million times she'd told it.

"Well, they lit a fire under him." Her own flare lit up. For a moment her eyes danced in the memory of the flames. "Old Gunda Singh must have known they weren't taking him to the Ganges and he was pretty darn shytie. All of a sudden, out of the blue, he bolted upright. There he was, sitting up if you please. Scared the bejeezus out of everyone." She laughed as much as her lungs would allow before the cough took over. "What a flamin' fright that was," she managed to add.

The phone rang down the hall as I pictured the spectators getting more than what they'd bargained for that day.

"Was he still alive?" This was the part she'd never explained. I tried to imagine being aware of my own body burning or being mad enough with everyone after I died that I'd do something unexpected like sitting up. I imagined Old Gunda Singh yelling, "You promised you'd take me to the Ganges, you cheaters."

"God, no! Dead as a doornail."

The phone rang again.

Granny got up to answer it. Even if the phone was ringing or Mars was falling from the sky, for that matter, I needed to know how or why he sat up when he was dead.

"What, then? How did he do it? How did he sit up?"

"I'll tell you when I get back," she said.

"I'm not letting you go until you tell me, Granny."

"When they cremated him, his muscles contracted and that made him sit up. Happens to everyone who's disposed of that way. Now are you satisfied? Don't burn me when I'm gone. And make sure they bury me in a lead-lined coffin. I don't want the worms and grubs getting to me either."

"You're not going to die," I said as if it were true.

"Just remember Gunda Singh. The dead don't like it when you cheat them out of their final wish," Granny warned.

The phone continued to ring in the background, with neither of us in a hurry to meet its demand.

"I'll get it," I said.

"No, I'll go." The telephone was one way to communicate that she still hung on to. She rarely made a phone call out, but she relished it when someone, anyone, called. Since she paid the phone bill, it was her right to make a production out of the experience.

"You'd better hurry then," I said.

"They'll phone back if it's important."

I rested my chin on my knuckles as Granny dropped more ashes, this time on the carpet. The elastic bandages strangling her legs reminded me of bindings that restrained Chinese girls' feet to stop them from growing.

I pictured the faithful old peddler making his last statement of glory and knew I would have jumped out of my skin if I'd seen his wrapped form sit up in the flames. The delightful terror made me shiver in a thrilling kind of way. I was ashamed of myself taking pleasure in the gruesomeness of Gunda Singh's cremation. But finally I understood.

Usually it was easy to hear Granny's side of the conversation when she was on the phone. I often listened and participated by imagining what the person on the other end was saying. It was more a case of overhearing than intentional listening. Today, I was absorbed with Gunda Singh.

I started peeling the potatoes. Potatoes were one of life's staples, like Granny's stories. As I sliced the skin with the sharp knife, delighting in how easily it shaved off, I wondered if I'd ever have a story as vivid as Gunda Singh's to tell my granddaughter.

By the time the third potato had been skinned, the house was unusually quiet. I decided Granny must have gone around the corner so as not to be heard. She did that when she was planning a surprise.

Chapter 33

THE LAST RACE

"We'll try and get on the Spirit of Progress tonight," I heard her say before hanging up.

"Who's getting on the Spirit of Progress tonight?" I called. My fondest memories still were of catching the train to Wagga Wagga and Lockhart with Granny. She didn't answer.

"Who was that?" I called again. She didn't hear so well lately.

"Aunty Fran."

"What did she want?" I knew things were better with Fran despite the playful comment Granny had just made about her sister, and I was glad they'd mended some fences during their recent visits.

"Michael had an accident." Granny's voice preceded her to the kitchen, where she stood with her hand over her mouth.

"What do you mean?" I jumped up, as if the action would help me understand.

"Michael had an accident," she repeated, waving me off as she headed for her seat. "Just give me a minute." She raised her hand as if to keep her shock away. I sat down.

"What do you mean he had an accident?"

"He's dead, Catherine."

That wasn't possible. Luck and determination had brought him safely back home, where only old people died.

"No he's not! He's down the south coast with Monica."

"His car spun out of control on the way back to their camping spot." Granny sat down at the kitchen table and cradled her head in her hands. For once, she didn't reach for her Viscounts. "Poor Fran," she moaned over and over again. "First Artie. Now Michael."

"What about Monica?"

"He was by himself," she answered. "Monica waited behind while he drove to the bottle shop to buy grog. Apparently, he started drinking heavily after he came back."

"Everybody drinks heavily," I said.

"Yes, well maybe they do." That perhaps explained why Granny's bottle of scotch emptied every other week, even though I rarely saw her drink.

I followed her to the front bedroom. She stretched up to the top shelf of her wardrobe, trying to reach the small suitcase she used for trips to Wagga Wagga.

"Can you get that down?" she asked, her fingers barely touching the brown leather. "It's too high for me."

She took two singlets out of the top drawer of her dressing table and placed them in the bag. "The police told Monica the news shortly after it happened. Her family stopped speaking to her when she left university and ran off with Michael. They're on their way to get her now. She's in a bit of a state."

This couldn't be happening. Granny must be mixed up. Old Gunda Singh's story had robbed her of her sanity. She must have confused Gunda Singh dying with Michael dying. Fran probably said he was *fine* and Granny thought she said he *died*. Her hearing was going, after all.

She'd been talking about being mad if we cremated her or buried her in anything other than a lead-lined coffin when Aunty Fran called. She turned everything upside down and got lost in the concept of death. But she'd also said something about an accident. And Michael.

Alive Michael. Not-here Michael. Not-there Michael. Survivor of the war. Cousin Michael who made me a pair of shoes when he was in the war, who offered to teach me how to drive, who drove too fast, who let me use his camera and his tape deck while he was away, whose letters I put off answering because there was always tomorrow.

Floating down the river on a burning bier, or was it a barge? Granny said *dead*. There was a mistake. Granny was sobbing. Unusual for her. I hadn't seen him since he came back. Hadn't even talked to him. He just disappeared down the coast. Left us all behind. And we let him! We were children down by the river, catching guppies. When did we grow up?

"I'll phone your mother. The train leaves Central at eight o'clock tonight. It doesn't give us much time," Granny said, focusing on the logistics of getting to Wagga Wagga.

How handsome Michael looked in his uniform the day we saw him off at Kingsford-Smith Airport. What was it he said to me?

"I'm not going with you tonight, Granny," I said. "I'll be there in a couple of days."

She continued packing as I slipped into where I needed to be. Alone.

How easy it is to fall into the trap of believing we have forever to figure things out and to lose track of the reality that the unexpected can strike at any time and turn our world upside down.

"Tomorrow's Saturday. I have to work," I said to Granny.

"Phone Lara and tell her we've had a tragedy in the family."

"I can't."

"Of course you can."

"There's no one else to work."

Granny's orders were beginning to tear at my nerves.

"She'll find someone else." Granny's pink and mauve polyester dress folded neatly into the suitcase that had tons of room when she closed it. "Now grab a few clothes and pack them in with mine, like you used to do when you were a little girl."

"We don't have tickets," I said.

"I'll phone the station after I talk to your mother."

I walked to the bedroom I shared with Mum. The butterfly brooch called from the jumble of junky jewellery I'd been given over the years. It wasn't there. I remembered I'd hidden it at the bottom of the top drawer of the dressing table. I rummaged around through worn out but still used pants, bras, and pantihose that should have been thrown out long ago.

I dumped the underwear, expired Commonwealth Bank deposit books, scribbled notes, and letters on the floor. The other two drawers were about to get the same treatment when it showed itself: the ugly butterfly brooch that was now the most beautiful treasure I'd ever seen. I stuck the pin into the shoulder of my sleeveless white lace dress and admired it in the mirror.

I slipped out of the sandals I'd worn all week and reached underneath the bed for the leather shoes Michael had made and I'd never worn. Looking down, I was greeted with two pigs' trotters stuffed into shoes two sizes too small. Michael had chosen the wood, the leather, the design, and the tools to create these beautiful shoes just for me. I would wear them whether they fit or not.

"Dearest." It was a long time since Granny had called me that. The insinuation she made that I was an accident of fate the day Mum went to Broughton Hall had left its mark. Everything seemed to go back to Broughton Hall, as if that day had begun a new chapter. "I phoned your mother and she wants to drive to Wagga. She's on her way home."

"I'm not going to Wagga. I'm working tomorrow; remember, Granny?"

"We've already discussed this. Just tell Lara that your cousin passed away," she said in her calmest voice.

"Stop saying that," I yelled. "I haven't had a chance to talk to him since he got back from Vietnam."

"Catherine, you're in shock." Granny moved closer and put her hand on my arm while I stared at the butterfly brooch looking back at me from the mirror above the dressing table.

"See, I'm wearing the brooch you gave me for my sixteenth birthday."

"And it looks lovely, dearest. Now we don't have much time. You need to pack a few things for Wagga." She did her 73-year-old best to steer me towards the wardrobe.

"I've already said I'm not going."

"Don't start that," she snapped.

"I'll catch the train down on Sunday night."

"Come on, Catherine, I don't like to leave you here on your own."

"I'm fine, Granny."

Mum bustled through the front door. "I'm home," she called.

"We're in here," Granny answered from around the corner.

Mum was ready to take charge, like a general who had no time for anything that didn't relate to the operation. Her clarity of vision shone like polished chrome: get her mother and her daughter to Wagga Wagga in order to help Fran process her grief.

"I'll just grab a few things and we'll get on the road. I've already filled the car with petrol." She hugged Granny, in whom I saw for a moment that flaxen-haired little girl. "The boys at Amoco checked the oil and tyres for me, so we're good to go."

It was my turn for a quick hug. Granny went to her room.

"What's wrong with you?" Mum asked, apparently incapable of figuring it out.

"Nothing," I replied.

Mum opened her overnight bag on the bed and accepted my response, which meant to her that everything was fine and normal, like the sun setting and the moon rising, followed by the moon setting and the sun rising. Nothing else mattered.

"What happened here?" Her hands flew to her hips and her mouth gaped.

"I was looking for the butterfly brooch you gave me."

"Did you have to make such a mess?" She sifted through the underwear on the floor. "How am I supposed to find anything in this disaster?"

"Is there a disaster?" The world was getting ready to go inland to Wagga Wagga. Maybe the communists had finally arrived from China and were about to invade Australia's coastline—exactly what the conflict in Vietnam was supposed to avoid but so far wasn't doing a very good job at. Everyone must be heading west to Wagga Wagga to avoid the first wave of the attack.

"Don't get smart with me, young lady." Mum pulled out what she needed from the rubble and stuffed the rest in the drawers before shoving them into the dresser.

"Got your things packed? We're leaving in a few minutes."

"I'm wearing the brooch. See, Mum?" She grunted in a frantic effort to close the flap of her bulging overnighter.

"Don't strain like that, Brenda. You'll bust a boiler," said Granny, standing at the door to announce she'd already checked that the iron was turned off and unplugged.

"And I'm wearing the shoes that Michael made me when he was in Vietnam," I pointed out as Mum continued to wrestle with the flap of her overnighter.

"They're too small for you," she said without looking. "They'll give you blisters."

"Why did my father leave, Mum?" It was about time she answered the question with something that made sense.

"God Almighty! I can't think about that now. I'm trying to get us all out of the house so we can get to Wagga." Despite packing excessively, she finally managed to subdue the flap.

"I just want to know," I said as if in the middle of a dream.

"How many times do I have to tell you? He didn't love us anymore and he wanted a boy."

"If I was a boy, would he have stayed?"

"For God's sake, Catherine, I don't have time for this now."

"I want an answer. Would he have stayed if I was a boy?"

"How do I know? Probably he would have."

"So he left because I was a girl?"

"That's right! Now stop mooning around and get on with it. There are more important things to think about. Poor Fran down there all by herself. I can't imagine what it must be like."

The problems of others created a sense of purpose for Mum. She couldn't face her own problems. My problems weren't worth the effort. I had no problems. Individual therapy and more group sessions could have helped her see things differently. Perhaps.

"I'm leaving," she announced loudly enough for everybody who lived on the street to hear as she pushed through the front door.

"Bye," I said, following her out to see them off. She was already rearranging a blanket, a pillow, and an umbrella to accommodate their bags.

"What do you mean *bye*?" Her patience began to steam like the pressure cooker when Granny boiled shin beef for the potted meat. "You're coming with us."

"No, I'm not, for the millionth time." A gorgeous butterfly, a real one with rich midnight blue wings sprinkled with orange, white, and yellow spots, landed on a bloom of one of the geranium bushes that lined the tiled path from the house to the front gate. He was beautiful. Why did I call him *he*? The butterfly's gender didn't matter, yet I'd thought *he*. He was free. He, no matter what species, was always free. Perhaps, if I wore the butterfly brooch long enough I would also become free.

"I have to work," I said, confident she'd understand, having brought me up to believe I'd have to support myself because I sure as hell couldn't rely on somebody else to do it.

"What about your cousin?" The dominant issues of loss and permanence evaded my mother just as they did when Mr Mann dropped dead on his front lawn. All she talked about was whether he'd been thoughtful enough to write her into his will.

"What about Michael?" she said, pressing the point.

"I'm wearing the shoes he made for me."

"You're going a bit off, I think," she wasted no time saying. "You're not making any sense." I sat down on the front step. "Are you taking any of those drugs they keep talking about on the news?" she demanded.

"No." Even though I had taken steps, lately, to shed the image of out-of-touch wholesome for in-touch cool. "But you're right, Mum. I think I'm *a bit off*, too."

"Well, whatever." She couldn't display my "off" condition to the neighbours like she could my huge appendix which Dr Morrison had placed in a bottle for public repulsion. That had put Mum in the spotlight and given her something to talk about for at least a month. "You can't stay here by yourself," she insisted.

"Why not?" If the chains weren't broken soon, I'd never fly. "Mum, I can stay home by myself."

A car boasting an illegally loud muffler screeched off Canterbury Road and sped towards the intersection of Chalmers and Haldon Streets where we'd come to expect the crash of a prang.

"Louts!" declared Mum after they'd sped out of sight.

"I don't understand how you can be so heartless. Not going to your cousin's funeral," she said. She threw up her arms. "Where did I go wrong? God knows I'm doing the best I can."

"You're doing fine, Mum."

"Trying to."

"I've already said I'll catch the train down on Sunday night."

"You'll have to book your own ticket," she warned. "You can't just get on the train, you know."

"I'll book it at the station when I go to work tomorrow. I might even walk down tonight."

I leaned on the front gate. Granny was already in the car. She hadn't lit a cigarette since talking to Fran.

"Let her stay, Brenda." Granny stared through the clean windshield. "You have to let go some time." Finally, she was freeing me from the warnings meant to ensure my safety but which in reality penned me up. *You're not going to let her do that, Brenda. Surely to God!* How could I grow if I wasn't free to make mistakes and learn what I needed to in my own way?

"I'd feel better if she came with us," insisted Mum.

Their bickering over what each one thought was best for me in that moment eradicated their power over me. Mum and Granny were changing. I was changing. Our relationships had begun their inevitable shift.

"It's only two days," said Granny. "She needs some time to sort things out."

The butterfly circled by again. Mum parked herself half in and half out of the car. She looked at her watch.

"All right then. Come and give your grandmother and me a kiss goodbye," she said, getting in behind the wheel.

I unlatched the gate and walked around the car to carry out my mother's request. I knew from the feel of it that she had tattooed a red smudge on my cheek.

"You be good now. I'll be there to pick you up when the train arrives at Wagga Station Monday morning. It gets in about six."

"Thanks," I said.

Granny inhaled from her puffer in the passenger seat. I walked behind the Morris Minor to the passenger side and leaned through the window to kiss the thinning hair on top of her head. The inside of the car burned.

"Roll down the back window for me, Catherine," Mum said, now the pilot, checking that all systems were ready. Granny covered her head with the pink scarf that had been resting on her lap and pulled it over her ears. The same one she wore the day we saw Michael off.

"Hate getting my head blown off in the wind," she said, tying it under her chin.

Mum threw her hands up. "We can't drive around in this heat with the windows rolled up."

Granny pulled the scarf further down on her forehead almost to the tip of her long straight German nose. Finally, Mum put the Morris in first gear and pulled away from the curb.

The little green car taking my mother and grandmother to Wagga Wagga reminded me of a tortoise, as it ambled up the street towards Canterbury Road. The speedster who had moments before commanded our attention made me think of the hare. Michael had also been that self-assured hare. Slow and steady might not win the race, but it was more likely to get there in the end.

Chapter 34

MICHAEL'S SHOES

I waited until they disappeared around the bend before going inside. I locked the glass door that turned people on the outside into apparitions. No one ever got around to installing the screen door when the extension was put on years before, so there was only the wooden door out the back to latch. I closed every window and entombed myself in the house where I'd grown up—a furnace without flames, noiseless except for the steady humming of the Kelvinator fridge in the kitchen, which echoed in every room except Granny's. The clutter that dominated even the smallest space felt as methodical as same-size jars placed in alphabetical order on a wooden rack.

I slumped into the kitchen nook and faced the spot where Michael had sat the morning he left for Vietnam. Self-assured and calm like a Western movie star who battled the odds and always won. I reached out to touch his face and saw his shyness the day I told him about Monica's crush on him.

The broken chime of the grandfather clock announced 4:30 the best way it could, its distress a testimony to having been ignored for a very long time. We'd all become accustomed to that broken sound and assimilated it into the household along with all the other broken parts. Did we each presume it was someone else's job to fix it? Was it unfixable and needed to be replaced? Or was it Granny's mantra—waste not, want not—that sealed its fate? With no answers, my own brokenness howled, inhaling and exhaling all the dimensions of brokenness and loss.

I carefully took Michael's letters and post cards from my bundles of letters. I sat down to read each word, determined to capture the details I might have missed or just not bothered to see before. More than just an account of his experience in Vietnam, his words were the legacy that would stay behind as a testimony to his being. Although his references to speeding and the trouble it got him into bothered me in a way I could not previously identify, I saw now that they were warning signs foreshadowing the inevitable. His personal challenge to out-perform the potential consequences of speed ultimately cost him his life. Speed would have the final say.

I thought back to the car rally when he took our lives into his hands. He was impatient when I asked *what if?* "An endless question with endless possibilities," he'd said. Now that he was gone, I could only wonder. What if he'd slowed down? A simple question with a logical probability: he would still be alive.

Wearing Michael's shoes to bed was as natural as covering myself in the letters he'd written. As natural as wearing the butterfly brooch, still attached to the white lace dress.

The phone awakened me from what might have been a moment of sleep. The raw fact that Michael was gone slashed at the four-way stop of rejection and acceptance, restraint and freedom. Opportunities to say all the things I wanted to say were gone forever, along with the assumption that "one day" would always be.

The annoying ring continued. I crawled to the foot of the bed and buried myself in the covers. When that didn't work, I flung them back and flew out of the room to end the racket.

"Yes," I said meekly.

"Dearest, I just wanted to check that you're all right." Pause. Nothing. "Are you all right?"

"I'm fine, Granny." I responded with what she wanted to hear. "How was your trip?"

"The run down here was uneventful," she answered. I could imagine many miles of silence between them. "Your mother is a marvellous driver," she added. "She's resting now, so I thought I'd give you a quick call." Pause. Nothing.

"How's Aunty Fran?" I asked.

"Not too good. She was waiting up for us when we arrived. She hasn't slept since the news."

"What time is it?" I asked.

"Eight fifteen. Are you ready for work?"

"I will be." The truth of it was that it wasn't work that had held me back from going to Wagga Wagga. Coming to terms with Michael's death was something I had to do in my own way without anyone else telling me how to do it.

"All right then. I'll let you get on with it. Goodbye, dearest."

"Bye, Granny."

I dragged myself through the shower and put the clothes back on I'd slept in. I phoned for a cab and forgot all about going to the station to get a ticket for Wagga Wagga.

Kings Cross grumbled like a sleepy child who'd suffered through the night with an illness she didn't understand. On Saturday and Sunday mornings, she awoke with blood on her face. A young man staggered out of the doorway across from the GI's Hut as the taxi pulled up.

"Two dollars, love." Beads of sweat dotted the cabbie's forehead, though it was still early in the day. "Hot as the hobs of hell," he declared, pulling at the neck of his short-sleeved shirt, already stained with garlic sweat. "Lots of fares to Bondi Beach today, that's for sure."

He whistled his own rendition of "Waltzing Matilda" while waiting for me to sort out the coins in my purse. His joviality contradicted the backdrop of human greed, violence, and victimisation that thrived behind the doors of Kings Cross. The underlying throb of the pain, disguised by outward glitter, only now came into focus. Pleasure had its price. I replaced the young man in the doorway with Carol and shuddered at the thought she might have tried to get my help the morning she'd collapsed.

Paul opened the front door as I stepped out of the cab.

"You're early," he said, blocking my way.

"So?" I pushed past him, as if he were a gate on a hinge. A thing not a person.

"Snappy this morning," he said. "Late night?"

"Late night. Early morning. It all rolls into one eventually, you know?"

The coffee shop had been closed for a few hours. The smell of grease loitered in its walls and carpet. I threw open the back door to let the rank air escape down the laneway.

Paul had already fired up the espresso machine and was sitting down to his first cup. Predictably, he perused the headlines and flipped through the pages for his morning read of the *Daily Mirror*. "You look like you slept in your clothes." With one eye on the paper and the other on me, he resumed his niggling. "Her Majesty's not going to like that."

"What's wrong with it? At least it doesn't look as bad as it stinks in here."

"She's particular about you girls wearing skirts and blouses. Looks more professional," added the man who paid no attention to his own grooming.

"Too bad. I'm tired of Her Majesty telling me what to do." I pulled the paper away. "This is what I'm wearing. If she doesn't like it, she can fire me."

"We're snappy this morning." He shook the paper to straighten out the words and lines. "I find that tone very becoming, by the way."

"Really? You don't find it becoming when Lara uses it."

"What's going on with you, Catherine?" he asked, putting down his morning read.

"Michael was killed in an accident," I said. "See the lovely brooch Mum and Granny gave me for my sixteenth birthday? And the great shoes Michael made for me when he was in Vietnam?"

"Steady on, Catherine," he said.

"They don't fit very well but I'll break them in," I continued.

"They're very cool shoes, but you're jumping all over the place," Paul said, lines tracking across his pudgy forehead.

"And this brooch," I said, ripping the lace as I pulled it away from my dress. "You might think it's a bit on the ugly side, but it has sentimental value." Paul stared. "We should look after the things people give us, don't you think, Paul?"

I let go of the brooch and grabbed his hand but quickly dropped it again, remembering the last time that happened. "I'm going to try harder in the future."

"Catherine!"

"Did I tell you my father left because I was a girl? The poor man only wanted a boy. People should be able to have what they want, too, don't you think, Paul? I'm sorry, Paul. I sound like my mother, throwing out all these questions without giving you a chance to answer."

"When did Michael die?" he asked.

"Did I tell you Michael died?" I asked, surprised to hear such a thing.

"Catherine, you just said it," he said.

The walls of self-doubt closed in, constricting and restricting the desperation of the rat in the maze I'd become.

"Yesterday."

"Take the day off," Paul said.

"Why?"

"You're under a lot of stress."

"I'm fine," I said.

"You're not fine. You've been working seven days a week for the last eleven months. And a lot of things have happened."

Until now, I hadn't noticed.

"I'll be fine," I insisted.

"Besides your work schedule, there was your mother's overdose. Then the business with Carol and Jefferson...and then Carol again." He leaned across the table. "To say nothing of your effort to have some kind of a connection with your father. And now Michael. Bloody hell, Catherine. That's a lot to try and digest in a short time."

Paul's summary of recent details shook me with a jolt. I had been sinking to the bottom of my worst nightmare. At least when the walls of the maze closed in, there was a chance I could push them back. There was no way I could bring myself up from a disaster that had taken me to the bottom of the ocean. Even when I wasn't, Paul was taking notice, listening and watching, absorbing the unseen. Just like I'd begun to do with Granny's stories. To be known in all the parts of your life, to be accepted without judgement or criticism, is a gift so profound it will free the butterfly from the hunter's net.

Paul stood up. His wisdom—or his fear—sat him back down.

"Who will work if I take the day off?" I asked.

"Grace or Lara could come in for you today." He doodled on the front page of the newspaper with the pen Grace used for taking orders. "I could work a double shift. Either Grace or Lara could waitress tonight."

"I was going to catch the train to Wagga tomorrow night," I said.

"Go tonight," he said directly.

"I hate to muck everybody up like that."

"You're not mucking anybody up. You've helped them out before. Remember New Years?" Paul asked.

I'd tried to forget the night I worked a double shift so Lara could go out to Leo's favourite Greek nightclub, coincidentally named Leo's, for a special bash. I ended up not going home that night. By the time Lara and Leo arrived back at the coffee shop, Sergeant Stan Peters was waiting and not about to leave. While they sorted out who wanted whom and who was cheating on whom, I continued to wait on tables.

Mum came looking for me and accused Lara of driving a hard bargain. Granny said we nearly put her in the grave.

"Lara will be in later with the clean table cloths. Ask her." Lara saved herself ten dollars a week by picking up the laundry ever since the Chinese laundry boy got sick.

Customers came in for breakfast. The familiar routine of taking orders and delivering them, making cappuccinos with the milk temperature just right so that it wouldn't boil and go flat brought order to chaos and skirted the minefield.

Things seemed almost normal when Lara and Grace appeared at the front entry, silhouetted by the bright sun outside.

"You look a bloody sight," Lara said without even a hello.

Her hair wasn't secured as efficiently as most days. The circles under her eyes hung on like the dark side of two half-moons. Grace went straight to the kitchen where Paul cut tomatoes and fried bacon for the BLTs the two Americans sitting at a table by the jukebox had ordered.

I poured two glasses of cold milk, took them to the table, and went to the kitchen to pick up the order. Grace was propped up against the stainless steel fridge with her arms folded and one leg crossed over the other. Paul wiped crumbs, tomato seeds, and lettuce strips off the preparation table. They had exchanged enough harsh words to open old wounds, judging by the look on her face. I grabbed the order.

If words were withheld in the kitchen they certainly tumbled out in the café section of the GI's Hut. Not unlike Mum, Lara's observation skills routinely missed nothing, except what a person was feeling.

"You can hardly walk in those shoes." She plonked herself down at the table. "Where'd you get them?" Lara demanded. "They're the ugliest things I've ever seen."

"My cousin made them for me." Her comment was an insult to Michael's workmanship. "They're a bit tight. But I'm breaking them in."

Grace, her arms still folded, strutted down the kitchen steps and stood by Lara. "Ready to go?" she asked.

Paul appeared at the top of the steps.

"Catherine needs the rest of the day off," he said.

"That's not possible," said Lara. "Grace and I have plans."

"You'll have to change them," Paul insisted.

"We can't. We're going to the markets, then to Bondi," said Grace, her tone more threatening than Lara's.

"It's okay, Paul." I grabbed his arm, caught the disapproval of Lara and Grace, and hung on.

"Her cousin died and she needs to go to Wagga tonight," he said.

"Well, I'm sorry about that, but..." She stood. "There's no one else to work."

"I can work a double shift," Paul said. "One of you can work now, and the other tonight, instead of both of you tonight."

"And who'll work tomorrow?" Grace asked.

"It's no different to the old days before Catherine came on board," replied Paul. "You and I'll work tomorrow."

"You don't listen do you, Paul?" said Lara, putting on her sunglasses.

"This is a special situation."

There was no need for Paul to risk his relationships and his job. The fog lifted.

"I need to go to Wagga to be with my family," I said.

"Leave and you don't come back," Lara responded as sharp as a knife.

"Lara?" Grace frowned at her friend.

"Okay then," I replied, feeling surprisingly relieved.

"Lara!" Paul said, using her name to make a statement, rather than ask a question. But it was too late.

"I apologise for the inconvenience I'm creating for you all." I emerged from the maze, the walls retreated, and the path got wider. I surfaced.

Lara, for once, was lost for words. The strength I'd so admired in Grace the day she told Ron off finally found its way under my skin. Courage seeped into the empty spaces in my backbone.

I straightened and turned to Paul. "Thank you for being the friend I never expected." I smiled and nodded to Grace. "Thanks for teaching me how to be a good waitress and for tending to my blister that day. Oh, and how to stand up to a bully."

Lara almost shook my hand when I offered it but pulled back at the last minute.

"Thank you, Lara," I said anyway, "for giving me the opportunity to work in your coffee shop and experience all of its on again off again drama; I've enjoyed the GI's Hut series. And ...I've learned a lot."

Out on the street, I waited for a cab and knew my days at Kings Cross had come to an end. After three years I was graduating with courses not listed in any university handbook. The knowledge about life and the strength I'd gained was far more valuable than anything I could have learned in a textbook or a lecture.

"Hi, Catherine."

I turned around to see Carol looking almost as good as her old self. Ron stood impatiently by her side.

"I heard you were in hospital," I said.

"I got out of rehab about a week ago."

"You look great." I was happy to see the smile of her former innocence back. Ron fidgeted with something in his pocket and looked nervously around.

"I feel great," she said.

"Yeah, yeah, come on," said Ron. "We'll be late!"

A vacant cab sped by. I wondered, but didn't ask, what she remembered from the last time we talked at the Whisky.

"I wanted to visit you," I said as an apology.

"Why didn't you?" she asked.

"I didn't know how," was all I could say.

"Oh," was all she could say.

I knew she didn't understand. There was neither the time nor the energy to try to explain. But then again, perhaps an explanation wasn't necessary.

"Come on, Carol. We're late." Ron grabbed her arm.

"What are you doing?" I asked.

"I'll manage myself better this time," was all she said.

I hailed down the next vacant cab. Before opening the door, I put my arms around Carol and pushed Ron out of the way.

"Bitch," he muttered under his breath.

"I'll never forget you," I said before sliding into the back seat.

"Oh, Christ!" Ron's disapproval floated down the street. They turned to leave.

"Wait!" I yelled to the cabbie as he pulled away. He slammed on the brakes, swearing obscenities at the car that almost rammed us from behind. I opened the door and jumped out.

"Carol, I want you to have these shoes," I said. "They're very special to me but they're way too small and I'll never be able to wear them comfortably."

She hesitated.

"I really would like you to try them on," I said.

"They're beautiful, but what are you going to wear?"

"I'll pick up a pair of thongs from Coles. Please take them."

"Okay," she said with the expectancy of a little girl about to try on her first pair of patent leather shoes.

"Come on, Carol. You don't need a bloody pair of shoes," Ron said.

"Just a minute." She stepped out of her platforms and into Michael's handmade wood and leather shoes. "They're perfect." Her smile said it all.

As the taxi drove off, I turned to look at Carol for the last time and was hopeful and afraid of the decisions that were hers to make. She was still on the curb when we turned down Williams Street, heading for Central Station. Just before she disappeared from view, I saw Ron put his arms around her in what looked like a tender embrace.

Chapter 35

THE SPIRIT OF PROGRESS

The sulphur smell of coal in the tender, the flawless sound of steel on steel, and the ghostly sight of steam trimming the fleeting bush soon rocked me to sleep with the familiarity I'd come to know and love as a little girl. The Spirit of Progress pulled into Wagga Wagga Station at six in the morning. It was Sunday. I'd arrived a day earlier than expected. I stepped onto the platform and looked up to the overhead bridge where Mum and Shirley used to park their bicycles after singing lessons and share their schoolgirl secrets.

"Collins Street, please," I said to the cab driver. The smell of bread toasting in the wood-burning stove greeted me at the gate. Aunty Fran opened the door. There were no words, just a knowing that our feeling of safety was wrapped in the arms of our grief.

"Flo! Brenda! Catherine's here," cried Aunty Fran. "Come and have some toast and jam with us, love."

* * *

St Michael's Cathedral was packed with family, friends, and many of the men Michael served with overseas. Michael's best mate Peter spoke of his skill with a rifle, the pet monkey he hid in their hooch, and how he always got a ribbing for going out of his way for the Vietnamese people he drove to and from Cat-lo.

Monica sat beside Fran in the front row and sobbed uncontrollably. Mum, Granny, and I sat shoulder to shoulder in a bond of genetically determined commitment, a bond that originated tens of thousands of years before we became specks in the grand scheme. Perhaps that DNA connection allowed us to put aside the differences that at times placed us light years away from each other. There was no time for differences in times like this. We sat united in the painful burn of Michael's absence. No one even noticed I was wearing my first pair of black rubber thongs.

Out of grief would come strength.

Father Keeble, the priest who had baptised and confirmed Michael, heard his First Confession, and given him his First Holy Communion, said the final farewell on our behalf.

As Michael's coffin was lowered into the ground, a six-gun salute thundered through the air. A bugle sounded the last post. Father Keeble recited a portion of the ode, "For the Fallen," by Robert Laurence Binyon.

> They shall grow not old
> As we that are left grow old
> Age shall not weary them
> Nor the years condemn.

At the going down of the sun
And in the morning,
We will remember them.

Smoke from the guns rose into the air. A butterfly fluttered by. Michael was free. He had completed his metamorphosis. The rest of us would continue on until our time came. And our time would come, regardless of whether we were driven by fate or our own choices. But in the meantime, equipped with the circumstances we had been dealt, we would search for our own version of freedom.

The ripped lace, now a tear, had let go of the butterfly brooch and let it fall off somewhere on my journey to say goodbye to Michael. I believed it had become real and flown away. I thought of Angela and hoped she'd have a gentle life.

So many people had taught me more than books could about the importance of relationship and change, love and kindness, forgiveness, compassion, acceptance, and letting go—perhaps none more than the soldiers who took the time to clap the net over the butterfly of the moment. Recording their thoughts, feelings, and wisdom while battling to stay alive. And sane. Words that shed light on young men thrown into the life and death reality of war.

With so much more to learn, I wondered what Michael knew that the rest of us didn't. *"Glad you've sorted yourself out. Now get on with it. By the way, maybe it's a good thing I didn't have time to teach you to drive,"* I heard him say.

Michael's death had crystallised a list of guiding principles to be embraced or ignored. I was old enough. It was time to leave the nest. Granny would get back her freedom, but not fully; Mum would never leave. One day I would find my father and ask him to tell me in his own words why he left. And if he said, "Because you're a girl," I would put aside his biased take on the sanctity of human life and thank him with every beat of my heart.

A reception followed at the RSL Club. Peter was refused admission because he was an Aborigine. He'd been included, though—the day he stood on the tarmac with his fellow servicemen—in the speech about pride and being one of Australia's sons. He was welcomed home to the world of contempt he'd known before the army and Vietnam. A painful slap in the face to his heritage as one of our nation's first inhabitants.

So Peter, Monica, and I turned our back on our country's racist hypocrisy and piled into Peter's car. We headed for Lockhart and the playground and the river to relive the days when Michael and I found refuge together in the uncomplicated innocence of childhood.

Peter stepped on the accelerator in his best mate's honour. The tyres kicked up red dirt, and the golden sun streaked through the towering gum trees.

As the speedometer tipped 100, I could hear Michael say for the last time, *Good one, Muffin.*

JANETTE BYRON STONE

Janette Byron Stone is one of those restless Aussies who went walkabout as soon as she could. Hungry to know what the rest of the world had to offer, her dream was to teach in different countries and cultures. She had no idea her venture would lead her to the Canadian prairie to raise her three children and then to the United States, permanently sealing her fate to live on the other side of the world. Now proud to call herself a citizen of three magnificent countries, she has never forgotten the privilege of growing up in the city with the world's most beautiful harbor.

Janette holds a diploma in teaching from Alexander Mackie College, Sydney, Australia, as well as a bachelor of education in secondary music and a master's degree in elementary curriculum from the University of Alberta, Edmonton, Canada. She has founded and directed award-winning choirs both in Australia and Canada. In addition, she is a published author and presenter and has performed in many amateur plays and musicals as well as professional TV and film.

Janette is the author of her debut novel *Please Write* (2019), a narrative fiction, and *Gifts from Time and Place* (2017), a collection of short stories, essays, and vignettes portraying the resilience of the human spirit. She also co-authored a children's book that showcases Key West through the eyes of a ten-year-old boy living on a sailboat.

When the northwest mountains of Idaho begin to chill, she and her husband Tom migrate to the tropical southeast.

You can visit her at www.janettecatherinestone.com

61728495R00183

Made in the USA
Columbia, SC
29 June 2019